D0389658

THE MAGICIAN'S KEY

Also by Matthew Cody

THE
MAGICIAN'S
KEY

THE SECRETS OF THE PIED PIPER

BOOK II

Matthew Cody

ALFRED A. KNOPF
NEW YORK

THIS IS A BORZOI BOOK PUBLISHED BY ALFRED A. KNOPF

Visit us on the Web! randomhousekids.com

Educators and librarians, for a variety of teaching tools,
visit us at RHTeachersLibrarians.com

Library of Congress Cataloging-in-Publication Data
Names: Cody, Matthew, author.
Title: The magician's key / Matthew Cody.
Description: First edition. | New York : Alfred A. Knopf, 2016. | Series: The secrets of
the Pied Piper ; book 2 | Summary: Max, nearly thirteen, is determined to find her way
back to Summer Isle to reunite with her brother and the children of Hamelin.
Identifiers: LCCN 2015035545 | ISBN 978-0-385-75526-9 (trade) |
ISBN 978-0-385-75527-6 (lib. bdg.) | ISBN 978-0-385-75528-3 (ebook)
Subjects: LCSH: Pied Piper of Hamelin (Legendary character)—Juvenile fiction. |
CYAC: Pied Piper of Hamelin (Legendary character)—Fiction. | Magic—Fiction. |
Brothers and sisters—Fiction. | Fantasy.
Classification: LCC PZ7.C654 Mag 2016 | DDC [Fic]—dc23
LC record available at http://lccn.loc.gov/2015035545

The text of this book is set in 12-point Requiem.

Printed in the United States of America
November 2016
10 9 8 7 6 5 4 3 2 1

First Edition

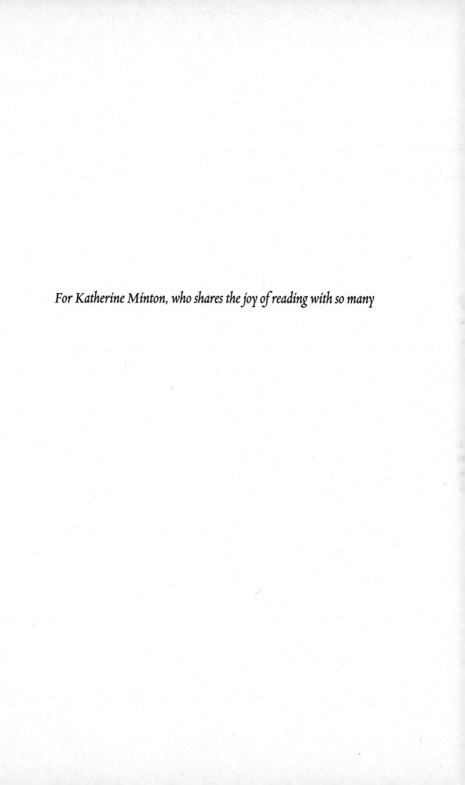

For Katherine Minton, who shares the joy of reading with so many

He plays up and down the street,
Then draws quickly to the stream,
A hundred and more children
A-moving away with him.
He plays them to a faraway land,
Of the type that is yet unknown,
Where milk and honey flow,
Thereto they advance cheerfully.
The pipe plays at all times.
The land—I don't know where it is.
Oh, you poor German youth,
How good it was at home.

—FROM A GERMAN FOLK SONG (1806)

The Rat King's Nest

The Peddler's Road

New Hamelin

The
Shimmering
Forest

A Troll Bridge

Shades
Harbor

The Summer Isle

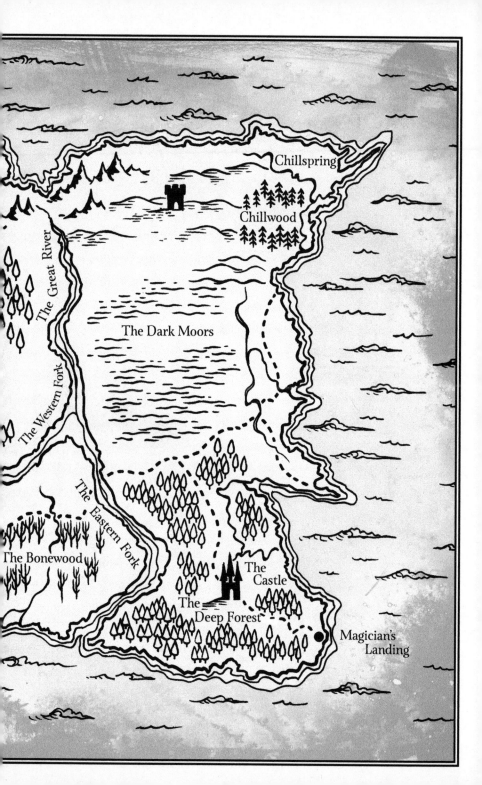

T he crow paced back and forth across Vodnik's desk, using stacks of paper as stepping-stones. Vodnik watched as it stumbled over a stapler, sending pens rolling off the edge. Yet the filthy bird strutted around like a little monarch, careless of the mess it was creating.

"Did you know," asked Vodnik, "that back in my day the peasants didn't stuff scarecrows with straw? Oh, no, they stuffed them with dead crows. Stitched them all together and hung them in the field as a warning. Can you imagine?"

The crow cawed at him, flapping its wings in agitation. Perhaps he shouldn't have goaded the creature so. Crows loved to gossip, and one could learn much if one knew how to listen. The crows had been talkative lately, and the talk was all about *magic*. Magic this world hadn't seen in centuries . . .

The crow grew quiet as something caught its attention—a cockroach scuttling across the office floor.

Vodnik leaned back in his chair and stroked his long beard, fingers absently working at the tangles. Magic had all but died out many centuries ago, when mankind stopped fearing the dark. A great exodus followed, and most of the magical creatures, or the Folk, as some called them, fled this world. There were pockets still here and there. Hints of the old powers lingered in certain bloodlines, but most of those lived in the shadows—descendants of beings too stubborn or too stupid to have made the journey to the last sanctuary of magic, the Summer Isle, back when the way was still open. Now the door was shut, and if you asked anyone, they would tell you: Vodnik had the only key.

But the crows were talking.

Poor wretched Vodnik. Once just a farmers' fable, a miserable hedge magician haunting mills and riverbeds, waiting for sailors to drown on the treacherous waterways so that he might jar their souls to fuel his petty magic. But that was long, long ago. Before Vodnik had discovered the key to real power, the Key of Everything.

His desktop exploded in a shower of papers as the crow suddenly launched itself after the unfortunate cockroach. Vodnik hurled a paperweight—a dead scorpion encased in cheap plastic—at the horrible bird, but he was a terrible aim. The crow dodged it easily, and flew out the open window, its meal clasped firmly in its beak.

Vodnik looked down at the mess the crow had left behind. Someone would need to clean up all these papers. "Mr. Twist!" he yelled.

Luckily, the bird hadn't disturbed Vodnik's precious box. He kept it on a little table against the back wall, safely out of the way. Vodnik loved the box with a mixture of nostalgia and obsession. It was an antique fisherman's tackle box, centuries old, and it had belonged to Vodnik's first victim. Fashioned from the wreckage of a sunken riverboat, it had a latch shaped in the likeness of drowned sailors, and the leather shoulder strap was worn soft with years of travel. The wood was thickly lacquered with varnish and blood, stained in sorcery, and when you opened the box, the little trays within expanded, but instead of fishing lures they held Vodnik's collection of jars. The oldest were opaque with dust and age; others were shiny and new. But inside each one was something precious.

These days he used the jars less and less, however. Magic was scarce in the modern world, and it had to be rationed. Vodnik's key was all the magic he needed to get anything he wanted. Those who dreamed of the Summer Isle, the desperate and afraid—those people had to come to Vodnik. He was their only option.

But now the crows were talking about strange new developments. They told Vodnik of two children who had left this world for the Summer Isle. They'd left the village of Hamelin and crossed over to the land of magic.

Without needing Vodnik's key.

The crows were saying that the two children had come to the continent with their father, a professor of some sort who'd been searching for a lost story. The search led them to Hamelin, an infamous place for children to go missing. Vodnik was old enough to remember the Pied Piper's vengeance upon that village, how he'd used his magic flute to lure all the children away. Vodnik hadn't been there himself, but word traveled fast among the Folk. A magician had stolen Hamelin's children.

Vodnik couldn't help but feel a pang of professional jealousy. The whole world knew of the Pied Piper, but few if any remembered Uncle Vodnik. And how many had Vodnik lured into the dark reeds near the riverbank? How many souls had he claimed over the centuries? Fame had eluded him.

But it was power, not fame, that mattered most to Vodnik, and now, nearly eight hundred years later, two more children had gone missing from Hamelin. Did that mean that *he* was at work again in the world? Was this modern world big enough for Uncle Vodnik *and* the Pied Piper? Was Vodnik's hard-earned power at risk?

The crows were garrulous but not always trustworthy, so Vodnik would have to gather more reliable information on his own. He had the children's name, Weber, and that was enough to start with.

"Mr. Twist!" Vodnik called again, exasperated. He needed new help, that much was obvious. He'd been putting it off for as long as he could, because he hated the idea of having to train a new man, but things around here were getting sloppy, and this was no time for sloppiness. Mr. Twist had been with Vodnik for so very long, and until recently he'd been dependable and efficient, slavishly so. But the years seemed to be catching up with poor Mr. Twist. Perhaps it was time for a fresh face.

There was a heavy-handed knock at the door, followed by the slow scraping of knuckles across wood. Finally.

"Enter," Vodnik called.

No response.

"Enter!" he called again, and still there was no answer. With an angry mutter, Vodnik crossed the room and opened the door himself.

Standing there in the doorway was Mr. Twist, his ancient face drawn and ghostly, his cloudy eyes staring off into nothing. A fly had landed on the tip of his nose, and it busied itself there, unnoticed. In one hand Twist held a stack of Vodnik's forgotten letters, ones he was supposed to have mailed days ago.

A family was waiting in the hall with Mr. Twist. Favor seekers. The crows' gossip would have to wait.

The father was a tall, broad-chested man—a blue-collar worker, judging by the rough calluses on his hands and the state of his work boots. And perfectly ordinary. But his little girl's skin was the color of birchwood, and her ears came to distinctive points that poked out well past her silver hair, marking her as one of the Folk. The mother was beautiful, though less exotic, and she wore a flowered hat with its brim pulled down low, hiding her own ears.

It's the mother's side of the family, then, thought Vodnik.

The man and woman were staring at Mr. Twist. They had polite enough manners to at least try and hide their revulsion, but their young daughter pinched her nose closed with her fingers as she made a face. Vodnik sighed. Poor Mr. Twist, he had taken on an odor these past few decades. How Vodnik had let him go this far was beyond him. But good help *was* hard to find.

"Ah, yes, you knocked, Mr. Twist?" said Vodnik, snapping his fingers in his man's face to get his attention. Twist seemed to come back to himself, at least somewhat, and grunted in the family's direction.

"Visitors?" said Vodnik. "Lovely. Be so kind as to fetch us a few candles, would you, Mr. Twist? Sun's nearly set."

Wordlessly, Mr. Twist began dragging himself back down the hallway, his feet scuffing the floor with that shambling walk of his.

"Why do we need candles?" asked the little girl. "Don't you have a light switch?" The mother quickly hushed her.

"It's all right," Vodnik reassured her with an unctuous smile. "This old mill hasn't had power for many years, my dear. And besides, there are customers of mine who prefer the dark."

Vodnik eased himself into his chair. The family stayed standing because there were no seats to offer them, which was entirely intentional on Vodnik's part. "I apologize for Mr. Twist. He's been in my employ for ages, and I suppose I'm too sentimental to let him go." That was true, he thought. Even beyond death. "So, what can I do for you?"

The man nervously cleared his throat. "Well, my name's Jon Wick, and my family and I, well, we were told by some . . . that you were, that is, they say you're a magician."

"Well, you were told wrong," answered Vodnik. "I'm not *a* magician, I'm *the* magician. And what else do they say about me?"

The man blanched. "There's stories, is all."

"Stories about Vodnik who traps souls in jars?" said Vodnik. "Vodnik who haunts an old mill near the North Sea, and has cold river water in his veins instead of warm blood? Those sorts of stories?"

"I'm sorry," said the man, nervously fumbling with his hat. "I don't mean to offend. Eh, I'm just not really sure how this works."

Vodnik smiled. "How this works is you tell me what you want, and I tell you what it'll cost you. Really, simple as hiring a plumber."

"Yeah," said the man. "Okay. See, it's about my daughter. You see, she's always taken after her mother, and we've managed so far. But lately . . ."

The man looked back at his little girl. It was funny, thought Vodnik, that the man seemed unable or unwilling to call his daughter what she was. An elfling. That he'd married an elfling woman and had an elfling child was obvious, yet the word eluded him. Still, there was genuine love in his eyes as he looked upon his child. And he'd braved a magician's dark den for her. People were such deliciously contradictory creatures.

"Yes, the elfling genes are recessive in some," said Vodnik. "Dominant in others. And they only grow more pronounced the closer the child comes to adulthood. But I cannot make your daughter human, Mr. Wick. I cannot change who she is."

"I never said anything about changing her!" snapped the man. Then he realized what he'd just said and quickly looked away. "I'm sorry, it's just she's perfect the way she is and I don't want anyone changing a hair on her head. That's why we're here."

Vodnik let him stand there for a moment in silence. He let Jon Wick wonder if he'd gone too far, raising his voice at the magician.

"What will Vodnik do?" he must be wondering. mused the magician. *"Add us all to his collection for our impudence?"*

"No, I apologize," said Vodnik at last. "Obviously, you love your family very much, and it was wrong of me to assume anything to the contrary."

Jon Wick and his wife let out sighs of relief. The daughter just stared wide-eyed at Vodnik. It took all of Vodnik's self-control to keep from laughing at their collective stupidity.

"Eh, it's all right," said the man. "Just hit a sore spot, is all. You see, we've managed this far, my wife and I, but now it's getting harder and harder and folks stare at our little girl. We're afraid that she might attract the wrong sort of attention."

"Secrecy is the best weapon we have," said Vodnik.

At this, the father looked down at his shoes and his cheeks darkened. "It's too late for that. See, the neighbors have been talking. We live in a small town, and folks there are superstitious. Last week a bunch of teenagers followed my girl home. They were shouting things."

"So you want me to take care of the teenagers?" asked Vodnik. "For a price I can send Mr. Twist..."

"No!" said the man. "Nothing like that! We just... we heard there's a place... a place where she wouldn't have to hide from anyone anymore."

Vodnik leaned back and steepled his fingers under his chin. Of course. They wanted Vodnik's key. They all wanted the key. "I, too, have heard of such a place."

The father exchanged a look with his wife and took a deep breath. "And we heard that you are the person to get us there."

"The name of the place is the Summer Isle," said Vodnik. "But it's very hard to get to. Nearly impossible. You see, the paths are all but forgotten. There's only one left that anyone knows of, and that door is locked."

"But they say you have the key," said the man. "Look, we can pay. I've got some savings."

"You'd have to take a long journey. The door is hidden across the ocean," said Vodnik, "beneath man's greatest city." He reached into his desk drawer and took out a small brass chest, tinged green with age. Vodnik flipped open the lid and spun the box around to face the family.

"Is that it?" asked the man.

"The Key of Everything," said Vodnik, nodding. "One key that can open any door, even the door to the Summer Isle. But if you want to use it, it'll cost you."

Vodnik picked up a chewed-on pencil and a sheet of paper off the floor, and scribbled down a figure. He scooted it across the desk to the man, then sat back and savored the moment the man's eyes grew wide as he read the price.

"We don't have . . . ," sputtered the man. "You must be joking!"

Vodnik shook his head. "There's only one Key of Everything. That means I can charge what I please. Supply and demand."

"But there has to be another way," the man pleaded. "Who can pay that much?"

"Few can," agreed Vodnik. "That's why I generously offer an alternative."

A spark of hope lit up in the man's eyes. "You mean like a payment plan?"

"I mean *servitude*," said Vodnik. He had been eyeing the width of the man's shoulders, the strength in those arms. Sometimes fortune smiled on him. "I told you that Mr. Twist is nearing retirement, and I just happen to be looking for a new employee to take his place."

"What? Work for you? For how long?"

"As long as it takes to pay off your debt," said Vodnik. "And in the meantime, I will provide safe passage for your wife and child to America. Safe and *secret*. I will lend them the use of my key."

"But we'll be without him?" For the first time, the wife spoke up. Her eyes were panicked, afraid. She was elfling, and she sensed more about Vodnik than her husband could.

Vodnik couldn't afford to let her spook her husband off. "Mr. Wick," he said, careful to soften his tone. "The truth is, you cannot go with them, even if you *could* pay. The Summer Isle is not a place for humans. But if you accept my offer, you can spend the rest of your days knowing that your family is safe, and in a place where they will never have to hide again."

"You can't," said the wife, but her husband interrupted her.

"Let me think a moment!" the man said.

Vodnik's sluggish breath caught in his throat. He nearly had him.

But just then the door swung open and Mr. Twist reappeared with the candles. Slowly he set a tarnished candelabra onto Vodnik's desk. He struck a match along the desktop and lit each candle deliberately, one by one. He didn't notice, or didn't care, that the match was burning down to his fingers, and by the time he was finished, his own thumb was on fire.

The room smelled like burning thumb.

Vodnik cursed silently. Of all the terrible timing! "Will you put yourself out?" he snapped.

Mr. Twist stared back at him blankly.

"Your thumb! Your thumb!"

Mr. Twist held up his other hand to his face, examining the wrong digit. There was a snap, like the crackle of a log in a fire, as Mr. Twist's blackened thumbnail popped off.

"The other thumb! The one on fire, you idiot!"

In the end, Vodnik had to scoot around the desk and put out Mr. Twist's thumb himself. Scowling, he shoved Mr. Twist back outside and slammed the office door behind him. After a moment to compose himself, he turned back to the Wick family and smiled. "Now, where were we?"

But the daughter, the little girl with silver hair and ears that were impossible to hide, took her father's hand. "Papa, no. I don't want you to. Not ever. Please, Papa."

The man wavered. His wife took his other hand and whispered something in his ear. Finally, he relented. "I'm sorry, Mr. Vodnik. But I can't take your offer."

Outwardly, Vodnik was all pleasant smiles, but inside he seethed. How dare this ordinary man say no to him? For a moment, he thought about having Mr. Twist drown the three of them in the river. Or perhaps he'd let them join the others in his box, those who'd displeased him over the centuries.

But he didn't do either. After all, there were complications to murdering someone in your own home.

And the father. Vodnik wasn't entirely convinced that he'd lost the man. He could see it in his eyes that he loved his family too much to think clearly. He was the sort that would sacrifice anything for them. Just the sort Vodnik could use.

"As you wish," said Vodnik, and he snapped the little chest shut and returned it to his desk drawer. The man's eyes followed the key as Vodnik hid it away. "But my offer still stands, should you change your mind. You know where to find me."

Especially, thought Vodnik, *after I cast a few curses on your home and rile up the neighbors a bit more. Maybe pets will start to go missing. Maybe people will get sick. Things will get worse for you, Mr. Wick, before they get better, and I'll be waiting here for you when they do.*

With a gracious bow, he opened the door and bid goodbye to the Wick family.

Once they'd left, his thoughts drifted back to children and the chatter of crows.

He would send Twist tonight. And there were others who owed him favors—so many who owed him favors. He didn't like to do things the messy way. Vodnik was as patient as the river outside his window. Slow and patient and strong. Vodnik was like that river, and the deeper one looked, the darker he became.

He would wait for Mr. Wick. And in the meantime, he would prepare for the Weber children to return, if they ever managed to. Perhaps a visit to the parents was in order. And then . . .

Well, Vodnik still had plenty of empty jars.

PART I

TWO WORLDS

CHAPTER ONE

The little cobbler's shop at the corner had no customers. At least, warned Mrs. Amsel, not customers *as such*. In their few weeks of journeying together, Max had learned that when Mrs. Amsel said something like that, it was almost always cause for alarm. The diminutive housekeeper was prone to dangerous understatements.

So when Mrs. Amsel came stumbling backward out of the cobbler's doorway, looking like she'd been standing downwind of a hurricane, Max wasn't exactly surprised. The old woman's flower-print cardigan sweater was matted with dust and bits of shoe leather, and her ever-present kerchief had been blown askew, so that her small pointed ears—a trademark of her peculiar lineage—peeked through hair that showed gray at the roots.

"Such rudeness!" exclaimed Mrs. Amsel in her thick

accent. She hastily rearranged the kerchief around her head, hiding those distinctive ears from view.

"Let me guess," said Max. "He doesn't know anything about elves and he's never heard of any place called the Summer Isle and he wants us to leave him alone and never come back. Pretty much sum it up?"

Mrs. Amsel muttered something in German under her breath, something that would make the woman blush if Max had been able to translate it. "And there is something else in there, protecting him," said the little woman. "I'm not sure—a poltergeist, maybe. Can you believe it? Not a strong one, I don't think. Just blows stuff around—but still, so very rude."

"I'm going in," said Max.

"What? No, *meine Liebe*," said Mrs. Amsel. "Forget him. We'll have better luck with the next one."

"That's what you said about the last three! I'm tired of everyone slamming the door in our faces and playing dumb. All we want to do is ask a few questions."

"They *are* rude," agreed Mrs. Amsel. "I always ask politely, but these provincial elflings have no manners."

"So maybe we need a change of strategy," said Max. She looked up at the closed door, the windows with the shades pulled low. Her mouth hardened to a straight line as she made up her mind. "Maybe we need someone who can be rude right back."

"But be careful! He is already angry."

"I've faced worse than him, believe me," said Max, and it was true. For the most part, Max's nearly thirteen years on this planet had been an uneventful stretch punctuated by fights with her younger brother and one impulsive morning when she'd decided to dye her hair bright pink. But in the last month, Max had traveled to a magic land, battled rat creatures and escaped a witch, walked over a troll bridge and bartered with ghosts. Now she was back on earth, but her brother was still trapped on the Summer Isle and her mother and father had mysteriously gone missing. All Max had was the little housekeeper for company. Like it or not, Max had packed a lot of experience into a very short amount of time. She felt confident she could handle a shoemaker and his magic wind.

The cobbler's shop was a single-story chateau nestled at the corner of a winding side street in a village so tiny it didn't appear on most maps. While the rest of the village could be called quaint, on this lone street the houses were either boarded up and abandoned or in such a state of disrepair that one had to wonder how anyone managed to live there at all. Weeds erupted through cracks in the brick sidewalk, desperate to reach the sunlight that failed to penetrate the seemingly endless shade. It was an odd place to find a shoe shop, but it was exactly the sort of place you'd expect to find a little hidden magic.

Mrs. Amsel had explained that those with magic blood lived in remote places because they eschewed technology, especially electronics. Electricity and magic were dual energies that did not mix well. Nothing could make a spell go awry like booting up a laptop. And Mrs. Amsel claimed that simply having elf blood in her veins was the whole reason she couldn't get her microwave clock to stop blinking twelve.

On this evening, on this particular street, Max and Mrs.

Amsel were the only souls in sight. This was good because, though she hadn't said anything yet to the little house-keeper, Max was pretty sure they were being followed. It was mostly a sense she had, the feeling of being watched that had gotten stronger over the past several days. A few times she thought she'd glimpsed a tall figure standing in the shadow of a building or in the shade of an alleyway. She'd seen such a figure before, back in Hamelin where their whole adventure had begun. Max hoped that this time the shadows were just shadows, and that her instinct was wrong. But she feared it wasn't.

All the more reason for urgency. Max wouldn't let them be turned away again. A little sign hung on the door that was the French equivalent of OUT FOR LUNCH. The sign had been hanging there unchanged since early in the morn-ing, and it was now nearing suppertime.

There was no doorbell chime to announce her entrance, which made sense because some elflings were superstitious and avoided things like cold iron and the chiming of bells, though they didn't seem to bother Mrs. Amsel in the slight-est. In fact, she often talked about how she missed listen-ing to the church bells of Hamelin. Not Max. She missed the sounds of traffic and people speaking English back in her own home in New York. She missed such things terribly. What had been intended as a short visit, just a quick research trip to Germany so that Max's father could work on his new book, had turned into something else entirely. Now her par-ents were missing and her brother was stranded in a land of magic, and Max didn't know how to help any of them.

She was not leaving this shop without some answers.

The inside of the shop smelled of leather and polish, and it was filled with racks of shoes in various states of disrepair. An antique cash register sat on the countertop, and across from it a small man sat hunched over his cobbler's workstation. He was as bald and knobby as an old potato, with two enormous pointy ears that twitched as he pried the soles off a pair of work boots.

The floor was covered with scraps of thread and flaps of leather that had been scattered everywhere, as if someone had left a window open in a storm.

The cobbler barked at Max in French without bothering to look up from his work.

"Excuse me," said Max. "Do you speak English?"

"Hmm?" answered the cobbler. "American? Are you with the old woman? I told her I don't have anything to say to you."

Max felt a very slight ruffling breeze brush past her. Little more than a sigh, but enough that it made her second-guess her decision to come in. She'd seen enough magic in her life to know that she didn't like it. A glance over her shoulder reassured her that Mrs. Amsel was waiting anxiously on the stoop.

"I just have a few questions," said Max, turning back to the cobbler. "It won't take any time at all."

The cobbler slammed one of the work boots down on his table and hopped off his stool. The seat had added a few much-needed inches of height to the little fellow, and now as he marched out from behind his counter, his head barely came up to Max's chin. His ears stuck out from his head like wings spread for takeoff.

"Don't take this the wrong way," said Max. "But don't people around here stare—"

"I don't usually get visitors," the little man snapped. "Most people *can* read the sign on the door."

"We're looking for information . . ."

Max's words were lost in a sudden gust that forced her to stumble backward. The front door blew open, and Max was pelted with a storm of shoe scraps. This must have been the poltergeist Mrs. Amsel had warned her about. It had blown the little woman right out the door, but Max wasn't Mrs. Amsel. She stood her ground, even though it meant she had to dodge a flying shoe or two.

"I'm . . . not budging . . . ," cried Max, shouting to be heard over the gale. "You awful . . . little . . . *shoe-elf*!"

All at once the wind ceased and a hush fell over the cobbler's shop. Though Max couldn't see the air spirit, she could feel its presence. Something was hanging about nearby, tense and expectant, like a child watching his parents fight. Judging by the shocked look on the cobbler's face, Max had just gotten in a zinger.

"I am *not* a shoe-elf!" the cobbler sputtered. "I am an elfling who happens to like fixing shoes. It's a hobby!"

"I really don't care who you are," said Max, brushing the dust off herself as best she could. "As long as you call off your attack wind, I'll leave you alone. *After* you answer a few questions."

"How do you know I won't sic my wind on you again?" said the cobbler. "Only, maybe this time I'll let it bite!"

Max swallowed. The truth was, she didn't know what

the cobbler might do; she was going on gut instinct here. That and a little bit of hard-earned experience.

"I guess you could do that," she said. "But it seems a lot more trouble than it's worth. Plus, I've never met an elf or elfling that mean."

The cobbler snorted. "Then you obviously haven't met that many."

As if summoned, Mrs. Amsel peeked through the open door. "Everyone getting along in here?" she asked sweetly.

Max kept her eyes on the cobbler. "You can knock me down or blow me right out of your shop, but I'll just come back in. Lock me out, and I'll knock so loud the whole village will come to see what the racket is."

The cobbler leveled a sour look at Max, then walked to the window and peered out. "Fine. But come in, the both of you, and shut the door. I don't want anyone else thinking I am open for business."

Mrs. Amsel stepped inside and closed the door behind her, but she didn't move any closer.

Every now and then Max could feel a tiny breeze blow past, like a dog sniffing her fingers.

The cobbler hopped back onto his stool so that he was more or less at eye level with Max. "So, what's your name, then?"

"Max."

"And there's your first mistake," said the cobbler, pointing a crooked finger at her. "Never give your true name to one of the Folk. Ever. Didn't your old lady elfling teach you anything about our kind?"

Mrs. Amsel tsked and shook her head. "Such rudeness," she murmured. "These country elflings are so superstitious."

"So, I guess that means you won't tell me *your* name," said Max.

Smugly, the cobbler shook his head. "No."

"Then I guess you're more afraid of me than I am of you." This part wasn't exactly true, especially not with an invisible spirit guard sniffing around her, but she wasn't about to let this tiny shoe-elf know how nervous she was.

The cobbler squinted at her for a moment, then leaned back on his stool. "What do you want to know?"

Max reached inside her backpack and took out a map. It wasn't just any map—this map was unique. In fact, there wasn't another one like it on *two* worlds. As she unrolled it across the cobbler's counter, she watched his expression. At first glance, it looked like a simple map of the Atlantic Ocean separating Europe and North America. But then, when you looked a little closer, you saw odd differences. The shapes of the landmasses were correct, but the usual borders of the nations had been redrawn and given names like *The Lost Duchy of the Gray Wild*. Where Belgium should be, it read *Here Once Dwelled the Hoofed Folk*. An arrow pointed across the ocean, with the words *West to the Winter Children*.

The Peddler's map, as it was called, was enchanted. It revealed what you needed to see, or where you needed to go. On the Summer Isle, it had shown Max and her friends the whole magical island. After Max returned to Hamelin, the map had shown her the world pretty much as it was, and seemed to be telling her that she needed to travel back to the States, to New York City. Lately the map had begun to change yet again, as it became a map of a world that no longer was. It revealed a world of magic that was long gone. It was a map of ghosts.

"Where did you get this?" breathed the cobbler, his eyes wide.

This was the part of Max's story that was hardest to tell. "I got it when I was on the Summer Isle," she said quietly. "My brother and I were kidnapped by the Pied Piper and taken there."

"The Piper of Hamelin?" asked the cobbler. "Like the story?"

"He's not just a story. Eight hundred years ago he stole Hamelin's children, and last month he came for my brother and me. Even though it's been centuries here in our world, on the Summer Isle the children of Hamelin are still just kids. Time doesn't really work there."

"Even if what you say is true, what would the Piper want with you?" asked the cobbler, and he glanced worriedly out his window. He probably thought Max was putting him in danger by just being there, and the truth was, she might have been. There was much still that she didn't understand about the Piper's plans.

"I don't know. We were in Hamelin because my dad was searching for some kind of lost story about the Piper, so maybe that had something to do with it. Maybe it got his attention or something. All I know for sure is the Piper came for us in Hamelin, and we woke up on the Summer Isle. Then the Piper used my brother to free himself from prison. I escaped, but Carter's still back there with the rest of the Hamelin children. When I got back, my father had gone missing. We can't reach my mother in New York, and I'm afraid someone has taken her, too, and I . . . I just want my family back."

Mrs. Amsel stepped up behind Max and gave her shoulder a reassuring squeeze. "Such a strong girl," she whispered.

The cobbler looked at Max for a few moments with unmistakable disbelief. Then he looked past her to Mrs. Amsel. "The Summer Isle? Can it really be?"

"It's true," she said, with a sad nod.

"But the land of magic has been lost to us for centuries," said the cobbler. "No one has crossed between the Summer Isle and this world since . . ."

"Not since the Pied Piper stole the children of Hamelin away," said Mrs. Amsel. "And left the Winter Children in their place. Not for nearly eight hundred years."

"He's back," said Max. "And this time he plans on stealing away *all* the children of earth, if he can. He was going to use a magic mirror, like a portal, to do it, but my brother stopped him. Carter smashed it to pieces just after I fell through. . . ." Max looked away and bit back the memory. "That's how I ended up here and Carter got trapped there. It should have been the reverse. It should have been me."

Even though Mrs. Amsel had told her time and again that it wasn't her fault, it still felt to Max that it was her failure that her little brother was alone. No, he wasn't alone. He had friends with him; he had Lukas, Emilie and Paul, all children of Hamelin. He even had Leetha, last child of the elves on the Summer Isle.

But he didn't have Max. He didn't have his big sister,

who'd looked after him his entire life, even on those occasions when he was a complete and utter pain in the backside, which was pretty often.

"Even if you are telling the truth," said the cobbler, "what can I do for you?"

"We've heard rumors," said Max. "A few of the other elflings we visited let some things slip before they kicked us out." She felt the air around her stir in agitation, and the cobbler held up his hand.

"It's all right now," he said to the invisible air. "Shush. Why don't you run along and play outside. Go on, now."

A breeze swirled around Max's head, whipping her hair in front of her face. Mrs. Amsel cried out in surprise as the door flew open and then slammed again. The inside of the shop was still. Despite the three of them, it felt empty somehow.

"He has been with my family for generations," explained the cobbler. "A minor air elemental who didn't make the journey to the Summer Isle when the Great Winds and the rest of his kind left this world. As the cities spread and the air grew dirty, my great-grandfather took him in, and he has looked after us ever since. Protective, but he can get overly excited."

"Like a family dog," said Max.

The cobbler actually chuckled. "Not nearly as much trouble as a dog. The wind doesn't get fleas."

"Please," said Max. "We heard rumors about a door to the Summer Isle."

"The door to the Summer Isle is just a fairy tale elflings tell their children."

"Well, I've learned to put a lot more trust in fairy tales," said Max. "Believe me."

The cobbler sighed. "I don't know much about it, other than the door's connected to stories about the Winter Children."

Max gave Mrs. Amsel a questioning look, but the old woman shrugged. "Sounds right."

"But they do say the door is locked," said the cobbler, glancing around warily, as if they were sharing secrets on a crowded street. "And Vodnik has the only key!"

"Who's Vodnik?" asked Max.

"He's a magician. Maybe the last one."

"A magician? You mean the kind that pulls rabbits out of a hat, or the real kind?"

"I mean the kind that traffics in dark powers and is best avoided!" said the cobbler. "He offers people things, he does favors, but they always come at a steep price. Few have dealt with him, and all those have lived to regret it."

Max ignored the cobbler's warning. "Where can we find him?"

"They say he lives in an abandoned mill near the coast. But again, I wouldn't go looking for him if I were you. Not unless I had no other choice. And maybe not even then."

Max studied the Peddler's map laid out in front of them. Indeed, in a dark forest along the coast of the North Sea were the tiny words *The Magician's Mill*. She couldn't remember seeing them there before. The Peddler's map grew stranger and stranger.

"Thank you," said Max.

"Don't thank me," said the cobbler. "Because if you're

going to be dealing with Vodnik, then you were better off when you were dodging my shoes. The nicest thing I could have done would have been to kick you out onto the street and lock my door."

"Well," said Max. "Thank you anyway."

"Petrof," said the cobbler.

"What?"

"My name's Petrof."

Max smiled at the lumpy little shoe-elf. "It was nice to meet you, Petrof."

"One more thing," said Petrof the cobbler. "That is . . . if you don't mind."

"Okay."

"What was it like?" said Petrof. "The Summer Isle, I mean. I've heard the tales of it. Every elfling grew up on them. The sun that never sets, and the trees that sing you to sleep. Did you see such wonders?"

Max hesitated before answering. She had seen wonders, that was true, but in her estimation the Summer Isle was more terrible than wonderful. The days of seemingly endless summer could change to frigid night in a matter of hours, and monsters roamed the land. The Summer Isle was every child's dream, until it turned to nightmare. "I met some really great people on the Summer Isle," said Max, finally. "And some of the worst. So, in that way, I guess it's a lot like any other place. It's funny how quickly strange can seem normal, huh?"

The answer seemed to satisfy the cobbler, and he nodded and bid them goodbye and a safe journey. As Max followed Mrs. Amsel out of the shop and into the fresh air, she watched a plastic bag blow in lazy circles along the street and wondered if it was just a breeze or an air elemental at play. A pair of crows perched on a nearby power line and cawed noisily at each other. The strange had become normal, and the normal had become strange.

She lingered there for a moment, then stepped back into the shop. She'd lost something on the Summer Isle, and it was about time she found a replacement.

"Well?" called the cobbler, without looking up. "You staying or going?"

"Going," answered Max. "But just one more question—are any of your boots for sale? I'm looking for a girl's size seven."

CHAPTER TWO

On the Summer Isle, for as long as any creature could remember, nearly every day was as hot as July. The trees stayed lush and green, and the flowers bloomed. In the evenings the sky would dim to early twilight, but the sun wouldn't go down. It hung low and orange until dawn, when it would rise again and resume its trek across the blue sky.

The Winter's Moon had always been the exception. On certain rare days, the seasons changed in a matter of hours, and that evening the sun would sink, exhausted, beneath the horizon and a cold moon would rise to take its place. True darkness would fall, and the land would suffer a single night of winter. Those nights could be deadly.

But dawn always came and the trees always blossomed, and by midday the near-constant summer would rule again. That had always been the magic of the Summer Isle, but now that magic was breaking. Summer was over, and autumn had come at last.

Carter and his companions stood in the middle of a young bonewood grove only days old and gazed down at the cause of the breaking. A pile of freshly upturned earth marked the Peddler's grave, and somewhere beneath the ground, his bones now fed a lone skeletal tree. An odd assortment of knickknacks, the odds and ends that had once stuffed the Peddler's pack near to bursting, hung in the branches, like ornaments on Christmas morning. A broken birdcage here, a lute with no strings dangling over there. It was a sorrowful grave marker for a person who'd sacrificed everything for the good of others.

For ages the Peddler's magic had kept the wildness of the Summer Isle in check; the Peddler's Road marked the boundaries evil dared not cross. Once, long, long ago, the Peddler and the Pied Piper had been close friends, teacher and student. But then the Piper kidnapped the children of Hamelin, stealing them away to the Summer Isle, and the Peddler had been forced into battle with his old pupil. Aided by the Princess of the Elves, the Peddler imprisoned the Piper inside a black tower as punishment for his crimes. Ages passed, and the Piper continued to scheme, even from within his dark tower cell. By making use of an enchanted mirror, he brought Carter and Max to the Summer Isle. He believed the siblings to be the descendants of the one child of Hamelin who'd been left behind. There was power in that bloodline, a prophecy that could return the children of Hamelin home and free him from his centuries-old captivity.

The Peddler went to battle once more, to help Max and the small band of New Hameliners rescue Carter from the Piper's clutches. They'd succeeded, but at great cost. Now Max was home, and Carter was stuck here on the Summer Isle along with the children of Hamelin. The Piper was free of his prison and the Peddler . . . the Peddler was dead, murdered on this very spot by the witch Grannie Yaga. The whole Summer Isle mourned the loss. The July days were gone, and the green leaves on the trees bled to orange and red. A chill wind blew even at noontime, and the past few evenings had grown so dark that the sun was hardly more than a dull pink glow in the west.

After untold centuries, the Summer Isle was changing.

Despite Leetha's warnings, Carter and his friends had made the dangerous journey to this new bonewood grove, to see the Peddler's grave for themselves. Though Carter had never actually met the old magician, Lukas revered him. Even Emilie and Paul seemed pained by his loss. Carter suspected that they'd hoped to find a miracle here, some evidence that the Peddler had survived his battle with Yaga. But all they'd found was the spot where he'd fallen, where the roots of the bonewood trees had sunk in deep, and the contents of the Peddler's pack were strung up like mementos.

Paul had wanted to set fire to the whole wood, though it seemed wrong to Carter to burn down trees out of spite, no matter how ugly. He couldn't believe that the trees themselves were malevolent, even if the witch who had planted them was.

But as it turned out, they had no time to debate burning

the grove because, as Leetha had feared, their side trek to visit the Peddler's grave had taken them dangerously close to rat territory. And the rats had picked up their trail.

As they climbed the hills that sheltered the new bonewood grove, they spotted the rats crossing the open moors less than a few hours' hike behind them. The rats of the Summer Isle weren't like rats back home. They were as big as a person and nearly as smart. Some even fought with knives. But they usually hid during the bright light of day, preferring to scavenge in the dimmer evenings. These rats, however, were traveling fast in the open sun, which meant they were hunting something, or someone.

As the six companions stood silently in the middle of the bonewood grove, Lukas, Emilie and Paul bowed their heads and paid their respects to the deceased magician. Leetha, the elf princess, kept her knives drawn and her eyes on the trail behind them, alert for the slightest sign of their pursuers. Carter hugged his arms around himself and wondered how long they had before the rats caught up with them. And Bandybulb wouldn't shut up.

It was by pure luck that they had stumbled upon Bandybulb. They'd found the furry kobold wandering the hills lost. Carter and Bandybulb had been prisoners together in Grannie Yaga's hut; after Yaga's hut was destroyed in her battle with the Peddler, Carter had feared he'd never see the kobold again. Now he was starting to wish that had been the case. Bandybulb liked to talk, and from what Carter could tell, he liked to talk exclusively about two things—the greatness of his king Tussleroot, and the obvious.

"If the rats find us, they will stab us with pointy things

until we stop moving," said Bandybulb. "Everyone knows this, yes?"

"Shh," whispered Carter. "Show some respect."

But Leetha glanced back over her shoulder. "The kobold's not wrong. We can't stay here much longer."

"If great King Tussleroot were here, I'm sure he could fend them off with his battle prowess," said Bandybulb. He pointed to Paul. "But all that boy has to fight with is a frying pan, which is best saved for cooking."

Paul cut the kobold off with a look, but it was true. He had lost his bow, and all he had to fight with was a cast-iron pan. Of course, Carter still had his little carving knife, but if there was one thing he'd learned on this adventure it was that he wasn't much of a fighter. That had been his sister's area of expertise. Except for Leetha, they were all fairly defenseless. And wasting time.

"It doesn't matter how fast we run," said Lukas. "The rats have our scent by now. I'd hoped that we'd find . . . help here. I didn't want to believe that the Peddler was really gone."

Emilie put her hand on Lukas's shoulder. "He didn't die in vain, but it will have been in vain if we don't escape the rats."

Lukas took a deep breath and wiped his eyes. "Leetha, you summoned the great North Wind to carry us away from the Piper's tower. Is there a chance he owes you another favor?"

The elf girl shook her head. "I'm afraid not. The only way we are escaping the rats is on our own legs."

"We can't outrun them," said Lukas. "We have an hour's

head start at the most, but they are quicker over land. And this grove isn't dense enough to lose them in."

"Will we have to fight them?" asked Emilie.

"I hope not," said Lukas. "We're not up to it."

Carter might not have been a fighter, but he *was* a problem solver. If they couldn't fight the rats and they couldn't outrun them, then there had to be a third way.

"Well, is there any place we could lose them in?" asked Carter. "Any place we could reach in an hour?"

Lukas and Paul exchanged a look. "There's the Chillwood just to the east of these hills," said Paul. "Doubt even the rats would venture in there."

Leetha barked out a laugh. Sometimes—most of the time, actually—Carter didn't get the elvish sense of humor.

"What's the Chillwood?" asked Carter.

"A cold, wet forest that'll freeze your toes off on a hot summer's day," said Paul. "Cursed place."

"Okay, sounds awful," said Carter. "But is it worse than fighting the rats?"

Leetha snorted. "The rats *would* be fools to follow us into the Chillwood, just as we'd be fools to go there in the first place."

"No, Carter's right," said Lukas. "Reaching the Chillwood before they catch us won't be easy, but we should try."

Carter knew what Lukas wasn't saying was that it would be doubly hard to escape the rats with him along. The others could at least run, but with his bad leg the best Carter could hope for was a fast limping walk. And that was on even ground, not these rocky hills.

Emilie pulled her shawl closer about her shoulders. "The

woods *might* be dangerous, but we *know* the rats are deadly. I say we do as Carter suggests."

Leetha the elf girl said nothing but nodded slightly, her wide eyes watching them all with something like amusement.

"Then we make for the woods," said Lukas. "We'll have to hurry."

This Chillwood forest sounded like one of the last places Carter wanted to visit, and yet now he and his friends were racing for it like barefoot children running for the ocean across hot sand. Lukas stayed near Carter, even though Carter's leg brace slowed him down. At Lukas's insistence, Paul scooped up Bandybulb and let the little kobold ride on his back, while Bandybulb shouted in Paul's ear what a fantastic sprinter King Tussleroot was.

Twice as they were fleeing, Carter's leg brace caught on some hidden rock, and Bandybulb was right there after Carter tripped, the lumpy little creature staring down at him.

"You fell over!" Bandybulb would say.

"You think?" Carter would respond through gritted teeth.

"Yes," Bandybulb would reply innocently. "I do."

This would usually be followed by the kobold's sage wisdom, passed on to him by his lost king Tussleroot (never mind that Bandybulb was his king's only servant and that the kingdom consisted of a five-foot by five-foot patch of toadstools). "You know what my wise king Tussleroot used to say about falling down?" Bandybulb would ask.

"It teaches us to get up again?"

"No, it is painful and best avoided."

The one consolation of being caught—if the rats caught up with them—at least, Bandybulb would become someone else's problem.

After an hour's hard march, they reached the outskirts of the forest known as the Chillwood. One could feel the unnatural cold radiating from the evergreen forest as a sickly mist hung over the treetops, subjecting everything beneath it to the constant drizzle of icy rain. Stepping beneath the branches was like opening a freezer on a balmy July day. The climb through the hills and subsequent sprint to the forest had left the children sweaty and overheated, and so at first the drastic drop in temperature came as a relief. As they passed beneath the boughs of the mighty fir trees, steam rose from their sweaty garments. Carter lifted his face to the sky and let the mist cool his burning cheeks.

Paul led the way as usual, scouting the trail ahead as the rest of them followed a few paces behind. Usually Lukas stayed near Carter, and Carter suspected that his sister had made the young Captain of the Watch promise to watch over him. At ten years old, Carter was the youngest, but he still resented being treated like a little kid. The rest of them looked no older than thirteen, and Leetha looked even younger, with her spindly legs and wide eyes. Carter had to constantly remind himself that these children were almost eight centuries old.

If the rats had dared to follow them into the Chillwood, there was no sign of them. Lukas now spent most of his time alongside Emilie. Carter had caught the two of them whispering to each other when they thought no one was paying attention, and by the looks on their faces, whatever they were discussing was serious. With Paul scouting ahead, and Emilie and Lukas conferring, that left Bandybulb or Leetha for Carter to walk with. Carter chose Leetha.

Leetha was a daughter of the elves, but other than the pointed ears, she wasn't what Carter had expected. She was small and earthy and dark, with hair of tangled leaves and clothing spun from vines. Her face was broad and childlike, but her eyes shone in the dark like a cat's, and when she smiled, she showed long, pointed teeth. This wasn't an elf from the movies; this was an elf of old folktales—the kind that stole away naughty children in the woods.

"Have you had your fill of looking at me?" asked Leetha.

Carter blushed. He hadn't realized he'd been staring so openly at the girl. "Sorry," he said. "I've just never seen a real-life elf before. Only stories."

"What do the stories where you come from say about us?" She cocked her head at Carter, curious.

"Well, in some of them elves are great warriors. In others they are mischievous, even dangerous."

Leetha nodded, as if this were as obvious as the sky is up and the ground is down.

"That's some of them," said Carter. "In others the elves are helpful."

"How so?" asked Leetha.

"Well, some make shoes and others make toys."

Leetha burst out laughing. She guffawed so loudly

that Lukas had to tell her to quiet down, while Bandybulb complained that no one had let him in on the joke. Eventually, once she'd wiped the tears from her eyes and managed to catch her breath, Leetha tried to explain.

"If you asked an elf of the Summer Isle to make you a toy," she said, "you'd end up tied by your toes to a tall tree branch and dangled as ogre-bait. But you are a very funny boy."

"I see," said Carter, although he really didn't. "Can I ask you a question?"

"I cannot laugh so hard again this soon," said Leetha, holding her stomach.

"It's not a joke," said Carter. At least, he hoped it wasn't. "I just wanted to know why you're coming with us. You helped rescue me from the Black Tower, and I'm really thankful for that, but you . . . ah . . . you don't seem to like people very much. No offense."

The smile drained from Leetha's face, and for a panicked moment Carter was afraid that he had offended her. What did elves do when you upset them? It couldn't be anything good. But when Leetha spoke next, there was no anger in her voice. "I was here when the Piper first brought the children of Hamelin to the Summer Isle, remember. *One hundred and thirty children, led away by a piper into a mountain.*"

"That's a line from the legend back home," said Carter.

"It isn't legend here. Here it is tragedy. When the Piper stole the children of Hamelin away from your world, he stole the children of the elves, the Winter Children, away from the Summer Isle. But he missed one."

"You."

"Me. So, you see, as the last daughter of the elves, I have an interest in you, the last son of Hamelin. For I, too, have heard the prophecy."

The prophecy again. Once, long ago, the Peddler had stolen a prophecy from a witch, which he in turn traded to Lukas for a joke. The prophecy said: *Only when the last son of Hamelin appears and the Black Tower found will the Piper's prison open and the children return safe and sound.*

Carter had memorized it, because just about everyone he met here on the Summer Isle believed that he was this last son of Hamelin. Certainly the Piper had believed it, or at least believed that Carter was the direct descendant of the boy who'd been left behind. The two were similar in temperament and in appearance, right down to the same useless clubfoot. For a while, Carter had even believed in the prophecy himself, had enjoyed thinking himself special, but now he knew better.

He'd learned that the Piper had stolen the children of Hamelin as revenge for being banished from the village as a small boy because the people there thought him the son of a witch. There was no grand purpose at work here, just one person's spite, which had caused the suffering of hundreds.

"I wouldn't put my trust in prophecies," said Carter. "You might not have noticed, but the children of Hamelin are all still trapped here on the Summer Isle. All I ended up doing was freeing the Piper for nothing."

Leetha watched him for a moment. "Maybe I just want to see what happens next."

The children continued their hike through the forest, but all talk died away as their clothes, still sweaty from the running, chilled their skin. They wrapped themselves in heavy wool cloaks from their packs, but the ever-present drizzle wouldn't allow them to dry off, and the cold stole into their bones.

It wouldn't matter whether they escaped the rats if they all succumbed to hypothermia. It wasn't long before they were wondering aloud, through chattering teeth, whether it would be safer to turn back, even though the rats could be waiting for them. The trail continued to wind deeper into the forest, and the farther they went the colder it turned, until the trees became heavy with dripping icicles and the drizzle thickened to sleet. Lukas and Paul searched for firewood as they went, but everything in this forest was too sodden to burn. When Carter looked over at Paul, he saw that their scout's lips were turning blue.

Carter became painfully aware that even if they turned back now, they would not make it out of the forest before the cold overcame them. They'd marched for hours beneath the heavy branches, and it would take just as many hours to march out again—only the trek back would be harder. Carter could no longer feel his fingers or toes, and his teeth were chattering so hard that he worried they would crack in his mouth. That, at least, was good. He'd read somewhere that if you were still shivering, then you weren't yet freezing to death. Not yet. They needed shelter and dry wood for a fire, or else they were all going to die here in the Chillwood. And it had been Carter's great idea to risk this forest.

In the end, it was Bandybulb the kobold who saved them all—or rather it was the kobold's stomach.

They'd come to a fork in the trail, and by this time they were all so frozen and miserable that no one could tell which trail led deeper into the forest and which might lead them out. Paul wanted to sit down and rest, but Lukas and Carter propped him up. To sit down in this weather would be dangerous. You might not get up again. It was Emilie who noticed the kobold had gone missing. The Chillwood had quieted the little creature, and Carter had forgotten all about him.

"Bandybulb!" called Emilie as she squinted at the trees. It was hard to see anything in the unending sleet. She called for him again, and this time they all heard his tiny voice, like a squeak box, answering from somewhere nearby. He was hungry, he called back, and would anyone mind if he stopped off for a quick meal?

Carter and his friends looked at each other, incredulous. Had the small-brained creature gone delusional from the cold? Carter had the worrying image of Bandybulb lying in the mud, freezing to death as he ate his hallucinatory dinner.

Lukas helped Paul along as the four of them left the trail to search for Bandybulb. They followed the sound of his voice as the kobold described the meal set out before him: mushroom soup and a loaf of warm berry-bread. And cider. Piping hot cider.

When they found him, he was not lying in a puddle, nor was he freezing to death. Quite the opposite. Bandybulb was standing in the doorway of a hovel that had been built into the roots of a giant fir tree. Light and warmth spilled out through the doorway, and Bandybulb stood there with a checkered dinner napkin tied neatly around his neck. His lips were sticky with honey and his cheeks were stuffed full.

"Oh! I'm sorry," he said, crumbs tumbling out of his mouth and all down his front. "Did you want some, too?"

CHAPTER THREE

Unlike most of his friends, Carter had no trouble sitting upright without banging his head on the ceiling of tangled roots and hard-packed soil. He could even kneel if he'd wanted to. All four of them had had to crawl inside the kobold burrow on hands and knees, but it was warm and it was dry and it was filled with surprisingly good smells for a hole in the ground.

They huddled together in a chamber the kobolds generously called the Great Hall, even though it barely fit the five children. A small stew pot hung over a tidy little fire pit dug into one wall. The fire itself was hardly more than kindling, but the walls of the burrow were so compact that the warmth stayed put, even as the smoke escaped through a small chimney vent up top. A kobold family lived in this burrow, and the mother and father waited on Bandybulb while casting suspicious glances at the children who'd invaded their home. Out of politeness, they'd offered food to Carter and his friends, but Carter stopped the rest from accepting. Five normal-sized stomachs would probably clean the tiny cupboards bare. The shelter and the warm fire were enough.

Several young kobolds peeked out of an adjoining tunnel that led to the back rooms, rooms far too small for even Carter to fit into. He winked at the little ones, and they shrieked in delight before scurrying away.

"We want to thank you again for opening your home to us," said Emilie as the father kobold cleared Bandybulb's plate away. He nodded, but said nothing.

"Bandybulb could sniff out a kobold home in a field of troll dung," said Bandybulb. He rubbed his round tummy and let out a little belch. "I thought you all could smell it, too, and just chose to ignore it."

"And why would we do that?" asked Paul.

Bandybulb scratched his head in thought. "You were enjoying the weather?"

Paul looked like he wanted to throttle the little creature, but Carter put a hand on the boy's shoulder. The thing about Bandybulb was that the creature was unusually honest for a kobold. Dim, but honest. If he said that he thought they were enjoying the freezing wet cold, then he meant it. Sarcasm was as alien to him as two suns in the sky.

"Bandybulb," said Carter. "While we were stumbling along in the cold, were there other kobold burrows on the trail that we passed by?"

"Three or four," said Bandybulb, nodding agreeably.

Paul put his head in his hands. "We almost froze to death out there," he murmured.

"The Chillwood is thick with kobolds near the out-skirts," said Bandybulb. "Many fewer the farther in you get."

"On account of the witch," said the little kobold wife, speaking for the first time.

Carter sat up straight. He could feel the others tensing as well. "What witch?"

The kobold wife blinked at Carter and tugged worriedly at one furry ear as she spoke. "Roga of the Wood. This forest is her home."

"Another witch?" asked Lukas.

Leetha snickered and shook her head. "You humans. Don't you listen to your own stories? There's *always* a witch in the woods."

"Roga and Yaga are sisters," said Bandybulb.

"How do you know that?" asked Paul.

"Bandybulb spent many days in Yaga's cage, and Yaga talked about her. She said terrible things about Roga that Bandybulb won't repeat. She sounded terrifying. I don't think they like each other very much."

"Well, she's of no concern to us," said Lukas. "If she haunts the Chillwood, then the sooner we leave it the better off we'll be."

"And then what?" asked Emilie. "If we escape the forest, and the rats who were following us, where do we go? We haven't talked about that."

No one answered right away. Emilie's question hung over them all like the mist over this cursed forest. Carter and his friends had been fleeing so fast ever since their escape from the Black Tower that there hadn't been the time for asking that simplest of questions. What next?

Carter was surprised when he realized that everyone seemed to be focused on him. "What? Why are you all looking at me?"

"You spent time with the Piper," said Emilie. "Did he tell you what he plans to do next?"

"No," said Carter. "I mean, not since we shattered his magic mirror. Without it, there's no way he can leave the Summer Isle." Even as the words came out of his mouth, he knew they weren't exactly true. The mirror was broken, yes, but it wasn't the only magic that could transport the Piper between worlds. He hadn't needed it when he first stole the children of Hamelin away, those hundreds of years ago. All he'd needed then was . . .

"His pipe," said Carter, as it dawned on him. "That's what's next."

Lukas's face darkened. "You mean the one he played to lure us all out of Hamelin?"

Carter nodded. "He kept talking about it. I think the Peddler took it away from him when they fought."

"The Peddler told us it was well hidden," said Emilie. "But he didn't say where."

"Well, I'd bet you anything that the Piper's looking for it now," said Carter. "That's his next move."

"But how's he going to find it?" asked Paul. "The Peddler hid it, and the Peddler's . . . well, you know."

"Well, at least if the pipe remains hidden, he won't be able to do any harm with it," said Lukas. "He can't find it if no one knows where it is."

"Someone knows where it is," said Bandybulb.

Carter sighed. Now wasn't the time to get into a debate

with the literal-minded kobold about what *someone* meant. "We're saying that no one here on the Summer Isle, no one living, knows where it is, Bandybulb. Don't worry about it."

"But the witch knows," said the kobold.

Paul sat up so fast that he banged his head on the low ceiling. "Ow! What's he talking about? What are you talking about, Bandybulb?"

But Bandybulb's normally wide-eyed, innocent face wasn't looking at them. He was looking away as he scratched at his furry belly nervously. "Roga will know where the pipe is," he said. "Won't she?"

The other kobolds slowly nodded.

"Everyone knows Grannie Yaga has the gift to see the future," explained Bandybulb. "But her sister, Roga, has the gift to see the present. Nothing that happens on the Summer Isle is beyond her gaze. No person can hide, and nothing can be hidden. Roga sees all."

"So she can find the Piper's magic pipe?" asked Carter.

Bandybulb and the other kobolds nodded.

This new information was at once both frightening and exciting. If the Piper got hold of his lost pipe, then he would be more dangerous than ever. He could travel freely between the Summer Isle and earth, stealing away children by the hundreds. Centuries ago the villagers of Hamelin cast the Piper and his mother out into a harsh and brutal winter, and the Piper's mother died because of their act. Those villagers were long dead, but the Piper's quest for vengeance lived on, twisting until it became, Carter suspected, a kind of madness. If the Piper couldn't punish those grown-ups who'd hurt him directly, then he'd punish grown-ups everywhere.

That was the frightening part of Bandybulb's revelation. It meant that their fight against the Piper might not be over. But it also meant that there was still a way back. As long as the pipe existed, there was a chance that Carter and all the children of Hamelin could go home again.

Carter looked around at his friends and saw the same exhaustion and worry that he felt—it was etched into their faces in the dark bags under tired eyes, in the faces that had grown unaccustomed to smiling.

"If Roga could tell us where the pipe is, we could get to it before the Piper does," said Carter.

"Wait," said Paul. "You are not actually suggesting that we visit this witch on purpose. Grannie Yaga's *scarier* sister?"

"It's a reckless idea and will most likely get us all tossed into a cook pot or worse," said Emilie.

"Thank you," said Paul.

"But it might be our best choice," she added.

"What?"

"Think about it, Paul," she said. "Use that wool-headed brain of yours. If the Piper doesn't already know that Roga can find his pipe, he will soon. And if he gets to it before we do, then our mission was in vain."

"Our mission? Our mission was to find the Black Tower, and we did. We also found a whole lot of rats, the Piper, a witch and a *gray man*! Does anyone remember him? Raggedy old corpse that tried to kill Carter? Hmm?" Paul tried sitting up again and only managed to crack his head that much harder against the ceiling. Cursing, he sat back down again and rubbed his skull.

Carter certainly remembered the gray man. The wraith clothed in tattered rags that had appeared in the Piper's chamber. Of course he remembered. He worried that he would remember forever, no matter how hard he tried to forget.

"We can't pass up an opportunity like this," said Carter. "Tell him, Lukas."

But Lukas shook his head. "No."

"What do you mean *no*?"

"I mean it's too dangerous. We set out from New Hamelin to find the Black Tower, and we did that, for all the good it's done us." Lukas put a hand on Carter's shoulder. "I'm glad that your sister found her way home, I truly am, but the rest of us are still stuck here, and now so are you. I wish we'd never left New Hamelin."

"But the quest isn't over!"

"Isn't it? The map is gone, the Peddler is dead and the Piper is free from his prison. I'm sorry, but I think we've done enough damage."

"The Piper said that his pipe could open doorways between worlds," said Carter. "Don't you see? That could be the key to getting everyone home again!"

"What about the prophecy, Lukas?" asked Emilie. *"Only when the last son of Hamelin appears and the Black Tower found will the Piper's prison open and the children return safe and sound."*

"A prophecy that was made by a witch!" replied Lukas. "The same witch that murdered the Peddler. He stole the prophecy from her, and she murdered him for it. This entire quest, this stupid dream that I led us on, turned out to be a giant lie. We were tricked, and then Grannie Yaga got the Peddler and the Piper got free. There is no way we are trusting another witch."

"Lukas—" said Emilie, but the boy cut her off.

"No! You were right at the start, Emilie. We should have stayed safe behind our village walls. Tomorrow we make for New Hamelin. I'll get the rest of you back safely, and then I'm finished. Finn will make a better Eldest Boy than I ever was."

For a moment, Carter thought Emilie was going to say something more, but she shut her mouth and looked away. Lukas had convinced them all to go on this quest. More than anyone, more even than Carter, he'd believed in the prophecy and the chance for them all to return home. Carter hadn't realized until that moment what sort of guilt Lukas must be feeling now that everything had fallen apart. Not one of them blamed him, but that wouldn't matter so long as he blamed himself.

"So it's settled," said Lukas through gritted teeth. "We'll set out in the morning. Leetha, you can come with us, or you can turn south to your own people. The choice is yours." The elf girl nodded but said nothing, her face expressionless. "Now, we should all us of get some sleep."

No one argued that point, and Carter knew that Lukas wasn't about to change his mind. The five companions made themselves as comfortable as they could in the kobolds' cramped little home, and thanked them again for their kindness and hospitality. Carter slipped off his leg brace and massaged his twisted foot. It throbbed, the pain a constant protest against all the punishment he was putting his body through. But it was less than before, so he felt he might be getting used to being an adventurer. An adventurer whose adventure was coming to an abrupt end.

While the rest curled up on the warm floor, Carter spied one of the smaller kobold children, who was eyeing his leg brace curiously. When the kobold saw Carter watching him, the little creature turned shy and began scurrying back to her room.

"It's okay," said Carter quietly. "Here, you can look." He held out the brace for the kobold to better see.

She took a few steps closer and peered at the plastic-and-metal brace. "Armor!" she whispered, impressed.

Carter smiled. "No, it's not armor. It's just that my foot turns the wrong way. This brace helps me walk—that's all."

The young kobold reached out and touched the teeth marks up and down the side. Teeth marks left there by a rat's bite. She looked up at Carter questioningly.

"Well," said Carter, "I guess it did protect me that one time. But I was just lucky."

The kobold sniffed the brace and looked back at Carter. "Your armor," she said definitively, and then turned and disappeared into the tunnel-like hallway.

Carter held his brace up and examined the bite marks and the many scratches it had earned both back home and on this journey. In a way, his history was etched into that leg brace. In every nick and in every notch.

Your armor. That's what Emilie had called it once, too.

As Carter settled down to sleep, he tried not to think too hard about the witch and the chance they were passing up. But his mind kept drifting back to Max, and to their father. The last time Carter had seen his dad was back in Hamelin, before the Piper had come for them. But more recently Carter had seen something else, a shade, perhaps his father's dreaming self, in a village called Shades Harbor. Dreamers sometimes wandered there in their sleep, but so did spirits. Even now, Carter didn't know if the person he'd spoken to there had been his dad dreaming or . . . his father's ghost. He tried to banish that frightening thought from his brain and instead imagined his sister on a plane next to their dad, alive and well, flying back to New York. He imagined his mother waiting for them at the airport. He imagined it, and hoped with all his heart that it was true. Then, without meaning to, he imagined the look on his mother's face when they got off the plane and Carter wasn't with them. Would he ever see any of them again? Was there still a way?

His eyes popped open. He knew what he had to do. He needed to stay awake until he was sure the others were asleep. Then he would quietly gather his things and . . . No, it was best not to think too deeply about it, or he might lose his nerve. It would be better just to act.

Their quest wasn't over. The others might be dispirited, and Lukas might even have lost all hope, but not Carter. His armor was dented, but it wasn't broken.

❧ CHAPTER FOUR ❧

I t had started with glimpses of movement outside the hotel room window at night, or the sound of heavy foot-steps echoing their own as they walked down an empty street. Other times it was the distant silhouette of someone standing too still in the shadows.

Up until this moment, Max had only suspected that they were being followed, but now she was positive.

Despite the cobbler's warning and Mrs. Amsel's misgivings, they were bound for the coast of the North Sea to find Vodnik the magician. Though the stories about the magician frightened her, Max had been looking forward to the peaceful train ride without any poltergeists or spirits or elflings (except for Mrs. Amsel, of course). However, that was before she'd decided to take a stroll outside the Eurail station, and before she'd caught the stranger watching her from across the street.

He was hiding in the shade of a building, which prevented Max from getting a very good look at him. But she saw enough to recognize the long, frayed coat and the filthy boots. She'd seen those boots back in Hamelin—they belonged to the same mysterious man who had spied on her and her brother before the Piper stole them away. For a panicked moment, Max had thought that it was the Piper himself, and that he'd followed her back to this world. But though the Piper was centuries old, by appearances he looked no more than fifteen or sixteen, and was slight of build. This person was enormous, easily the largest man Max had ever seen. Back in Hamelin, Mrs. Amsel had dismissed him as just another vagrant wandering the streets, but there was no dismissing him now. A simple vagrant wouldn't have followed them halfway across Europe.

Max was about to go inside the station to find Mrs. Amsel when the stranger did something he'd never done before—he stepped into the light. Despite the summer heat, he had a hood drawn up over his head, hiding his face, and his hands were shoved deep into his pockets. He had to be close to seven feet tall. He was a literal giant, a giant who shunned the sunlight.

For a moment, Max felt his eyes upon her, even though she couldn't make out the face beneath the hood. Something small but important passed between them, like a whispered secret, and Max knew beyond any doubt that he was here for her. The stranger started forward, hesitantly at first as he kept his face hidden from sun overhead, but with growing confidence as he began dodging cars along the busy street. He was coming her way.

Max wasn't about to wait for him to reach her. She bolted for the station door, shouldering her way past commuters and ignoring their protests as she pushed by. The Eurail station here was small, with a few ticket counters and some benches arranged like church pews in the center. A woman's bored voice made announcements in French over a crackly speaker system. Max found Mrs. Amsel next to a ticket window, counting her change.

"Ah, there you are," she said. "I bought two one-way tickets to Wilhemshaven. I'm sorry, but I could only afford coach seats. I am only a housekeeper, after all."

"I don't care about the seats," said Max. "We have to get on the train, now!"

Mrs. Amsel took a step back as a look of concern washed over her face. "Ah, *meine Liebe*, what is the rush? The train does not leave for another five minutes."

"I saw someone watching me," said Max. "He was outside and he looked dangerous."

As if summoned by the thought of him, the stranger came striding into the station. Several people hurried out of his way, casting fearful looks at the seven-foot-tall hooded man wearing an overcoat in the middle of summer.

Mrs. Amsel noticed him immediately. "Oh my, that one? He does look like trouble."

Max slowly nodded as the stranger's hooded face turned this way and that, searching the station for her. "He's been following us since Hamelin."

"What? All this way? How do you know?"

"Remember the man in the shadows that Carter and I told you about? Well, that's the same man, I'm positive.

And I've seen him since. Just glimpses, but I think he's been trailing us this whole time."

"That man has been following us and you didn't say anything!" said Mrs. Amsel, her face aghast. "He could have snatched you up while my back was turned and I wouldn't have known anything. Ah, this is getting far too dangerous for one so young and reckless—"

Max interrupted her. "I didn't tell you because I knew you'd just do what you are doing now—lecture me!" She tugged on the housekeeper's arm. "Come on! We need to get on board the train. Now!"

Together Max and Mrs. Amsel started to weave their way through the crowd of people filing out of the station and onto the train platform. Mrs. Amsel offered apologies in German as they cut in line and stepped on people's feet, but Max kept her eyes on the tall stranger. He was moving along with them now, keeping pace even though he was still on the other side of the station waiting room. The crowd of passengers cleared out of the giant's path like water against a ship's prow. Still, Max and Mrs. Amsel had managed to cut their way to the front of the line, and suddenly they were out the door and onto the train platform.

Stepping from the air-conditioned station into the summer heat was like opening an oven door. They made it outside just as the train was coming to a stop, with a squeal of metal grinding on metal and the ozone smell of electricity and oil. Mrs. Amsel was surprisingly spry for her age, and she managed to keep up with Max as the girl bounded across the platform toward the nearest train door. They brandished their tickets at the conductor, but he held them back with an outstretched hand. The passengers were going to be allowed to disembark before Max and Mrs. Amsel could board.

Max watched impatiently as a line of businesspeople and a few families lumbered off the train, in no particular hurry. She heard Mrs. Amsel let out a little gasp, and she looked over her shoulder to see the giant, who'd emerged from the station and was striding right for them.

Surely he won't do anything to us with all these people around, thought Max. Then a thick-necked man with tattoos all up and down his muscled arms, who wasn't watching where he was going, collided with the giant on the platform. The tattooed man might as well have walked into a solid brick wall. He fell backward, dazed and holding his nose as the giant merely stepped by him. He didn't even slow down.

By now the hooded giant had gotten the conductor's attention as well, and the conductor glanced worriedly at him as he drew near. Max wasn't going to wait any longer. She shoved their tickets into the conductor's face and pulled Mrs. Amsel onto the train.

The giant was right behind them, but luckily the conductor took his job seriously. He stepped in front of the giant and, in French, politely asked him for his ticket.

This time the giant paused to glance down at the conductor. Max and Mrs. Amsel took the opportunity to grab a pair of seats in the second car, where they hunkered down by the window and watched and waited. The giant was looking from the conductor to the train and back again.

"I don't think he has a ticket!" whispered Mrs. Amsel, but Max worried that the giant wouldn't care about tickets.

He could just shove the conductor aside and board the train. Then where would they run to?

Go, go, go, Max thought, willing the train to leave the station.

The train's intercom came on and a bell dinged. The conductor hopped aboard just in time as the doors slid shut behind him. The giant stranger was left on the platform while the train started to roll away from the station. Max didn't think he could see her through the glass, but for the second time she felt those eyes. As he lifted his face to look for her, Max caught a glimpse of pale flesh under his hood.

Mrs. Amsel collapsed back into her seat, her hand pressed against her heart. "Oh, I am not made for such excitement!"

"Did you see the size of him?" said Max. "And the way he hid from the sunlight? I'll bet you he isn't even human."

"Well, he is not an elfling, that's for sure. We do not grow so big!"

"But why's he after us?"

Mrs. Amsel patted Max on the arm. "You say he only watched you and your brother back in Hamelin?"

"Yeah. I mean, we never got close enough to let him do much else."

"And he has been following us this whole way, always watching but never doing anything. So what is different about today?"

Max thought for a minute. What had changed?

"Vodnik," she said. "You think he doesn't want us to find Vodnik?"

"Could be. Why else would he come after us like that

in the open daylight and in a train station full of people?" Mrs. Amsel rested her head wearily against the window. "Whatever the reason, I hope we can put many kilometers between us and him. Meanwhile, I need to take a little nap."

The little woman shut her eyes and was soon snoring away, lulled to sleep by the hum of the train. Max watched the lush countryside fly by their window in a verdant blur as the train barreled north. She couldn't imagine falling asleep herself, but she was actually glad Mrs. Amsel was getting some extra rest. She worried about someone her age (and she claimed to be well over a hundred) running around like this. She worried about her, but she also knew that it was pointless to ask her to remain behind. The woman insisted on staying with her, and secretly Max was glad of it. As infuriating as she could be with all her fussing and lecturing, Max had grown quite fond of Mrs. Amsel over the past few weeks. With Max's parents missing and Carter trapped on the Summer Isle, the little elfling housekeeper was the closest thing to family that the girl had.

Max was glad of the company, because she felt certain that they would see their mysterious hooded giant again. The question that worried her was, could they reach Vodnik first?

CHAPTER FIVE

Poor Bandybulb looked miserable being out in the Chillwood when everyone else was sleeping, warm and cozy, by the kobolds' fire. The sky overhead might have been bright blue or purple twilight, but it didn't matter much in this mist-shrouded forest of pine trees. It was always gloomy in the Chillwood.

Carter had worried that Bandybulb would wake everyone with his complaining as they snuck out of the kobolds' home, but Carter needed some kind of guide if he was going to set off into the Chillwood, and the kobold seemed the most knowledgeable about the witch they called Roga of the Wood.

Finding her would be easy, claimed Bandybulb. Being a witch's wood, the Chillwood was a cursed place, and every path led to Roga if you followed it long enough. You never knew if her cave was just around the next bend, or if it was directly behind you. The witch was an ancient creature who had made her home here when the Summer Isle was young, and the Chillwood had grown up around her. The mist that clung to the trees was Roga's breath, the kobolds said, and the dripping ice was the blood of her veins, for she was the coldest of all witches, untouched by joy or laughter. Where Yaga might delight in a story or song, or in the hunt or the suffering of others, her sister found joy in nothing. Yaga plotted and planned. Roga simply *was*.

How Carter was going to bargain with such a creature was the part of his plan he hadn't figured out yet, but he hoped to think of something along the way. Odds were that the Piper would come calling on Roga sooner or later, looking for his lost pipe. And Carter felt sure that their only hope of defeating the Piper, and of getting home, was to find the pipe before he did.

In the dark, the forest looked more menacing than ever, and what little nighttime light made its way through the trees was caught and strangled by the foul mist. A heavy ground fog had settled in, and Carter could barely see where to place his own feet. He walked in fear of stepping in a ditch or sinkhole. His woolen cloak was already soaked again from the constant drizzle.

Bandybulb marched steadfastly behind Carter, but the gloom of the forest had even gotten to the normally loquacious kobold. Neither spoke, and there wasn't so much as a birdcall to keep them company—just sounds of crunching twigs beneath their feet. Carter started to worry about other dangers besides the witch—what if wolves hunted this forest? But these were fears he should have considered before sneaking away from the others, and it was too late now to change what he'd done. He was out here in the wood, and his protectors didn't even know it. So he gripped his little knife in his hand and kept on walking.

He was on the verge of telling Bandybulb that they should turn back when they happened upon a dank and dreary clearing. Carter thought forest glades were supposed to be bright and cheery, open patches where you could see the sky past the thick trees. But the clearing here only made the frigid drizzle heavier, and slushy puddles of mud and ice covered the ground, drowning the undergrowth. An enormous mound of rock and earth sat in the center of the frozen glade.

"What is that?" whispered Carter.

"Roga's barrow," answered Bandybulb.

"Her what?"

"It was once the tomb of an ancient king of legend, a king who was to return when his kingdom needed him the most."

"Is that true?"

Bandybulb shrugged. "It doesn't matter. Roga broke in ages ago and gobbled him up. She calls the barrow home now, surrounded by all his treasures."

"What a horrible place to live," said Carter.

"She cannot escape it," said the kobold.

"Is she under some kind of curse?"

"No," answered the kobold. "Over the years Roga has devoured many creatures; because of that she has grown very fat. Now she cannot fit through the door anymore. She is like a field mouse who crawled inside a bottle and can't get out again."

"If she's stuck in there, how does she still eat?"

"Her food comes to her," said Bandybulb, staring pointedly at Carter.

Carter shivered, and this time it had nothing to do with the weather. Grannie Yaga was a hunter. She'd used her enchanted hut to chase down her prey, but Roga was more like a fat spider in a web, waiting for flies. Carter couldn't decide which was more frightening. "Maybe we should take a closer look. If she can't get out, then I guess we'll be safe enough if we don't go inside."

Bandybulb nodded enthusiastically. "And when you are devoured, I will make sure King Tussleroot hears of your bravery."

"And where will you be?" asked Carter.

"Sitting here," answered Bandybulb. "Admiring your bravery from afar."

At the foot of the massive barrow was a small entrance, barely large enough to allow a grown man to enter if he stooped low. It was too dark to see inside.

Carter stepped cautiously into the clearing but stayed well back from the cave. Bandybulb had said the witch couldn't leave her lair, but Carter didn't want to take a chance that the kobold might have his information wrong. Bandybulb was Bandybulb, after all.

"Hello?" he called. At first there was no answer, no sound whatsoever from inside the barrow. But he *felt* something moving around in the darkness. It was a sense in the air, of something large shifting, not unlike the displacement of water when one shifts in the bathtub. It was followed by a loud scraping noise, the sound of something soft and flabby, like heavy flesh dragging across stone. The air coming out of that dark mound smelled like someone's morning breath.

"Who's come to visit Roga?" asked a husky voice from within the cave.

"I've come to ask Roga a question," Carter called back, his voice faltering a little. It was hard not to turn and run. He could feel the unspoken menace in the air.

Silence. Then, "Can't hear you very well, child. Come closer."

Carter could see Bandybulb in his peripheral vision standing at the edge of the glade and shaking his head emphatically, *no.*

Not that Carter needed to be told that. "This is as far as I'll come, I think."

Then something enormous drew near the cave entrance. Carter couldn't get a good look—it was too hidden by the deep shadows. But he did get a glimpse of pale mottled flesh before it retreated again into the lightless barrow, like a shark breaking the surface of some great dark ocean and then diving again. The barrow groaned and shook as something massive shifted inside of it.

Carter prayed that Bandybulb had been right. "I'm looking for the pipe of the Pied Piper. It's hidden, and I think you know where it is."

"And why should old Roga tell you?" the witch asked from the darkness. "I am the cold witch of the Chillwood, and I don't grant favors."

"Okay. What do you want in return?"

"Nothing you'd care to part with" came the witch's reply.

"There must be something," said Carter. "I was thinking that since you can't leave your cave, I could give you food maybe." He searched in his pack. "I have some salted pork."

"You are my food, boy."

"You know," said Carter, taking another step back for good measure, "I'm getting a little tired of people telling me how much they want to eat me. I heard enough of that in Grannie Yaga's hut."

"Yaga!" cried the witch. "What do you know of Yaga?" Her voice rose to such a fury that the barrow shook and Carter retreated yet another few steps, this time nearly slipping on a patch of hidden ice. The ground fog was getting so thick that he couldn't even see his own feet. But he couldn't run away, not before trying to get the information they needed.

"Grannie Yaga kept me prisoner," said Carter.

"And she didn't eat you? How like her, the skinny hag."

Of course. Roga and Yaga were sisters, the kobolds said. And these two had a sisterly rivalry in a way that only witches could. Carter wondered if he might be able to use it to his advantage now. He knew something about sibling rivalry.

"Well, obviously she didn't eat me," he said. "She gave me to the Piper instead."

Again Roga said nothing at first. There was only the sound of her enormous body shifting around. "Yes, I see her now. Poor dear's lost her foolish chicken hut. Serves her right. Piper's free as well! I suspect he'll be coming to see Roga, yes, he will."

"The Piper? Where is he?"

"Come into my cave and I'll show you."

This wasn't working. There was absolutely no way Carter was going to go into Roga's cave, and she had no desire to help him—her only interest in Carter was as a main course. His only hope lay in Roga's jealousy toward her sister.

"Yes, I can see the pipe now, in my mind's eye," she said. "Lovely little thing."

"You can't tell him where it is," said Carter.

"And why not? Perhaps he will play Roga a sweet tune and lure children to her cave! Oh, wouldn't that be a tasty treat."

"If you help him, you'll be helping Yaga," said Carter. "She gave me to him. She wants him free."

"Why would she want that?"

"I don't know," admitted Carter. "But I bet if I got to that magic pipe first, it would upset her. Drive her crazy, I'll bet."

"Clever boy," said Roga after a moment. "Perhaps I can see why Yaga didn't gobble you up right away. Wonder if she regrets it now. Must stick in the old hag's craw that you are running loose. Must annoy her something terrible!"

"Tell me where the pipe is and I promise I'll go on annoying Yaga as much as I can."

Roga's ugly whitish eye appeared at the doorway. "Let's put it to the test. I'll tell you where to look for the pipe, but whether you can use the information—well, that'll be the test."

"Okay," said Carter. Of course he could use the information. Once he knew for sure where the pipe was, then surely his friends would follow him.

"Go south," said the witch. "South to the coast. The pipe is hidden where it all began. The pipe is hidden in the isthmus of rock known as Magician's Landing."

Magician's Landing! Carter vaguely remembered the name from the Peddler's map. Though the map was lost, surely Lukas would remember it. He had memorized every detail.

"Thank you," said Carter, backing up. "And in return, I promise to be a royal pain in the butt to your sister every chance I get. I've had experience annoying siblings."

"Is that all you want to know?"

Carter paused. "What do you mean?"

"I have more secrets, boy. Would you like to hear some?"

"No, I don't think I—"

"The New Hameliners are still alive. The ones thought dead and gone are not."

Out of the corner of his eye, Carter saw Bandybulb waving at him to hurry up, but he turned back to Roga's cave instead.

"What are you talking about?"

"One hundred and thirty children were stolen from Hamelin by the Pied Piper, but there are far fewer today, yes?"

Lukas had told them over the years they'd lost New Hameliners to the rats. Leon, Marc. Carter had assumed that meant they'd been killed in battle, but maybe not.

"Are you trying to tell me that there are New Hameliners alive somewhere else? Outside of the village?"

"Oh, yes!" said Roga. "So many children lost to the darkness, and now in darkness they live, as slaves to the rat king. They wait for rescue, but they wait in vain. So come, boy, stay a while and chat with me and I'll tell you exactly where to find them. If I cannot eat you, then at least offer me a little conversation."

So the lost New Hameliners were alive? If Roga was to be believed, they were captives of the rats. Slaves.

"Okay," said Carter. "Where are they?"

"The rat king keeps them underground in his nest, in the mountains north of New Hamelin. Chained to do his bidding."

"But the rat king is dead." Though Carter hadn't seen it happen, he'd heard Lukas and Emilie talk of their fight with Marrow the rat king outside the doors to the Black Tower. That fight had ended with Leetha's knife in the rat's back.

From somewhere in her cave, Roga let out a low sigh. "The king may be dead, but a new rat sits on his throne, more dangerous than Marrow ever was. The king is dead, long live the king!"

Carter wondered how his friends would take this news. That their companions were alive was cause for hope, but he shuddered to think what their lives must be like as slaves, much less slaves of the rat king.

"Okay," said Carter. "Thanks, I guess. But I'd really better be going."

With a nod to the witch's cave, Carter turned—and fell on his face. He hadn't tripped, though; something had pulled him off his feet. He looked around, but all he saw was the drifting mist and mud.

"Lose your step?" called Roga. Carter didn't like the note he detected in her voice.

He started to pull himself up to his feet when suddenly something yanked him by the ankle. Tendrils of ground fog had wrapped themselves around his feet and were pulling him, slowly, inexorably, backward through the mud. He'd been right: Roga was a spider and this forest was her web. Now he was trapped in the center of it.

"Help! Bandybulb!" Carter tried to hold on to something, but all his fingers found was icy mud. The dutiful kobold appeared at his side, but when the little creature tugged at the misty tendrils, they were as tough as rope.

"Not so clever a boy as it turns out, eh?" called Roga. "Chats with Roga and keeps well clear of her cave, but all the time he forgets the most important thing—Roga is a witch, and witches know magic!"

Bandybulb was whimpering as he tugged fruitlessly at Carter's bonds. The kobold was loyal enough to get himself killed along with Carter. The mouth of Roga's barrow was only feet away now.

"Help!" Carter cried again. He tried to think, but he was panicking. He could hear Roga moving around in the darkness. She was making smacking noises with her lips.

Then there was a flash of movement, something so fast that Carter could hardly glimpse it, and his legs were suddenly free. From deep in the darkness, Roga bellowed in rage.

"Get up and run, human boy," said a voice in his ear, and Carter looked up to see Leetha yanking him to his feet. The tendrils of fog shrank back from her flashing knife.

"Wait! We can't leave Bandybulb!"

"Don't worry about him," said Leetha, and she shoved Carter forward as she pointed the way. The round little kobold was already well ahead of them and making for the forest as fast as his chubby legs would take him.

With Leetha's help, Carter stumbled out of the deadly clearing dragging his leg brace through the frozen mud. As he did so, he was vaguely aware of Leetha hacking at more shapes appearing out of the mist. But once they reached the safety of the trees, the mist began to dissipate. Still, they ran on until Roga's cave was well behind them.

"How'd . . . How'd you find me?"

"We elves are very light sleepers," said Leetha. "You were easy to follow."

"Then why didn't you stop me?"

Leetha shrugged. "I wanted to see what would happen."

"Well," said Carter, massaging his leg. "You saved my life. I owe you one."

At that, Leetha broke into a huge, pointy-toothed grin. "That's true! Ah, you poor boy. It's never good to owe an elf."

"Better than being witch food."

"We shall see." As Leetha smiled, her eyes glinted in the half-light. Like a cat eyeing its prey. "That was a very foolish thing you did, seeking out the witch all alone."

"Carter wasn't alone," squeaked the little kobold. "Bandybulb was there the whole time."

"A lot of good you did him," replied Leetha.

Bandybulb held out his stocky little arms and smiled up at her. "Perhaps Bandybulb should start to exercise. Then one day he can be strong like a girl elf!"

She rolled her eyes at the little creature. "Kobolds," she muttered.

"Leetha," said Carter. "You understand why I had to do it, don't you? Lukas has become just like Max, and now he's so worried about protecting me that he's not making the right decisions. I'm smaller than the rest of you and my foot is twisted all the wrong way, but I'm not fragile. I'm not made of glass!"

"I don't think you're fragile at all," said Leetha. "And size is relative. You're shorter than Lukas, but you are a giant to Bandybulb here."

"Oh, Bandybulb cannot but get dizzy when he looks up your nose, Carter, sir," said the kobold.

"But you won't win on your own," continued Leetha. "The Summer Isle is too dangerous to be without friends for long."

Carter thought he detected a note of sadness in the elf girl's voice. She'd helped to rescue him from the tower because that's what the Peddler would have wanted her to do. But he'd wondered why she chose to stay with them now. Finally, he thought that he understood. Leetha was the last elf child in all the Summer Isle, so how long had she been without friends?

"You're right," said Carter. "Thanks, Leetha. I mean it."

The elf girl nodded. "Come, let's gather up your kobold and get back. You, I suspect, are going to be in a lot of trouble, and I don't want to miss that!"

CHAPTER SIX

*L*ukas called a halt at midday, and Carter and his friends rested in the shade of an enormous troll hill. Like the troll bridge they'd crossed at the start of their journey, this massive mound of rock had once been a flesh-and-blood troll. But if the stone troll that served as a bridge over the Western Fork of the Great River had been enormous, this slumbering giant had been even bigger. And ancient. Great swaths of tough wind grass now grew along his top and sides, and the years of wind and rain had smoothed his features until they were almost indistinguishable from regular stone. If Emilie hadn't pointed out the overhanging shelf of rock that looked suspiciously noselike, Carter might not have believed that this was a troll hill at all. But here it was, a giant of ages past. Carter wondered if this one had been caught unawares by the daylight, or if he'd simply grown tired of hiding beneath the ground. Either way, today he provided welcome shelter for tired travelers.

After happily leaving the Chillwood behind, they'd followed the coast south along the sea. Leetha called it the Sea of Troubles, and it was an impressive sight. Like the rest of the Summer Isle, it was so much wilder and more beautiful than any sea back home. When the water was calm, it shone like blue-green glass, slowly undulating beneath the cloudless sky. When the tide was high and the wind picked up, waves the size of houses broke against massive stone reefs where schools of mermaids played. A few of the creatures dared to swim close when they spotted the travelers, and Carter, Lukas and Paul had to stop up their ears with their fingers to shut out the mermaids' siren song, while Leetha and Emilie stood at the water's edge and shouted insults at the mermaids until they gave up their singing and went off to frolic in the waves.

The sun reflected off the water, and beat down on their heads. Paul and Leetha found a freshwater stream not far from the coast where they filled up their water skins. Lukas made sure everyone drank their fill before leaving. Better to carry the water inside their bodies than out, he told them.

After two days' worth of scrambling over rocky beaches and navigating narrow cliffs, they could finally see the Peddler's Road in the distance, a winding path of cobblestones and dirt meandering south as far as could be seen. The road beckoned, but first they stopped to rest in the shade of the troll's nose.

Spirits had been low ever since Carter shared what Roga

had told him. The revelation that the Piper's pipe was hidden at Magician's Landing paled in comparison to the discovery that New Hameliners were being held by the rats as slaves. Lukas had taken it particularly hard, and Carter remembered that both Leon and Marc, the two Eldest Boys before Lukas—both of whom had disappeared mysteriously in the night—might have been among the captives. After hearing the news, Lukas had been too preoccupied to continue to scold Carter about sneaking away to find the witch in the first place, despite Bandybulb's insistence on telling everyone how close Carter had come to being eaten. Over and over again.

Carter couldn't help but feel responsible for the pall that had settled over the group, even though all he'd done was deliver the news.

As he leaned against the troll's stone nostril, he took his foot out of its brace and massaged it. It hurt, but not much more than every other muscle in his body. Still, it felt good to take his shoes off and let both his feet breathe a little.

Emilie sat down next to him and handed him a plate of hardtack bread and a few nuts. "Lunch," she said.

"Thanks," said Carter. "Not much left of our trail rations, is there?"

"Leetha will hunt again this evening, and she'll find something. Now that we're well south of the Chillwood, there's bound to be game about. It kills Paul that he can't go with her, but without his bow and arrows he'd be useless."

Carter nodded. "Can't really hunt with a frying pan, can you?"

Emilie gave a soft laugh. "Now, that is truly putting your cart before your horse."

Carter smiled. It was nice to hear someone laughing again. Leetha sat sharpening her knives while Paul absently poked holes into the dirt with a twig. Lukas used a piece of charcoal to sketch on an empty wineskin. Carter knew that he'd been trying to re-create the Peddler's map from memory. No one else was talking.

"Are they okay?" asked Carter quietly.

Emilie sighed. "It's been a hard couple of days for all of us. What the witch told you about our friends . . . It's difficult."

"But I thought you'd all be happy to hear they're alive."

"We are," said Emilie. "But you have to understand, we mourned for them long ago. There were those of us, Lukas included, who dreamed that they might not be dead, but no one really believed it. Now . . . it's an old wound picked open again."

Emilie dabbed at her eyes and took a deep breath. "I can't imagine what they have been going through all these years."

Carter took a bite of hard, stale cracker. Suddenly he understood what was really happening, why the New Hameliners had been so sullen these past few days. "You're going after them, aren't you?"

Emilie shook her head. "We would never take you into the rat king's nest, into such danger. Lukas made a promise to your sister to look after you."

"But you want to," said Carter. "All you want to do is go

back and save your friends." Carter hadn't realized it, but he was no longer talking quietly.

At this, Lukas looked up from his sketching, and Paul stopped fiddling with his sticks. All eyes were on him.

"You should do it," said Carter, addressing them all. "You should go save your friends, just like you saved me from the Black Tower."

"We are not dragging you into the mountains," said Lukas.

"You don't have to," said Carter. "I'll . . . I'll keep going south along the road. I can go to Magician's Landing alone. I want to."

"Forget it," said Lukas.

"You should listen to the boy," said Leetha. "If you are worried about him, then sending him south is the safest choice. The road leads into the Deep Forest, and to my princess's castle."

"The Deep Forest?" said Paul. "What do you think your elf friends will do with him when they find him wandering their forest? String him up by one foot or two?"

"They won't harm him if I'm with him," said Leetha.

Lukas paused. "What are you saying, Leetha?"

"I will go with Carter to the castle. There, we can ask the Princess for help; she can send a team of outriders with us to Magician's Landing. We will find the Piper's magic flute."

Emilie scoffed. "You asked your princess for help once, remember?"

Leetha turned her eyes on Emilie, and Carter felt the tension between the two girls. The elf princess was a sore spot for Emilie, though Carter didn't know why. "Things have changed since then," said Leetha.

"What? Now that the Piper's free she'll help?" said Emilie. "A little late, I think."

"The Peddler's dead," said Lukas. "That's it, isn't it?"

Leetha slowly nodded. "There was a bond between the Peddler and the Princess. Not exactly friendship but respect. They were allies, and she did not come to his aid."

Thus far Carter had only ever witnessed two emotions in the elf girl—calm and laughter. But now a flicker of something new passed across her face, something darker, and less human.

"A broken promise is powerful magic among my kind," said Leetha. "The Princess will have to help us now."

"Then we'll all go to the Princess," said Lukas. "We'll stay with Carter."

"What?" said Paul, standing up. "Didn't you hear what Leetha just said? She'll take him there; all they have to do is follow the road. There's no need for us to go, too."

Lukas stood now, too, and faced Paul, his expression serious. "I made Max a promise to keep her brother safe."

"And what about your promise to us?" said Paul. "What about your promise as Eldest Boy to keep New Hamelin safe?"

"That's Finn's responsibility now."

"No, it's yours. You're Eldest Boy whether you want to be or not. Not only are our friends being used as slaves, but there's a new rat king, and you can't tell me that this one's going to sit by and not try that village wall again. Maybe the next true night. He might have already done it! The whole village might be in irons for all we know and you're worried about *Carter?*"

"I didn't ask to be Eldest Boy!" shouted Lukas. "I never wanted it!"

"Who cares?" said Paul. "You are. It's your responsibility. You know, I've done a lot of silly things and I may get into trouble, but I've never tried to run away. Stop using Carter as an excuse because you're afraid to go back."

Suddenly Lukas turned around and punched Paul. Paul fell backward onto his butt, and the rest of them sat in stunned silence as he rolled to a sitting position and rubbed his jaw.

Lukas looked aghast at what he'd done. "Paul, I'm sorry," he said, offering the boy a hand up. "I didn't mean—"

Before Lukas could finish his apology, Paul grabbed his hand and yanked him to the ground. Then the two boys were rolling through the dirt, punching and cursing at each other. Leetha was laughing and Bandybulb covered his eyes and Carter thought they looked just like kids in a schoolyard fight.

"Oh, for heaven's sake!" said Emilie, and she reached down to pull the two boys apart. Someone, and it was lucky for that person that no one could say exactly who, threw back a fist to line up a punch . . . and hit Emilie square in the nose instead.

The girl stumbled backward but did not fall. If there had been silence when Lukas had struck Paul, it seemed that time itself had taken a pause now. Even Leetha's laughter dried up in an instant, and the elf girl looked at Emilie, wide-eyed and almost fearful.

The two brawling boys leaped off each other and scrambled to their feet, tripping over each other in a race to apologize.

Emilie gingerly examined her nose as she blinked away tears. "You boys, ow!" She sighed. "Well, it does not appear to be broken."

Lukas and Paul stood at attention, their heads bowed. Carter had never seen such looks of terror on their faces, not even when they'd fought the rats.

"Emilie—" Lukas began, but Emilie cut him off with a wave of her hand.

"You be quiet," she said. "And you stop your smirking, Paul."

"But I'm not!" protested Paul.

"You are on the inside, so stop it," said Emilie. "Now, if all your empty-headed foolishness is done for the day, I want to hear from the one person that really matters in this debate. Carter, what do you want to do?"

The sudden shift of everyone's attention back to him was startling, but Carter took a breath and began. "I think Paul's right."

"Now wait a minute," said Lukas, but Emilie shushed him again.

"I don't agree with everything he said," added Carter. "But I do think you have a responsibility to New Hamelin that is bigger than your promise to my sister. You all saved me from the Black Tower. That's enough. And honestly, I'm tired of being treated like I'm just a kid, by a bunch of *other kids*!

"I'm going south to Magician's Landing," he continued.

"Leetha said she'd show me the way. I can't stop the rest of you from coming with me, but I think it would be a big mistake. You rescued me already; now there are other people who need your help."

Lukas stared at Carter for a moment. "Paul? Can you find a way across the moors west to the river?"

The other boy nodded. "And beyond into New Hamelin, or north to the mountains."

Lukas walked over and put a hand on Carter's shoulder. "I told you once that you reminded me of my best friend back in old Hamelin. It's true, and never so much so as right now."

"Thanks," said Carter.

"Emilie," said Lukas, "you can go with us or stay with Carter."

"I'm following Paul," she replied. Then, suddenly blushing, she quickly added, "Someone needs to keep him out of trouble."

"That settles it, then," said Lukas. "After lunch we'll say our goodbyes and head west. Carter and Leetha will go south to the Princess. Leetha, after you've found the pipe, if you can convince her . . . well, I think we could use help in New Hamelin. Our people are in trouble."

Leetha nodded. "I will do what I can. But I, at least, will come. I've grown quite fond of watching you humans quarrel."

"And, Carter," said Lukas. "We will meet again."

Carter smiled and nodded, but he found he couldn't quite get the words out to say a proper goodbye. He was too close to crying, and the last thing he wanted them to see was his tears. So he was shocked to hear sobs coming from nearby.

Bandybulb was crying noisily into a small rag that already needed a good washing.

"You're taking him with you, right?" asked Paul. "Please say you're taking him with you."

Grudgingly, Carter nodded, and Bandybulb let out a little shout of joy. Then the rest of them packed their things. Lukas and Emilie took the lion's share of the rations, since Leetha promised that she could hunt along the way. Bandybulb packed up a pile of small stones that he'd taken a liking to, wrapping them in the same snot-nosed rag he'd been using and tying the bundle to a small stick that he slung over his shoulder.

Soon there was nothing left to do but accept Emilie's hugs and the boys' pats on the shoulder, and then Carter watched the three of them hike off into the wilderness, until their backs were mere dots in the distance, and then they were gone.

"I was right, you know," said Leetha, coming to stand next to him. "Size is relative, and you, Carter, are very tall today. Very tall indeed."

Carter didn't say anything. Instead, he turned and put one foot in front of the other, and began walking south, with Leetha and Bandybulb by his side.

CHAPTER SEVEN

Max sat in the passenger seat of their rented car and stared out at the decrepit old mill, supposed home of Vodnik the magician. The dilapidated building stood precariously on the bank of the Elbe River, not far from the German coast of the North Sea. The whole building seemed to lean away from the land, as if it might soon sag into the river. Someone had once tried to warm the place up by adding a coat of paint—Max could still see the turquoise flakes peeling in places—but it would take more than paint to make the building look anything less than desolate. A dock extended from the building past the river's edge, where a great waterwheel turned with the slow draw of the river's current. Max wondered with a shiver if there was a giant stone-grinding wheel somewhere inside. The image of the empty wheel grinding away by itself unnerved her, because there was something so terribly lonely about this place already. She'd learned in her travels with Mrs. Amsel that what little magic was left in the world hid in seemingly abandoned places, but this was often just a facade. Like the cobbler's closed-up little shop, there was life inside. But this place wasn't a facade. If there was magic here in this old mill, it wasn't the kind that welcomed people. It was bitter and content to be alone.

"What a place is this?" said Mrs. Amsel, peering over the steering wheel. The little woman could barely reach the pedals. "Perhaps the map is wrong."

"The map is never wrong," said Max, but just this once she wished it would be. "Besides, doesn't this creepy old building look exactly like the kind of place you'd expect to find this Vodnik guy? Also, I think our notorious magician drives a Prius."

Max pointed to a small car parked in the shade of the mill's carport. "Someone's home, at least."

"I want you to be very careful," said Mrs. Amsel. "I think Vodnik is not to be trusted. Stay back and let me do the talking."

They got out of their car and trudged up the gravel driveway. A crow rested on a stump pecking at a piece of something nasty as it watched them approach. Since coming back from the Summer Isle, Max had decided she didn't like crows. She didn't like the way they looked at you—it was too . . . *familiar.* Like they knew something you didn't.

"Why don't you go back to your roadkill, you stupid bird," said Max, but the crow just kept staring as they passed by.

When they got close, Max spotted someone sitting in

the driver's seat of the little parked car. It looked like a man with his head resting on the steering wheel.

"Do you think it's Vodnik?" whispered Max.

"What's he doing sitting in his car?" asked Mrs. Amsel.

"One way to find out," said Max, and before the house-keeper could stop her, she walked over to the car and rapped on the glass.

Let Mrs. Amsel do the talking? thought Max. *Right.*

The man's head jerked up. Startled, he looked first at Max and then at Mrs. Amsel, and seemed to relax. When he got out of the car, Max saw he was broad-shouldered and dressed in well-worn work clothes, as if he'd just come off a shift doing construction work. His face was friendly, despite the worry lines etched there. He greeted them in German.

"Do you speak any English?" asked Max.

"English? *Naa,*" said the man, shrugging.

"You see?" said Mrs. Amsel, shouldering her way past Max. "You let me do the talking."

Mrs. Amsel and the man spoke quietly for a few minutes. The man looked nervous, and he kept stealing glances at Max, but then Mrs. Amsel did something unexpected. She took off her kerchief, exposing her delicately pointed ears. For some reason, that seemed to calm the man, and suddenly he was talking quickly and with obvious emotion while Mrs. Amsel patted his arm reassuringly. All the while, Max paced impatiently. At least, back on the Summer Isle there was only one language, a magic language that everyone spoke, whether they realized it or not. Back there she didn't have to rely on tiny housekeepers to translate.

"So, I guess he's not Vodnik," Max called to Mrs. Amsel.

At the mention of the magician's name, the man gave a start. Mrs. Amsel shot Max a look, and went on talking.

After a time, the man let out a long sigh and Mrs. Amsel gave him a hug. They exchanged a few more words before he got back into his car and drove away.

"What was that about?" Max asked. "Who was that?"

"Just a father worried about his daughter," said Mrs. Amsel. "So worried that I think he was getting ready to do something foolish, but I hope I talked some sense into him." She shook her head and glanced up at the darkened windows of the mill. "I think we should do as the man has done and drive away from this place and never return."

"What?" said Max. "After coming all this way?"

"This Vodnik is not a good person," said Mrs. Amsel. "That man—his name is Jon Wick—came here to get passage for his wife and daughter to America. He said that Vodnik has a key that will unlock the last door to the Summer Isle—"

"You see?" said Max, cutting her off. "It's true, then! We came to the right person."

"No!" said Mrs. Amsel. "You did not let me finish. I don't know how, but I think Vodnik was going to do something awful to that poor man."

But Max was no longer listening. There was a door to the Summer Isle and there was a key, and that was all that mattered. She ignored Mrs. Amsel's protests as she ran back around to the front of the mill, and pounded on the door.

Mrs. Amsel came trailing after her. "Maxine!" she called in a fierce whisper. "You must stop and listen to me. This is a very bad idea!"

Nobody called her *Maxine*. She didn't care how angry the woman was—Max hated that name. She knocked on the door again. Harder.

Mrs. Amsel reached her just as the door started to creak open. *Too late now,* thought Max.

The front door of the old river mill opened to reveal a tall man, so gaunt that his paper-white skin stretched taut over his protruding cheekbones. He gazed out the doorway with cloudy, unfocused eyes.

And the smell. He smelled like milk curdling in the sun.

The gaunt man said nothing, and Max wasn't even sure at first if he was aware they were there. But then he grunted and cocked his head slowly toward them.

"Oh!" squeaked Mrs. Amsel as the unblinking eyes came to rest on her. "So sorry! Wrong house . . . We'll be on our way."

The little woman tugged on Max's arm, but Max yanked it back. She dared to look up into the man's dead eyes. "We're looking for Vodnik the magician. Does he live here?"

The man continued to stare.

"Come on—let's go," whispered Mrs. Amsel.

Without a word, the man turned and walked back inside. But he left the door wide open, which Max took to be an invitation. She followed him, with Mrs. Amsel reluctantly at her side.

The front door opened onto a spacious hall. It must have been some kind of work floor back before the mill had turned derelict. Max thought she could hear the grindstone turning in the distance. Or perhaps she just imagined it, because the mood inside this place made it easy to let your fears run away with you. Someone had turned the front room into a kind of museum. Woodcuts hung along the walls, and bits of broken statuary, all of which looked very old, were displayed on pillars lining the hall. It was hard to tell what the statues had once been, but Max thought she could make out a large claw here, part of a leering face there. The woodcuts were even more disturbing. Most were waterfront scenes of lakes and rivers, and all of them showed drownings. In one, sailors tried in vain to swim to shore as the river pulled them under. In another, a witch was tied and being dunked into a pond by angry villagers. They added to the oppressive ghoulishness of the place.

"Just to be safe," whispered Max, "let's stay away from the river. Far, *far* away."

Mrs. Amsel nodded as she inspected one of the ancient etchings. It depicted a scraggly-bearded man sitting atop a waterwheel. He was holding several jars in his arms and chatting with a horned devil. "There's writing on this one."

"Can you read it?"

Mrs. Amsel slipped on her reading glasses. *"Vodyanoi."*

"Sounds Russian."

Meanwhile, their gaunt butler—at least that's how Max had started thinking of him—began a slow climb up a flight of steps at the end of the hall. "Let's follow him," she said, taking the reluctant Mrs. Amsel by the hand.

The stairs groaned as the butler dragged himself step by step. Halfway up, he paused, as if he'd forgotten what he was doing. He just stood there for a long moment, unmoving.

Finally, Max spoke up. "Excuse me, but were you taking us to see Vodnik?"

The sound of her voice seemed to bring the man back to life, and he resumed his halting climb. Several minutes later, they found themselves at the end of a long hallway in front of a closed door. The butler moved like his arms and legs were made of rusty wire, but he eventually knocked on the door. Three loud raps.

No one answered, and the butler didn't bother knocking again. Instead, he turned and, without sparing Max and Mrs. Amsel another glance, began the slow trek back down the hallway to the stairs.

"This is getting ridiculous," said Max, and she went ahead and knocked again. When there was still no answer, she tried the doorknob. The door was unlocked.

It was a plain office, with a single desk and a tall-backed chair behind it. There were no decorations, and the only other furniture was a small table against the far wall. Atop the table was some kind of antique box.

"No one here," said Mrs. Amsel, poking her head into the doorway but no farther. "Let's go."

"Just hold on," said Max, and she started to explore the room. "Keep a lookout in case he comes back."

If this was indeed the office of a magician, then it was very disappointing. There were no spell books or black candles, no pentagrams drawn on the floor. The desk itself was empty except for some sheaves of blank paper and a few pens. The only thing unusual about the room was the old box, which was done in the same hideous style as the wood-carvings downstairs, with the same nautical motif. When she looked closely, Max saw the latch had been carved into the likeness of drowning men clawing to stay above the waves. Cautiously, she reached for it, but she stopped just inches from the wooden face of a man, mouth open and eyes bulging in horror. The detail was terribly lifelike.

Loath as she was to touch it, she felt drawn to see whatever was inside. An urgent curiosity drove her forward, and she grasped the latch.

Then she gave a start as Mrs. Amsel whispered her name. The housekeeper was leaning against the door, listening. "Someone's coming!"

Max hesitated. If she could just get a peek at what was inside . . .

"It's not the butler," said Mrs. Amsel. "They're coming up the steps!"

With an effort, Max tore her hand away and left the box unopened. She padded across the room as quickly and quietly as she could in her boots, but it was already too late.

The door swung open to reveal a portly man in a tattered suit. His beard was brownish grey, the color of river water, and hung all the way to his stomach, and his bushy eyebrows curled up like two horns protruding from his angry brow.

"Maxine Weber," said the man in perfect English. "My name is Vodnik, and I have been waiting for you."

CHAPTER EIGHT

Vodnik shut the door behind them. Just before it closed, Max caught a glimpse of the butler on the other side, standing guard. Vodnik was plainly annoyed at the butler for leaving them unsupervised, but he put on a polite face for his visitors.

"Well, what can I do for you, Maxine?"

"It's just Max, and how do you know my name, anyway?" asked Max as the magician took his seat behind his desk. The clothes were different, more modern, but otherwise Vodnik looked just like the bearded man from the wood etchings. The man who'd been conversing with the devil. The *vodyanoi*.

"As I'm sure you know, I'm a magician," replied Vodnik. "And we magicians have ways of knowing things."

"Spies, you mean."

"Well, the pink hair does make you stand out."

"Okay," said Max. "Then I guess you already know why we're here."

"You need a favor?"

"Yeah."

Mrs. Amsel whispered something under her breath; it might have been a prayer. Max didn't like dealing with this man, and just being in his home made her feel dirty, tainted. It was as if everything she touched left an oily sheen. The air in his office didn't only smell bad, it *tasted* bad. She took shallow little breaths, trying to inhale as little of the foulness as possible.

Vodnik leaned back in his chair and stroked his beard. "What is it you want?" he asked. "Need help house-training your elfling?"

Mrs. Amsel gasped. "Well! I never."

"Mrs. Amsel is my friend!" said Max. She almost said *housekeeper* out of habit.

Vodnik chuckled. "Have a sense of humor. So, what did you want to see me about?"

The sooner Max got what she wanted, the sooner they could get out of there. "I need to get back to the Summer Isle, and we heard that you have the only key."

Vodnik sat forward in his chair. "*Back* to the Summer Isle? So you want me to help you get *back*?"

Max didn't answer. She'd said only what she'd needed to, but she was already worried it was too much.

The magician stroked his beard again and fixed his eyes on Max. He didn't sound surprised by what she had told him, but he was clearly interested. "You know, only one other being has managed to make that crossing and come back again. Only one other person has ever managed such a thing. Remarkable. I suppose you didn't tell your parents."

"My parents? No." What did her parents have to do with anything? Just how much did Vodnik know about her?

"And what about your brother—Carter, isn't it? Maybe he came back, too. Is he skulking around here somewhere? Outside perhaps? I thought I heard something moving around in the trees on my way in."

"No, Carter's . . ." Max looked at Mrs. Amsel for support. How did Vodnik know all of this? But the old woman looked as confused as she was.

"Her brother is the reason we need to go to the Summer Isle," said Mrs. Amsel. "He's still there."

Vodnik considered this for a moment, and then he opened the top drawer of his desk and withdrew a small brass chest. "I do have the key you heard about. It's called the Key of Everything. One of the last bits of real magic left in this world, and it has the power to unlock the last door to the Summer Isle."

He flipped the chest around so that Max could see the little brass key sitting in the box's cushioned interior. It looked too plain against the rich silk lining.

"For many centuries, I have controlled the only way into the Summer Isle. It's a service only I can provide. Now suddenly children are coming and going as they please! You can see why that would be bad for my business."

"But I *can't* come and go as I please," said Max. "That's the whole reason I'm here. My brother and I were kidnapped by the Pied Piper and woke up on the Summer Isle. But I don't even know how he took us there! And to get back, I came through a magic mirror in the Black Tower, but I'm pretty much sure that's broken now—"

Mrs. Amsel suddenly cleared her throat, and Max realized she was rambling. "Sorry."

"The Piper!" said Vodnik, sneering. "It was the Piper who locked the last door to the Summer Isle. A greedy magician, he laid a curse upon it so that only he could travel back and forth between this world and the world of magic."

"But you can open it," said Max.

"Yes, thank goodness for my magic key," said Vodnik, but he wasn't smiling. "And I suppose you would have me unlock the door and let just anyone cross over. Elflings, trollsons and goblinfolk. All the miserable descendants of magic. Why stop at emigration? What about vacations? I already have the slogan—*This year, summer on the Summer Isle!*"

Max didn't know what the magician was going on about, but he was obviously getting himself worked up. He stopped pacing and leveled his gaze at Max. "You are a very dangerous girl."

Then he turned his back to Max and walked over to the hideous box, the one that Max had very nearly opened. "Mr. Twist!" he called.

The office door swung slowly open and the ghastly butler appeared in the doorway. Then Vodnik opened the box so that Max finally got to see what was inside. Glass jars sat in rows on wooden trays, and in each floated a ghostly mist, a gently swirling vapor. Max wasn't sure what she'd expected to see, but this wasn't it. In contrast to the horrible images etched on the outside of the box, the little jars of mist looked peaceful—beautiful, even.

Vodnik chose two of the newer-looking jars and set them on the desk in front of Max, angling them so that she could get a good look. Inside the jars, the mists began to solidify into shapes.

When Max saw her parents' faces in the jars, she screamed.

Max screamed until Mr. Twist's long fingers grabbed her neck from behind, and shoved her toward Vodnik's desk. Out of the corner of her watering eye, she saw the butler had Mrs. Amsel in a similar hold, even as the little elfling woman pummeled him with her handbag. At least, the old lady did that much. Max couldn't even summon the will to fight. The truth had leached all the strength out of her—somehow, those were her *parents* in those jars.

Mr. Twist forced Max and Mrs. Amsel to their knees so that they were eye level with the desktop. Vodnik was using a clean rag to wipe two brand-new, lidless jars. "This is nothing personal, you understand," he was saying. "Just business. People pay what I charge only because they believe I control the only way into the Summer Isle. People's desperation brings them to me, but you represent an alternative. You represent hope, and hope is a thing I cannot abide."

Max was hardly listening. She was barely paying attention to anything other than her parents' faces floating in the jars. "What have you done to my mom and dad?"

"They're not dead, if that's what you're worried about," said Vodnik. "We're not living in the Dark Ages anymore. No, I've jarred their souls, but their bodies are just sleeping in a hospital—the victims of unexplained comas. An enchanted slumber, actually, a trick as old as those fairy tales your father is so fond of. I thought they might know how you and your brother had managed to cross over to the Summer Isle, but they turned out to be as ignorant about magic as the rest of humanity. It's such a shame when parents don't know what their own kids are up to.

"They'll stay that way until their bodies grow old and die. Oh, if this were the old days, I could keep them right here, and with their souls in my possession I could command their bodies to do my bidding, just as I command Mr. Twist there. But too many mindless zombies walking around attract attention. I prefer to stick with one 'butler' at a time."

"You are a monster!" cried Mrs. Amsel.

Vodnik leered at her. "These are modern times. These days I'm just a businessman." The way the shadows fell across his pointed eyebrows and tangled beard, he didn't look human. "And in business, as in magic, you should always negotiate from a position of strength."

"What do you want?" asked Max.

"Easy," said Vodnik. "I want you. The girl who came back!"

Max's tears of sadness for her parents turned to tears of anger. She fought against Mr. Twist, but the undead servant held her tightly with fingers of iron.

"That doesn't make any sense!" said Max. "Why me?"

Vodnik, however, didn't have a chance to answer, because at that moment there was a loud crash from downstairs, like the sound of wood splintering, followed by the pounding of heavy feet running up stairs. He looked up, alarmed, and stepped back from his desk as his office door flew open.

At first Max's heart sank when she saw the giant hooded figure standing there. *Of course,* she thought. *He's caught up with us just in time to gloat.*

Then the unexpected happened. Mr. Twist turned his head slightly, as if dimly aware that someone else had entered the room. Vodnik barked an order at Twist, and for a moment Max couldn't understand why the magician would be ordering one of his servants to attack another one. But Twist obeyed, and he released Max and Mrs. Amsel at the same time that the giant closed the distance between them in two great steps. Twist reached for the giant instead. The giant appeared uncertain, but when the zombie butler reached for his throat, the giant fought back.

He grabbed Twist's delicate-looking wrists before those long fingers could reach his neck. For a moment, there was a struggle as Twist tried to break the giant's grip, and Max was shocked to see how equally matched the two seemed to be. But the giant used his weight to his advantage and shoved his body into Twist, knocking him backward. Pale fingers clawed at the giant's face and his hood was thrown back, revealing a shock of red hair.

Vodnik had retreated into a corner and he glared at the giant. That's when Max realized that she was free and no one was watching the desk. With a swipe of her arms she grabbed the two jars containing her parents' souls.

"Let's go!" she shouted.

At the sound of Max's voice, Vodnik seemed to come to his senses. He lunged for Max, but the desk was in the way.

At that very same moment, Max heard a sickening snap, and suddenly the red-haired giant came stumbling backward, holding one of Twist's arms in his hand. It had broken off, like a dry twig, at the elbow.

For a moment, everyone stood perfectly still. The giant looked in horror at the broken limb in his hand, and Mr. Twist glanced down, expressionless, at his missing arm. There was no blood, just a small cloud of dust where the brittle skin had crumbled into nothing.

"Kill them, you idiot!" shouted Vodnik.

"Come on!" cried Max, and she shoved Mrs. Amsel out the door as the giant followed.

The three of them sprinted down the steps and out the front door and made a dash for the car. The giant realized that he was still holding Twist's arm and hurled it away in disgust before pulling his hood back down over his face. For just an instant, Max caught a glimpse of boyish pale cheeks and bright blue eyes.

Mrs. Amsel hopped into the driver's seat, and Max scrambled in beside her. There was no way the giant, their rescuer, was going to fit into that small car. He looked anxiously over his shoulder as Twist appeared in the mill doorway. The undead butler was slow but in pursuit.

"Grab the top!" shouted Max.

"Huh?" said the giant.

"Can you hold on?"

The giant crawled onto the trunk of the car, his legs curled up underneath him. His arm span was so wide that he could grip the roof through the open windows on either side.

"Are you on?" asked Max.

As if in answer, the roof sagged ominously and the entire car groaned underneath the giant's weight.

Mrs. Amsel pressed the pedal to the floor and they sped off along the gravel road, an elfling behind the wheel, a pink-haired girl riding shotgun and a giant clinging to the roof.

CHAPTER NINE

They drove until they'd put miles between them and
Vodnik's horrible mill. They kept going until they
were no longer the only car on those back roads,
until they realized people were staring at the giant on top
of their car.

Max clutched the two glass jars tightly in her hands. It
looked like a trick; her parents' faces were too gauzy and
transparent to be real. Maybe it was the magic, maybe it was
a daughter's bond with her parents, but she could feel deep
down in her heart that the jars were genuine. She literally
held her parents' lives in the palms of her hands.

What would happen if she opened the lids? Would their
souls fly back to their bodies and they'd wake up in their
hospital beds and tell the surprised nurses that they'd just
had the strangest dream?

Or would her parents just fade away? And what about

Carter? Max had failed to get the Key of Everything, which meant that even if they did find the Winter Children, even if there was a door to the Summer Isle, she wouldn't be able to open it. She wouldn't be able to rescue her brother without Vodnik's key.

It was a few moments before Max realized that Mrs. Amsel had stopped the car. They were in the parking lot of an abandoned gas station, and the giant had slid off the roof and was now standing several feet away, in the building's shade. Mrs. Amsel watched Max, with eyes that were red and puffy from crying.

"We will save them, *meine Liebe.* We will find a way." Mrs. Amsel reached out and stroked Max's hair. "You have already rescued them from that awful magician. That was very brave."

"It's my fault they were in danger in the first place."

"How can you say that?" asked Mrs. Amsel. "This is not your fault and not your brother's. You know whose fault this is. You know who started all of it."

Max did know. In fact, she'd made a promise to the Peddler back on the Summer Isle. In exchange for his help in rescuing Carter from the Black Tower, she'd promised to spare the Pied Piper's life, if ever given the chance. It had been an easy promise to make, and she'd never regretted it. Until now.

"Keep them safe," said Mrs. Amsel. "This is powerful magic we are dealing with, and I don't want to do anything rash until we know more about the curse Vodnik has laid upon your parents. So, for now, keep them safe."

Max opened her backpack and tucked the jars safely next to the scroll case that held the Peddler's map.

"In the meantime," said Mrs. Amsel, "I think we owe someone a big thank-you."

They looked toward the giant stranger, who was rocking back and forth on his feet, as if unsure whether he should leave or stay.

Max got out of the car and slung her backpack over her shoulders—she wasn't about to go anywhere without it now. She took a few steps toward the stranger but didn't get too close. After all, this person might have just saved their lives, but he'd also been spying on them for weeks.

"Who are you?" asked Max.

The hood turned from side to side as the giant glanced in each direction. He looked like he might bolt.

"Let me try," whispered Mrs. Amsel, and she said something to him in German in a considerably gentler tone of voice.

"I don't really speak that much German," answered the giant, in English. "I'm Dutch."

His voice was surprisingly high-pitched for someone so big.

"Why don't you show us who you are?" asked Max. "It would be easier to talk if we could see your face."

The stranger, after a moment's hesitation, drew back his hood. While she'd gotten a glimpse of him back at the mill—the red hair, the pale skin—she was still surprised by what she saw. This person, this seven-foot-tall giant, was just a boy. Beneath that mop of curly red hair was a heavy brow, but his cheeks were round and plump like her brother's. A faint sprinkle of freckles dotted his nose. He squinted at them, even though he was standing in the shade.

"Is that good enough?" said the giant boy. "I have a thing about the sun."

"What?" said Max. "You're just a kid! But you're, like, twice as big as—"

Mrs. Amsel cut her off with a sudden gasp. "Oh, *mein Gott!*" she whispered. "Your size! And the sunlight! You're a trollson, aren't you?"

The boy nodded. "Yeah."

"What's a trollson?" asked Max. Vodnik had mentioned the word, but that had been the first Max had heard of such a thing.

Mrs. Amsel clapped her hands in delight. "I knew it! You see, Max, trollsons are like elflings, but instead of having elf blood in their veins, they are part troll. Stories say they are descendants of a lost clan of trolls who refused to leave earth for the Summer Isle. I've heard of such persons, of course, every elfling has, but I've never seen one! I thought you were all . . ."

"You thought we were all stone?" said the boy. "No. Most of us can move around in daylight. But those who can't have gone into hiding below ground or . . . you know."

Max suddenly remembered the massive bridge they'd crossed back on the Summer Isle. That bridge had once been a living, breathing troll before the sunlight turned it into stone.

"I'm sorry," said Max. "But you don't look much like a troll. You're big, sure—like, really big—but that's it. Trolls are all bumpy and toothy and stuff."

The boy shrugged. "My great-great-great-grandfather was full-blooded troll, although according to the family stories he was kind of a runt. Since I'm only one-eighth troll, I can walk around in the daylight, but I try not to because I get really itchy and break out in hives. Also, as you all keep saying, I'm big."

"Whoa," said Max, stepping closer for a better look. He really did look like a seven-foot-tall kid.

"Manners," chided Mrs. Amsel.

"It's all right," said the boy. "I'm used to people staring."

For just a moment, Max felt like she was talking to her brother again. He'd grown up with people staring, too, and he'd usually handled it with the same nonchalance as this trollson boy. But because Max knew Carter better than anyone, she also knew what an act that was. You never got used to the stares, not really.

Max quickly looked away. It was odd that a trollson boy could make her miss Carter so terribly, and make her feel ashamed at the same time. "That was rude, and I'm sorry," said Max. "My name's Max. This is Mrs. Amsel."

"Harold," said the boy.

"No offense," said Max, "but that's a terrible troll name."

"My great-great-great-grandfather was named Bigsnout Stonemuncher, so I think I got lucky."

"Well, Harold," said Mrs. Amsel, "thank you for saving our lives."

The boy looked uncomfortable and scuffed his enormous feet along the ground. "That's all right."

"But you've also been following us, haven't you?" asked Max. "Ever since Hamelin."

The boy's pale cheeks turned pink. "I wanted to talk to you," he said. "But I wasn't sure what you'd do. I'm . . . I'm not real good with people. I tried to work up the courage in the station, but then you ran away. So I . . . I hopped onto the train as it was leaving."

"They let you on?" asked Mrs. Amsel.

"I stowed away. I've ridden lots of trains that way. Sometimes I have to ride on top, but that's okay."

Just like he'd ridden on top of their car, although *holding on for dear life* might have been a better way to describe it. What a strange way to live, being too big for most things and too young to do anything about it.

"Where are your parents, Harold?"

"I have a mom and a dad, but they left for the mountains when I was nine. They'd gotten so big that people were getting scared of them."

"How old are you now?" asked Max.

"Eleven," he answered simply. Then, noticing the shocked looks on Max's and Mrs. Amsel's faces, he quickly added, "But it's all right. That's what trollsons do. We spend time out in the world while we can. No one bothers me. But . . . it's been lonelier than I expected."

Mrs. Amsel made a little clucking sound with her tongue, like she had just found a lost puppy. "You poor thing."

"Wait a minute," said Max, stepping in before Mrs. Amsel started trying to feed him from her handbag. "We do appreciate what you did back there, but you still haven't explained why you were following us in the first place."

"I wasn't at first. I was just following the rats. Hundreds of them—thousands, even. I was down under the bridge in Hamelin when I noticed them, scurrying by in single file like an army. I got curious, so I followed them to your house."

Max remembered that day, when she'd seen Harold for the first time. He'd been hiding in the shade of a grocer's awning, across the street from the house her father had rented. She'd seen rats playing there, too—ordinary rats, not like the giant creatures on the Summer Isle. And that night thousands more of the creatures came bursting from the vents inside the house. They'd tunneled into the house through the basement.

"I saw the rats come, and I saw how the rats left," said Harold. "I knew there had to be strange magic going on. I got curious."

"You followed us all the way from Hamelin because you were curious?"

"At first," said Harold. "Then I heard you were asking around about Vodnik. He has a bad reputation among the trollsons. Very bad. That's when I decided to try and talk to you. To warn you not to look for him."

"At the train station?" asked Mrs. Amsel.

Harold nodded. "That didn't work out so well. I didn't mean to scare you. Honest."

"Harold," said Mrs. Amsel. "Back in Hamelin, you were sleeping under that bridge, weren't you? Because you have nowhere else to go."

"It's not so bad. We trollsons kind of have a thing about bridges anyway."

"Oh, you poor thing," said Mrs. Amsel again. She reached up like she wanted to pat him on the cheek, but there was no way she could possibly reach that high. She settled for taking his hand instead.

"No," said Max. She saw where this was heading. The last thing they needed was for Mrs. Amsel to start picking up strays. "No way."

The little woman gave Max a sharp look. "He has nowhere to go. And we owe him a hot meal at least." She patted Harold's stomach. "Bet you have a good appetite, yes?"

Harold nodded as his belly gave a rumble.

"Look," said Max. "Maybe we can buy you some food, but then you have to go back to . . . wherever you came from. It's not that I don't appreciate what you did—I really do. But we are on a sort of quest. We need to fly to America to find the Winter Children, because that's where the door is and well . . ."

"I don't fit on planes," said Harold.

"Sorry."

"But if you're looking for the Winter Children, you can't take a plane anyway. You have to go by boat."

"What do you know about it?"

"I told you Vodnik has a bad reputation among the trollsons," said Harold. "That's because so many of us try to make deals with him. Some of us get sort of *trollier* the older we get. I know what Vodnik promises, that the Winter Children are protecting a door to the land of magic where trollsons won't have to hide, and the magician has the only key."

"Yeah, we heard pretty much the same story," said Max.

"Some trollsons get desperate enough to deal with the magician," said Harold. "My cousin Geldorf did."

"And what happened to your cousin?" asked Mrs. Amsel.

The giant frowned. "I don't know. But I got a postcard from him before I left home. Look, I still have it."

Harold dug around in one of his massive pockets and produced a wrinkled postcard with a picture of seagulls flying over a blue bay. "He wrote that he was getting on a boat for America. See?" He pointed to a messy scrawl on the back and started reading. *"Don't worry about me. Got what I needed from Vodnik, but still don't trust him, so I'm arranging my own transportation. I've found sailors here who know the way. All will be well."*

"Can I see that?" asked Max, and Harold handed her the card. She could barely make heads or tails of the handwriting, but she could clearly make out where the card was from. "Cuxhaven?"

"It's a fishing town on the coast," said Mrs. Amsel. "Not far from here."

Max undid her backpack and took out the map. Harold's eyes went wide as she unrolled it on the ground in front of them.

"There!" said Max, and she pointed to a little dot near the sea. "Shipwreck Way."

"Doesn't sound promising," said Mrs. Amsel.

"That's just its old name," said Max. "That's how the map works. Call it Cuxhaven or Shipwreck Way, the map is leading us there."

"Is that a magic map?" asked Harold.

"Yeah. It shows us where we need to go."

"I'm impressed."

"Don't be," said Max. "Even if you're right, even if there is a boat in Cuxhaven that can take us to the Winter Children, we still need the key. And Vodnik has it."

"You can't go back there," said Harold.

"I have to!" said Max. "I don't have any other choice."

Mrs. Amsel cleared her throat. "Actually, you do." The old woman held a small brass chest in her hand. Very gently she opened the lid, and Max saw the key inside.

"The Key of Everything!" breathed Max. "But how did you get it?"

"During the fighting, when you grabbed your parents, I grabbed the chest," said Mrs. Amsel, smiling. "Not bad for an old lady, eh?"

Max hugged the little woman until she complained she couldn't breathe. Max's parents were still trapped, but they were no longer in Vodnik's possession and Max would find a way to free them. She knew where to find the door to the Summer Isle. Apparently, she even had a part-troll bodyguard, whether she wanted one or not. And now she had the magician's key.

PART II

BY LAND AND SEA

"Where's a troll bridge when you need one, eh?" said Paul as they gazed down upon the vast expanse of the Great River laid out before them. Emilie shushed him, but Lukas silently agreed with the scout's sentiment. After a week of hard travel, they'd finally reached the Great River. Here at the narrow crossing, the river was only fifty or so feet across, as opposed to a quarter of a mile in most other places. To travel south to try the shallower forks would take days, and their passage north was blocked by mountains. This stretch of river was their best bet to get across safely and without losing additional days.

But the Great River was not their greatest worry at the moment—the ogres were.

Paul's keen ears had identified the booming crashes and heaving grunts long before the others were aware of them.

What Lukas might have mistaken for distant thunder, the experienced scout recognized almost immediately. Emilie and Lukas had refused to believe him at first, because ogres rarely strayed far from their homes in the Bonewood (they needed a ready supply of trees to club each other with), but Paul had insisted they follow the sounds until they found a steep rise that looked down on the river valley. There they crawled to the summit on their bellies so that they could take advantage of the natural cover as they peeked over the top.

Paul was right. There were ogres down near the river-bank. Four of them, which by ogre terms was practically an army, since the brutes were not known to get along in pairs, much less in groups. It was often said that two ogres would beat each other for fun, and three would beat each other to death.

The two pressing questions now were what were these ogres doing so far from home, and what force was keeping them together without killing each other? Emilie wanted to forget about the ogres altogether and follow the river south to the forks, but Lukas's curiosity was piqued. And more, his intuition was telling him that spotting four ogres this far north was cause for concern. What sort of concern, he could not yet say, but he was content to wait and watch awhile.

At first Paul found watching the ogres exciting. Every now and again two of them would get into a shoving match, and Lukas and he started placing bets on which one would be pushed into the river first. With nothing else to bet, they traded chores: "If the great big fat one with the bald patch wins, you have to dig the fire pit at camp for the next three nights. If the stupid-looking one with half an ear wins, I'll do it."

But after a few hours, even betting on ogre fights grew tiresome, and soon Paul was siding with Emilie's plan to give up on the ogres and head for the forks, just because it was something to do. So Lukas kept watch alone. Not a one of them was seriously considering trying to sneak past. Ogres had terrible eyesight, but there was nowhere to hide down there. They would surely be spotted if they tried to cross.

Still, Lukas didn't want to leave just yet. The ogres had spent the day doing what ogres do—hitting each other and trying to eat things that aren't usually eatable, like rocks. There was nothing more to see here and yet, even as the afternoon gave way to evening, he couldn't bring himself to leave. His instinct told him that these ogres were waiting for something, and that something was important.

This meant Lukas was left with ample time to worry about Carter, and to second-guess his decision to let the boy go south with Leetha to the Princess's castle. On the surface, Carter's argument had made sense. It was a far more treacherous path that Lukas and the others were on now. Even if they could find a way to rescue their fellow New Hameliners from the rat king, there was no telling what dangers they would face along the way. The ogres down below were proof enough of that. And yet, just as Lukas's instincts told him to watch the ogres, his instincts also said that Carter's own road would be more dangerous than any of them expected. It was a nagging worry he'd had ever since they'd split up, and one he tried to ignore. Carter was better off with Leetha and the elves, he told himself, and he worked hard to believe it.

It was well into evening by the time Lukas discovered what the ogres had been waiting for. He'd been trying to ignore Paul, who climbed back up the rise to whisper to Lukas what a terrible idea it would be to make camp this close to the ogres and that they should move on while they still could, when Lukas spotted new figures approaching. They were following the river down from the north, and Lukas had to squint to see them in the evening gloom.

The newcomers were too small to be ogres, and it wasn't long before Lukas recognized their odd loping gait—sometimes on four legs, sometimes on two, with their noses high in the air to sniff out the path ahead of them. Rats. Lukas counted six of them, each bigger than a boy. When he pointed the creatures out to Paul, the scout smiled and rubbed his hands together in anticipation. He naturally assumed that the rats would stumble upon the ogres and he'd get the pleasure of watching them get squashed flat by the brutes. But Lukas feared otherwise. The ogres weren't waiting in ambush, but they were waiting.

As the rats drew near to the narrow crossing, the one in the lead continued on while his companions held back. Then one of the ogres, the fat one who'd won his fair share of the day's fights, stomped out to meet him.

"What are they doing?" whispered Paul, incredulous.

"They're talking," said Lukas.

After a few moments, the rat went back to his companions and the six of them made for the river crossing, in the company of the four ogres. Rats and ogres were traveling together, and what's more, they'd been expecting each other. This was a planned meeting.

Paul shook his head. "I've never seen anything like it. Ogres not killing each other—and now they're friendly with rats? What's the world coming to?"

"Things are changing," said Lukas. "The leaves have turned, and the days are colder. The Piper's loose, the Peddler's dead and, if that witch Roga is to be believed, there is a new rat king on the throne. Bad things are happening everywhere."

"So, what do we do?" asked Paul. "I'd hate to make camp on that side of the river knowing that there's rats and ogres about."

Lukas thought for a minute. The rats had come down from the north and the ogres up from the south—why did they choose to meet here in the middle?

"Those ogres cross the river, and the rats could lead them north to the mountains. To the rat king's nest."

"Why would they go there? Rats inviting them over for supper?"

"That's exactly what I'm afraid of," said Lukas. "Ogres and rats working together. What if this is the start of some kind of alliance?"

Paul let out a low whistle. "That would be bad. Really bad."

"We should follow them," said Lukas. "If they're headed to the rat king's nest, then let's find out why. Go get Emilie and tell her to get ready to cross the river."

Paul nodded and ran back down the hill. Something

about this was wrong, and they didn't even have the whole story yet. As Lukas tightened his knife belt and stared out at the dark river, he was struck by another troubling thought, but one that he couldn't help now. His instincts about the ogres had been right—they were up to something.

So what about his instincts about Carter, about the feeling he'd had but ignored? Just how much danger had Lukas left the boy in?

ᚃ CHAPTER ELEVEN ᚄ

After nearly two days at sea, Max was finally able to stomach a slice of toast with jam and a cup of hot tea. She'd gotten sick that first evening aboard the dilapidated little steamer, ironically named the *Leviathan,* and spent the next twenty-four hours in their cabin, which was really just a small storage room that was currently being used to store passengers instead of cargo. She remembered hearing, in between bouts of throwing up, Mrs. Amsel question one of the sailors about the seaworthiness of their vessel. His only reply had been a barking laugh.

Cuxhaven had turned out to be a charming fishing town, although the shipwreck museum failed to inspire confidence in the journey ahead. Mrs. Amsel had quickly and rightly identified the people they needed to talk to by their sheer ugliness. The sailors were hard men, and Max guessed that a life spent at sea led to a tough demeanor and more than a few wrinkles. But the crew of the *Leviathan* were beyond weather-beaten. First off, they were short. Some smaller even than Mrs. Amsel, with long buck-toothed faces and scraggly beards. And a few of them, if the light hit them just right, looked positively *greenish*.

One glance and Mrs. Amsel declared that these little men were just too ugly to be entirely human. And the elfling woman was right. The *Leviathan* was crewed by goblinfolk, a sort of magical half blood descended from, of course, goblins. Goblins were great sailors, so the sailors said, which Mrs. Amsel warned was a very goblinish claim. Goblinfolk had rather inflated opinions of themselves, but they were not inherently dangerous. The *Leviathan*'s captain never showed his face, but after a bit of negotiation with the first mate, plus what cash Mrs. Amsel could afford, the sailors agreed to take on Max and her friends as working passengers, as they were bound for New York anyhow. And yes, they remembered Harold's cousin because he had nearly cleaned their galley bare on the voyage to America. Trollsons were not timid eaters.

At first the blue water and the salt breeze were a welcome change, but the never-ending motion of the *Leviathan* tossing about on the ocean soon drove Max from the deck and back to their cabin, where she traded the ocean view for the bottom of a bucket. She spent the entire second day at sea nauseous and swearing that she'd never set foot on a boat again.

She felt terrible that her friends had to spend those first few days at sea working—Harold on deck and Mrs. Amsel in the kitchen—while she lay sick on her back in a hammock. She rarely saw Harold during the daylight hours and Mrs. Amsel only when she brought Max tea and tried to get her to eat. But in the evenings the two would return to the cabin exhausted from their duties, and Harold would tell Max and Mrs. Amsel stories about his family's history. The once-shy trollson had really opened up since joining them on the boat, and Max learned the hard way that Harold prided himself on being an amateur genealogist (apparently, trolls were very serious about their family trees). He loved to go on about his ancestors. And on.

And on.

"My great-grandfather was named Makefist Stonemuncher," he explained one evening. "And he married a giant daughter—that's what we call our females—named Gwenda Lakestrider, and they had two trollsons and a giant daughter, which was unusual because many giant and troll folk only have a single child, and even more remain childless. Not enough room for more, you see."

"Oh my," said Mrs. Amsel. "So your full name is Harold Stonemuncher?"

"No," laughed Harold. "My grandfather changed his last name to Van Dam. Had to get with the times, I guess. Anyway, Gwenda could trace her ancestry all the way back to the terrible giant Gogmagog of Great Britain. Legends say that Gogmagog was killed by a Trojan warrior, but family history states that he actually settled down in Iceland, where he became an authority on sheep husbandry. . . ."

While Max appreciated the company, having to listen to Harold and Mrs. Amsel talk about the trollson's exhaustive family tree only made her desperate to get better that much sooner. It turned out there were few things duller than troll history.

When she was alone, if she wasn't getting sick into a bucket, she dug out the glass jars from her backpack and stared at her parents' sleeping faces floating in the mist. Were they dreaming? she wondered. Back in the Summer Isle, Max had visited Shades Harbor, a town of ghosts and dreams. Carter claimed that he had seen their father there and that he'd been looking for Max and her brother. Was that what her parents were doing now? Were they searching for their children in their dreams?

By the second evening, she was finally well enough to take a turn on deck, which felt wonderful, although Mrs. Amsel had warned her that some of the sailors were not very welcoming of the passengers. The captain still hadn't emerged from his cabin the entire time they'd been at sea. Harold and Mrs. Amsel were late returning to the cabin, even though Harold had promised them all a lecture on the Scandinavian Stonemuncher clan and their successful transition from pillaging to soy cropping. Max worried that something was up.

She slung her backpack over her shoulders—now that it carried her parents' souls, she wouldn't let it out of her sight—and set out to find her friends. It turned out Harold was still on deck hauling barrels, even though the sun had nearly set. A few of the sailors were sitting around on crates and laughing at him while they cracked jokes. Max watched as Harold hauled the barrels to one side of the ship, and then the sailors would snicker and point to a different spot on deck and he'd be forced to move them all over again.

"Harold, what are you doing?" she asked as he hefted a barrel for what seemed like the fourth or fifth time.

"Balancing the boat," he answered, out of breath.

"You're what?"

"Dridge over there said that the ship is off balance and if we don't get it just right, the whole thing could capsize."

"Who's Dridge?"

Harold gestured to the group of snickering goblinfolk sailors. "Glad you're up, Max. You look one-hundred-percent better."

The sailors were laughing even harder now, and one was making faces. Max felt her ears burning with anger.

"Wait here for a minute," said Max.

"Max, don't," said Harold.

"Just wait here."

She hadn't been of much use these past couple of days, but now that she was feeling better, she wasn't about to stand around and let these goblin sailors turn Harold into the butt of a joke. She was still weak, however, and she'd yet to get her sea legs. She stumbled a few times, and the sailors laughed all the harder when they spotted her wobbling their way.

Max steadied herself as best she could and planted her hands on her hips. "Which one of you is Dridge?"

Two of the goblinfolk just shrugged, but the middle one, a pointy-nosed fellow with an eye patch and a crusty red cap, answered her in heavily accented English. "I am Dridge."

"You're making my friend *balance the boat*?" she asked. "Is this how you treat all your passengers?"

"No," said Dridge, smirking. "Just him."

"Well, how about cutting it out," said Max. "The joke's over and you've had your fun."

"Fun's not started yet," said Dridge. "Days' more fun to be had." He stood up tiptoe on his crate so that he was more or less eye to eye with Max. "Young girl is careful, or her friends maybe swim rest of way to port, yes?"

Max understood the threat perfectly. If she didn't bite her tongue, they could all pay the price. Grudgingly, she swallowed her temper and turned her back on Dridge and his buddies and rejoined Harold. A lot of help she had been.

"Can I get you anything? Are you thirsty?"

"No, I'm fine," said Harold. "I've got plenty of fresh water nearby—what do you think these barrels are filled with, anyway?"

From across the deck Dridge shouted, "Troll boy! Hurry with those barrels. This side of boat is tilting." Then he and his friends went from snickering to outright guffaws. They laughed so hard one of them rolled off his crate, and this just made his friends laugh harder.

Max felt her blood rising again.

"It's okay," whispered Harold, seeing the look on her face. "Goblinfolk have a mean sense of humor, but there's worse things than moving barrels around all day. Eventually they'll get tired of it. I'll see you back at the cabin soon."

Harold knew. He knew what was really going on, and what's more he knew the danger they would all be in if he caused trouble. For some reason, this just made Max feel worse. But she wasn't helping him by standing around, and the truth was that after barely eating for two days, she was too weak to help him move barrels.

She searched for Mrs. Amsel and found the little woman coming out of the galley with a tray of food—cheese sandwiches and sliced apples. She was happy to see Max up and about, and gave her a sandwich and some apple slices for her supper.

"Mrs. Amsel," said Max. "What do they have you doing?"

Mrs. Amsel shrugged the question away. "These men need a little extra help around the kitchen, that's all. Dinner is running late tonight, but I'll be along shortly. In the meantime, you eat. Get your strength back."

Max didn't believe her, but she didn't want to press the issue any further for fear of wounding the old woman's pride. But Max was sure that the extra help Mrs. Amsel was providing meant that she was now doing all the cooking for the entire crew. Judging by the slovenly habits of the sailors, Max could only imagine what state the kitchen must be in. The poor woman looked like she wanted nothing more than a nap, but with a solid grin, she patted Max on the cheek. "Now, I'd better get back to the galley. There will soon be a horde of hungry sailors to feed!"

Hours later Harold and Mrs. Amsel finally returned to the cabin. Mrs. Amsel was nearly asleep on her feet, and Harold so worn out that he didn't even feel like talking. Max helped Mrs. Amsel into her hammock while Harold, who was far too large for any hammock, curled up on the floor with a flour sack as a pillow. Soon the both of them were fast asleep. Harold the trollson slept as quietly as a baby, while the dainty elfling housekeeper snored like a wood saw.

But after two days of lying around, Max could not sleep. Her body craved exercise. The sea was calm, and a bright gibbous moon shone in brightly through the porthole. All was quiet, so Max decided to risk a nighttime stroll on the deck. After all, no one had told her *not* to walk around, and if all the crew were asleep in their bunks, what would be a safer time?

Max stepped outside and breathed in the salty air. With the ocean before her and the stars overhead, and with the gentle hum of the *Leviathan*'s engine, she was almost able to enjoy the moment—but that would mean forgetting how these sailors were treating her friends. She stepped carefully along the deck, staying well away from the edge. If she somehow fell overboard out here in the dark, no one would even notice she was missing until dawn.

As she explored, she heard sounds coming from the rear, or the stern, of the ship. Max had once heard that you could sometimes find dolphins playing in the wakes of ships at sea, so she decided to watch the water from the boat's aft. But she paused when she saw a small figure step out of the shadows.

Max backed away as quietly as she could—she didn't want to deal with any of the sailors. This sailor's back was turned to her, his face hidden from view, but he kept glancing around, as if he was afraid of being seen. Max stayed hidden behind a smokestack. Something told her to watch and wait, and after a few minutes, a large bird flew out of the night and landed on the sailor's outstretched arm. It was a crow, and when it cawed at him, he shushed it and started whispering into its ear. Then it took flight again, and the sailor watched it disappear, before slipping back into the shadows himself.

Max waited for a few heartbeats, until she knew the sailor was gone, then ran all the way back to her cabin and slammed the door behind her. Poor Harold and Mrs. Amsel were both so exhausted from their day's work that neither one of them even stirred at the sound.

Max sat in her hammock and tried to process what she'd seen. That sailor had been talking to a crow and then he let it loose. Why? Why bring a bird on board just to let it fly away in the middle of the ocean? There weren't any islands this far out for it to fly to, nowhere to go unless . . .

Unless there was another boat.

Unless they were being followed.

Sleep was a long time coming, and when she did finally drift off, she was haunted by dreams of leering goblin faces staring out at her from inside glass jars.

❧ CHAPTER TWELVE ❧

At some point during the night, Max's nightmares turned from fears of goblins to worries about her brother. In the dream, Max and her father were looking all over the house in Hamelin for Carter, but whenever they entered a room, they would just catch a glimpse of him going out another door.

When Max awoke, she was all alone in the cabin. Harold and Mrs. Amsel had snuck out early without disturbing her. It made her angry that they would be worried about waking her up when they were the ones who had to slave away all day. In her frustration, she tried to clean their little storeroom cabin, but there wasn't much to tidy up. Two hammocks and Harold's little pallet of smelly blankets was all there really was. Back home, when she was mad at her mom or dad, Max would make and remake the bed, just to give her hands something to do while she grumbled about how unfair parents were.

"This whole thing is stupid," she murmured to herself as she refolded Harold's blankets a third time. "I don't want them worrying about me. Everyone tiptoeing around treating me like a—"

Max stopped herself. She'd almost said *like a cripple.* That was a word they didn't use in her family, and she felt ashamed that she could even think it when Carter could be in who knew what kind of danger. But they were in danger, too. Someone on the ship was sending messages by bird. He was doing it in secret, and Max had a pretty good idea who he was sending those messages to.

She felt considerably stronger today, and she stepped out onto the deck determined to make herself useful. Unfortunately, the day had already taken a turn for the worse. A crowd had gathered around Mrs. Amsel as the sailor named Dridge yelled at her in a language Max couldn't place. Harold stood behind her, fists balled in anger, but Mrs. Amsel held him back with a hand on his chest.

She stood there, stoically taking the sailor's abuse as he waved a bowl of something in her face. Dridge, it seemed, was unhappy with his breakfast. As Max rushed over to the scene, Dridge switched to English.

"Slop!" he growled. "You feed us slop when you give troll boy whatever he wants! I see you sneak him food."

"I will cook you something special," said Mrs. Amsel calmly. "Just let Harold go back to work and I will go into the kitchen and—"

Dridge cut the little housekeeper off by emptying the contents of his bowl onto her head. Most of his crewmates shook their heads in disapproval, but a few of his buddies laughed. With as much dignity as she could muster, Mrs. Amsel wiped the porridge out of her eyes. Max expected her to unleash such a tongue-lashing as to make the sailors hide for a week, but she stayed quiet.

Not Harold. Apparently, the boy could handle all the abuse these sailors could dish out just so long as it was aimed at him, but seeing them humiliate Mrs. Amsel was too much.

With a monstrous—Max might even describe it as *trollish*—roar he grabbed Dridge by the collar and hefted the little sailor off his feet. Most of the sailors cried out in alarm, but a few actually cheered.

"As foolish a thing as I ever saw!" boomed a deep voice, and all at once the mob turned quiet as the door to the captain's cabin creaked open.

The captain of the *Leviathan* differed from his crew in that most of them could at least pass for human if you didn't already know their true nature—ugly little humans, but humans nonetheless. The captain was another matter. Dressed as a fisherman he might have been, in his long-shoreman's coat and hat, but his face was more animal than human, with a turned-up nose much like a bat's and two round dark eyes like pools of ink. His fingers ended in long black claws. And he was big, nearly as tall as an ordinary man, but broader in the shoulders and powerfully built. Harold may have still towered over him, but the captain had a dangerous look about him that said he'd seen plenty of trouble.

Max scurried backward from the horrible captain, and the rest of the crew quickly parted to let him pass. His black-eyed gaze drifted over each of his men in turn until he got to Harold, who dropped Dridge to the deck.

"My boys sometimes claw at each other, but I don't take kindly to passengers gettin' into spats with 'em," he said.

"The troll boy's a menace, captain!" cried Dridge.

"And what do you say to that, trollson?" said the captain. "What should I do with someone who picks fights with my crew?"

Either Harold was too scared to say anything or he didn't want to cause trouble for Max and Mrs. Amsel. But Max wasn't going to stand by and watch. "He didn't pick the fight," she said. "Dridge did."

She pushed her way through the crowd of sailors and took Mrs. Amsel by the arm. "Dridge poured his breakfast over her head. Look." Mrs. Amsel still had lumps of oatmeal in her hair to prove it.

"Hmm," said the captain. "And who are you?"

"Max."

"Toss troll boy overboard, Captain Hob!" said Dridge.

"You should keep that mouth of yours quiet, Dridge," said the captain.

"But, curse them, Captain, they started it!"

"The elfling poured her porridge on her own head, then?" Captain Hob asked.

"Aw, it was just a bit of fun, is all," said Dridge.

Captain Hob stared down at the goblinfolk sailor. "You want to have fun, go back to poking bilge rats with a stick. Let the passengers be."

Dridge looked away and muttered something under his breath, but he nodded.

"And you all," said the captain, pointing to Max and her friends. "You're confined to your cabin from here on out. I see you on deck riling up my crew and I *will* let you swim the rest of the way. Understand?"

Max and the others nodded, then hurried back to their cabin. Although the captain had pronounced it like a punishment, Max couldn't help but wonder if he hadn't just made the voyage easier for them on purpose. Confined to their cabin meant that Harold wouldn't have to haul barrels and Mrs. Amsel wouldn't have to cook.

As for Dridge, the captain gave him his own punishment, and that evening Dridge grudgingly delivered the dinner tray to Max's cabin, while the next morning he was out on deck "balancing the boat" as his crewmates laughed.

❧ CHAPTER THIRTEEN ❧

The Peddler's Road had changed much since Carter and Leetha had last seen it. The road's path through the Summer Isle was long, and at different points it was a grand stone highway, while at others little more than a dirt trail. But wherever the road reached, no weeds troubled it, and trees had a mysterious habit of falling over next to it but never across it. It was said that the Peddler's Road couldn't be blocked. Until now.

With the Peddler gone, his road was falling into ruin. The cobblestones here were cracked and ruined, and wicked-looking vines, covered in inch-long thorns, snaked across the ground, ready to trip the unwary traveler. Bridges that crossed streams and creeks had all crumbled, and these were hard crossing because the waters flowed fast and angry now. The Peddler was dead, and other, less pleasant forces were gobbling up the road's power with alarming speed, and soon there would be nothing left.

Worst of all, the Peddler's Road hadn't simply been a road; it had served as a fence to keep the wilderness in check. But now all was breaking its bounds, and the few bright spots of civilization would be in peril as the wild spread. Leetha warned Carter that unwholesome lands like the Dark Moors, even the Bonewood, might spread unchecked without the Peddler's magic to keep them at bay. She worried that they might even threaten the Deep Forest, home of the elves.

Still, what was left of the road offered the safest route, even if it was more perilous than it once had been. Better to follow a road, no matter how treacherous, than to risk getting lost in the wilderness.

After several days of traveling together, the three companions fell into a rhythm. Leetha kept the lead and cleared away the brush and intruding weeds that seemed particularly dangerous. Carter and Bandybulb followed close behind, and Carter told Bandybulb stories about famous people from back home. This was mainly to keep the little kobold from lecturing him on the great exploits of King Tussleroot the Wise. Carter began with George Washington, Amelia Earhart and Gandhi, but he eventually moved on to the true adventures of Luke Skywalker, Bruce Wayne and Bilbo Baggins. Bandybulb, needless to say, was impressed.

The three of them were sheltering for the evening in a small ruined watchtower when it started to rain. Leetha didn't know who'd built the old tower, and Carter was just glad that there was enough of a roof intact to provide some cover from the rain, which was getting heavier. Soon the sky grew dark and great thunderclouds lit up with dueling forks of lightning. The wind blew sheets of rain in through the holes in the tower roof, and their little fire sputtered as it struggled to stay lit. Carter kept expecting the storm to blow over as most summer storms do, but this one lasted throughout the evening. More than once, he imagined he could hear the playing of pipes beneath the cracking peals of thunder. At least, he thought it was his imagination, until he saw Leetha listening at the window and staring worriedly at the storm.

The next day there was less conversation as they picked up their pace. Though no one spoke of it, not even Bandy-bulb, the previous night's queer storm had unnerved them all. The strange music and the storm itself had left them distracted and scared, and that evening they unknowingly made camp too near a hangman's tree, and they were forced to threaten the tree with fire when it tried to loop one of its ropelike branches around Bandybulb's neck. Fleeing the tree meant that they had to camp out in the open, and they were harassed by gusting winds that tore at their cloaks and blew dirt into their eyes. That night there was no mistaking the pipes. When the wind died down for a few seconds, they could hear the haunting music, louder than before.

They were being pursued.

By now their fear gave way to short tempers, and they argued about whether to keep following the road or take their chances in the wild. It was afternoon of the following day when Leetha finally called a halt to their march. Carter and Bandybulb sank to their knees, exhausted. Leetha had been keeping a brutal pace.

"It's time we accepted the truth," she said. "We cannot run fast enough to escape that which follows us. And we all know who it is."

"The Piper," said Carter.

Leetha shook her head in frustration. "But how can it be? I thought you said that his magic pipe was hidden away? Even if he knew where it was, he couldn't have gotten to it so fast."

Carter had been asking himself the very same question. "He carved up the furniture in his cell to make the flute that he used to lure my sister and me here. Maybe he's carved another. It won't be as good as his original pipe, the one hidden at Magician's Landing, but it looks like it's enough to do some magic at least. These storms and winds are not natural."

"That still doesn't explain why he's chasing us," said Leetha.

"Maybe he knows we talked to Roga. Maybe he visited her himself."

"It's a shame she didn't eat him," said Leetha.

Carter let out a tired laugh, which only earned him a stern look from the elf girl. "That wasn't a joke."

Leetha stomped over to the side of the road, where she plopped down, crossing her arms over her chest in a pout. "There are likely beasts about, so there's still a chance he'll get eaten. I live in hope."

Carter rested his chin on his knee. It would be so easy

to go to sleep right there in the middle of the road. He felt someone standing over him, and he looked up to see Bandybulb. The kobold stuck out his foot, practically shoving his big toe in Carter's face. "Bandybulb has a splinter."

"Oh, who cares?" snapped Carter, and he hauled himself up to standing.

The little kobold frowned. "But it's a big one."

Carter looked at the road ahead, then back the way they'd come. The road was empty for miles in either direction, curling through the rolling fields and tall grasses that bordered the eastern coast. "How far are we from the Deep Forest?"

Leetha sighed. "If we stick to the road, we should reach it in a day or so. Longer if we try to cut across the moors. But in the wild we'd have a better chance of losing the Piper."

"Well, let's assume, for the sake of argument, that the Piper manages not to get himself eaten," said Carter. "That leaves us with a problem of what to do about tonight."

"We can stand and fight," said Leetha.

"You're the only one of us any good at that," said Carter. "And we're all exhausted. If the Piper's going to make his move soon, he did a good job softening us up first. And he might not be alone."

"Rats?" asked Leetha.

Carter nodded. "He might have help. We're in no shape to risk getting lost in the moors, and we need a better option than fighting."

"Even if we keep marching through the night, he'll likely catch us."

"Maybe we can slow him down, at least," said Carter. "I

have an idea. It's a long shot, but luckily we have the perfect person to make it work."

At that moment, the little kobold, who'd been digging furiously at the splinter in his toe, let out a cry of pain. "Ow! Now it's in my thumb!"

Bandybulb stuck his wounded thumb in his mouth and glanced up at them. "Why is everyone looking at me?"

Kobold magic was small magic. So small as to be easily overlooked, which was often the point, as most kobolds worked hard not to be seen. While it was true that kobolds produced no great magicians, it was well known that some were knowledgeable in charms, illusions and even minor curses.

Bandybulb, it turned out, was not one of those kobolds.

While King Tussleroot accounted himself a powerful sorcerer, so powerful that his own magic was so imperceptible as to be ineffectual, poor Bandybulb simply didn't possess the gift. But he did possess another gift, one that Carter had witnessed back in the Chillwood, in the home of the kobold family that had sheltered them. For whatever reason, Bandybulb was well liked by other kobolds, even respected. Carter was counting on that now.

As the sun set in the western sky, Carter and Leetha hiked south along the road, not bothering to make camp. Carter's legs felt like they were made of wobbly rubber, and his eyes stung from lack of sleep. Leetha didn't look much better, and from all the grumbling she'd done throughout the day it was obvious she didn't think much of Carter's plan. But she didn't have a better one. Everything now depended on Bandybulb.

They hiked for several more hours, and the evening, unlike the past several, was quiet and cloudless. No wind blew, not even a breeze to ruffle the tall prairie grass. Everything was still, as if the Summer Isle was holding its breath, waiting for what was to come. For a little while, Carter dared to hope that they would pass the evening safely.

That hope was dashed when a bank of storm clouds rolled in from the north, driven toward them by music on the wind. The Piper was close. And this time, along with the storm came the rats. The clouds hung heavy in the sky, but the flashes of lightning revealed several sleek bodies scurrying their way, not far behind them on the road. The rats weren't bothering with stealth anymore; this was an open charge into battle.

"How many can you see?" asked Carter.

"Seven, eight," said Leetha, her eyes shining, cat-like, in the dark. "No, wait, there are more . . . a dozen at least."

Carter's stomach did a turn. *A dozen?* Up until now, Carter had actually felt somewhat confident that his plan might just work. But he hadn't anticipated a small army to contend with.

"Do you see the Piper anywhere?" he asked.

"No. . . . Is that a good thing or bad?"

"Bad," answered Carter. "If we don't know what he's up to, then it's definitely bad. Come on."

They turned their march into a run. All they could do

now was make for the Deep Forest, still miles away, and hope that Bandybulb did his part well. Leetha offered her arm to help Carter along, but he brushed her away.

"I'm fine," he said. "I can keep up. Just keep moving!"

The clouds darkened the sky overhead almost to true night, and even though the storm was blowing in from the north, throwing rain and pellets of hail at their backs, great gusting headwinds would suddenly shift and slam into them from the south, slowing their progress and at times knocking them off their feet. There was definitely sorcery at the heart of this storm.

The rats were gaining on them, and Carter could hear their rasping voices calling taunts and jeers at their prey. Soon they would be upon them. He took out his little carving knife. He wasn't much good at violence, but he wouldn't let Leetha fight alone.

"Where . . . ," gasped Leetha. "Where is the kobold?"

Carter shook his head. Bandybulb should have been here by now.

The rats were thirty yards away. . . . Twenty.

"Bandybulb!" Carter shouted against the storm.

A small furry head poked itself out of the tall grass on the side of the road. "Yes?"

Carter stared at the little kobold for a moment, dumbfounded. "Bandybulb! The rats!"

"Oh! Now?"

"Yes, now!" cried Carter.

Bandybulb disappeared again into the grass and for another moment nothing happened, except the rats closed on them until they were within spitting distance. Then they slowed down and began to stalk forward on all fours, teeth bared.

"Can't keep running, children," snarled their leader, a big black one with a scar across his snout. "Time to pay the—"

He didn't get to finish his sentence, because at that moment the tall grasses around them erupted with a chorus of squeaky little voices as a shower of small rocks and sticks was launched at the rats. The leader rat was hit in the eye with a stone the size of a strawberry. He cursed and shook his snout and pawed at his eye.

"Ambush!" he cried.

Then the grass parted, and the rats were met with at least thirty naked little butts. Carter had experienced this himself once, being mooned by kobolds, and it wasn't a pretty experience.

"Don't worry," Carter said to Leetha as she scrunched up her face in disgust. "Those butts are on our side!"

"Kobolds," she muttered.

The rats, outraged and in pain from the assault of tiny projectiles, dashed into the grass after the kobolds, but the kobolds were faster and, in the grass, nearly impossible to spot. Fewer than half the rats heeded their leader's orders to stay put and capture the children, and as those loyal few started forward, a new wave of kobolds led by Bandybulb himself dashed out from the grass, carrying long twines of ropewood. They ran beneath the rats' feet, tangling them up in the ropewood and tripping them over themselves. More rats fell as the kobolds cheered.

But the leader deftly dodged the ropes and kept on

coming. Lightning flashed overhead and a peal of thunder rang in Carter's ears as the rat stood back on his hind legs and produced a long leather whip in his hands. Thorns were tied into the lash like barbs.

Leetha stepped forward, a knife in each hand and a wicked elfish grin on her face. Her canines were bared.

"Go, Carter—keep running," she said.

"I won't leave you here," he said.

Then the rat lunged, snapping his whip at Leetha's face. She was nearly struck trying to keep her own body between the rat and Carter. Carter tried to dodge away, but his leg tripped him up and he stumbled. His foot twisted beneath him, and he cried out in pain.

"I can't fight and protect you at the same time," Leetha shouted. "Go! I'll catch up!"

Leetha was right. If Carter wasn't a fighter, he would just be another target—one that Leetha could get hurt trying to protect.

He turned and started limping away from the fight, feeling cowardly and useless, even though it had been his plan to have Bandybulb summon the kobolds. A plan that had, so far, taken eleven rats out of the fight, but all he saw was his own leg, dragging through the mud.

If he hadn't been looking down, he might have seen the hand reaching out of the darkness. He might have had time to dodge, or at least cry out for help before it wrapped itself around his mouth. He might have caught a glimpse of the pied cloak.

But it was too late.

⇥ CHAPTER FOURTEEN ⇤

As Max had hoped, being confined to quarters had turned into a blessing for Mrs. Amsel and Harold, who were finally able to rest. It was harder on Max, who'd already spent most of the voyage stuck indoors. She'd traded seasickness for an acute case of cabin fever. Meals were delivered by Dridge, although whenever the sailor served them, he looked like he would like nothing better than to beat everyone senseless with the dinner tray. But his fear of the captain must have outweighed his hate for Max and her friends, because the food was always hot and the plates were cleared promptly.

Max took advantage of their time together to tell Harold and Mrs. Amsel about the mysterious figure she'd seen on deck the night past. The news was worrisome, and everyone agreed that the presence of a crow this far out at sea was even more ominous. If it had simply been the pet of one of the sailors, then Harold or Mrs. Amsel would have seen it when they were working on deck. Max told them she suspected they were being followed by another ship, but all they could do about it was hope that the *Leviathan* was faster than its pursuer.

On the morning of the fourth day of their five-day voyage across the Atlantic, the ship's engine died. A steady rain had pelted their cabin all through the night and into the morning, so it had taken Max and the others a while to realize that the once-constant hum of the ship's engine had gone quiet. The first indications that something was really wrong were the anxious shouts and the stomping of footsteps outside their door. Max peered out the porthole and saw that they'd come to a complete stop. The ocean was dimpled by raindrops, but the *Leviathan* wasn't making its own waves. It was dead in the water.

It wasn't long before they heard a heavy knock at their door. When Harold answered it, Dridge stood outside, drenched and miserable-looking in the rain.

"The captain wants you," he said, pointing past Harold to Max. "Just you."

"What's he want her for?" asked Harold, but Dridge ignored him and continued to stare at Max.

"He said come, now," said Dridge.

"Whatever for?" asked Mrs. Amsel.

"Ship's engine's broke," said Dridge. "And someone broke it."

"Sabotage?" said Max, and the three friends exchanged worried looks. "He can't think we had anything to do with that. We've been locked up in here."

"Maybe you sneak out during the night," said Dridge. "The captain will question *everyone*, passengers and crew."

"Then we'll all go together," said Mrs. Amsel. "He can talk to all of us at once."

"You think I want to come out into rain and fetch you?" snapped Dridge. "For two days I am cabin boy because of you. *Clean this, Dridge. Scrub that.* But I do it because captain says do it. Now you, girl, must come with me—alone— because captain says do it!"

Dridge snatched his red cap off his head and wrung the water out of it as he glared up at the rain. "I am soaked to come fetch you. But fine, you want to stay here, I will tell the captain you say no."

"Wait," said Max. "I'm coming." The last thing she wanted to do was make the captain suspicious by refusing to be questioned, and he'd been right before when he'd said this was his ship. While they were out here on the water, his word was the only law.

"You shouldn't go alone," said Harold.

"We don't have anything to hide," said Max. "But look after my backpack while I'm gone, okay?"

Harold gave her a knowing nod. "I won't let it out of my sight."

Mrs. Amsel insisted she wear her jacket, and she wrapped one of her scarves around Max's head. "You will catch your death out there in this weather!"

Dridge stamped his foot. "The captain is waiting!" he barked. They hadn't invited the soggy sailor inside, and he was getting more and more drenched by the minute.

Max felt silly wearing Mrs. Amsel's headscarf, but once

she stepped outside she was thankful for it. Storm clouds darkened the sky and the rain was soon coming down in sheets. Max could see whitecaps among the waves as the wind picked up. The morning's calm sea was turning rough. Men gathered around the engine room, and thick black smoke was billowing out of the hatch. The situation looked even worse than Max had imagined.

"Is the ship on fire?" she asked, alarmed.

"Engine, but is under control," said Dridge. "Come."

Dridge led her away from the smoke and around to the ship's starboard side. This close to the railing, Max could feel the sea spray of the crashing waves mixing with the pounding rain. Lightning flashed overhead, followed by a rumble of thunder.

"Can the engine be fixed?" asked Max.

"Yes."

"How long will it take?"

"Long enough," he said.

Too late, Max saw the ugly grin on Dridge's face, and she realized that they were alone at the railing. Everyone else was helping to put out the engine fire.

Before Max could call out, Dridge threw his shoulder into her and she hit the railing. For a moment, she tottered there, off balance, but then he put his hands on her back and shoved, hard. She toppled over the side of the *Leviathan*, but she didn't hit water. She landed, stomach first, on something hard, knocking the breath out of her. She managed to roll over, gasping for air, just in time to see Dridge above her, using a rope to rappel down the ship's hull.

Max was in a lifeboat tied to the ship. She tried sitting

up, but her head was spinning. Dridge reached the lifeboat and shoved her aside.

"Sick of taking orders," Dridge was saying. "For you, Vodnik will pay me enough to get my own boat. I give orders from now on!"

That's when Max spotted, off in the distance, the small silhouette of a second ship cutting through the waves. This far away she couldn't tell what kind, but whatever it was, it wasn't adrift like the *Leviathan*.

Dridge drew a long knife from his belt and cut the rope, severing their lifeboat from the *Leviathan*. Just then a wave rose beneath them and slammed the boat against the hull. Dridge nearly fell overboard, but unfortunately he managed to hold on.

"Call for help and I'll gut you like a fish," he warned, and he scrambled past Max to the lifeboat's little outboard motor. He turned the ignition switch, then cursed as sparks suddenly shot out, followed by a small puff of smoke. It looked like their lifeboat was having its own engine troubles.

As Max rubbed her sore chest—she was getting her breath back slowly—she remembered what Mrs. Amsel had said about magic creatures and electricity. The two didn't generally get along. That was probably why the *Leviathan* was a steamer.

Dridge growled and slammed his fist down on the useless motor. If they didn't pull away from the *Leviathan* soon, the waves would smash their little craft to pieces against the ship's hull.

Dridge pulled out the lifeboat's oars and slotted them through the oarlocks on either side, and then he began to row. He was trying to make it to the other ship before the rest of the crew discovered they had gone missing. He rowed into an oncoming wave and Max held her breath as it crashed over them, threatening to capsize their little vessel. Cursing all the way, Dridge was struggling to row against the storm and the storm was winning. Just then, on the deck of the *Leviathan,* Max saw a light shining, like a flashlight, searching the waves. People were gathered at the railing.

"Over here!" she screamed as she stood and waved her arms. Dridge could do his worst. She wasn't going to let herself be kidnapped again. Never again.

The goblinfolk sailor roared at her to shut up and whirled around in his seat, knife appearing in his hand as he dropped the oars. That turned out to be his mistake because at that very same moment the lifeboat hit another wave and the oars, sitting loose in their oarlocks, were torn free. Instinctively, Dridge reached for them to keep them from washing away. He'd lowered his guard, and Max kicked him in the face with everything she had. The cobbler's boots were thick-soled and solid, and Dridge's nose was not. He screamed in pain as he dropped the knife overboard.

But the force of Max's kick knocked her off balance as well, and she was already standing in a boat on a choppy sea. There was a moment where she was balanced on one foot; then the boat rocked and she followed Dridge's knife into the water.

The world disappeared in the roar of the great churning ocean around her. She swallowed salt water and gagged as she struggled to keep her head above the waves, but they washed over her, and the heavy boots she'd been so thankful for just moments ago weighed her feet down like they were lead. She was sinking.

She held her breath until she felt her lungs would burst, but it was no use. She was drowning.

Then she wasn't. Something had her. Arms wrapped around her middle and she was swiftly hauled to the surface, where she took in the sweetest gasp of air she'd ever tasted, before vomiting up a lungful of seawater. She was dimly aware of a face next to hers. Dridge? No, this was someone else. This sailor had her in his arms, cradling her head to keep it above water as he held on to a life preserver that was being pulled back toward the *Leviathan*. The next thing she knew, strong hands were hauling her aboard. Harold had her, and Mrs. Amsel helped him lower Max gently onto the deck.

Max lay there, coughing and sputtering and surprised to be alive. Captain Hob stood over her, but he didn't seem concerned about her. He was peering through a pair of binoculars at the distant ship, which was getting nearer. Max pulled herself up to sitting and saw that Dridge and the stolen lifeboat were nowhere to be seen, but then she thought she spotted a flash of a lone red cap being tossed about on the waves.

"We got worried when we saw the engine smoke through the porthole," explained Mrs. Amsel. "When we went outside, we bumped into the captain, and it was obvious that he never sent for you. We were so worried. It was lucky his men spotted you."

"Thank you," said Max. Her voice was ragged from coughing up salt water.

The captain lowered his binoculars and looked down at her, unsmiling. "Why does that other ship follow us? Dridge has always been spiteful, but he has been with my crew for years. Now I suspect that he sabotaged my ship to get you off it. Why? What's so important about you that would drive one of my men to mutiny?"

He knelt down until he was face to face with her. "No more stories now, or I will toss you back into the drink like an underweight fish. Tell me."

Max looked to Mrs. Amsel and Harold, but they didn't say anything. This was Max's mission. Her decision.

"Better than that, let me get my backpack," she said. "And I'll show you."

CHAPTER FIFTEEN

The captain's quarters were surprisingly well furnished and clean. Max didn't know what she'd been expecting, but given Hob's appearance, she was surprised to learn that the captain of the *Leviathan* was something of a neat freak. His bunk was impeccably made, the sheets turned back and folded with a crisp crease, and his desk had been varnished to a shine. There were shelves of antique nautical instruments on one wall—a brass compass, a spyglass—and they were spotless. You could give this room the white-glove test and not find a speck of dust.

Captain Hob insisted on questioning Max alone, so Harold and Mrs. Amsel were made to wait outside, which they didn't like at all. But they were just on the other side of the door should Max need them. She hoped that she wouldn't.

Captain Hob offered her a chair, but he stayed standing. "Well?" he said. "What do you have to show me?"

Max dug around in her backpack while trying to stay calm and not think about the captain's black-eyed stare. She could only hope that she was doing the right thing by trusting the captain. It was hard to put faith in strangers, but she didn't see any other choice. Her simply being on his ship had put them all in a dangerous spot, adrift in the ocean with a mysterious vessel closing in. If he even suspected her of lying now, he'd just toss her overboard. Max had to hope the truth was enough to win her some sympathy.

Gently she placed the two jars on the captain's desk and angled them so that he could see the floating, misty faces within. He bent down to get a closer look.

"This a trick?" he asked.

"No," said Max. "That's my mom and dad. Vodnik the magician stole their souls and put them in these jars, and I'm stealing them back."

"That him in the other ship? The one that's headed toward us?"

"I think so," said Max. "Dridge said that Vodnik was paying him to kidnap me."

The captain folded his arms across his chest and stared down at her. "Perhaps the magician will pay me instead. Maybe more for all three of you? You think of that?"

Yes, she had thought of that, and that's why she was glad her friends were right outside the door. Though if it came down to a fight with the entire crew, they wouldn't stand a chance. But this captain felt like a different sort than Dridge, and Max was betting everything on that being true.

"I think . . . ," she began, forcing herself to meet the captain's stare head-on. "I think that if you could be bought, Vodnik wouldn't have bothered with Dridge. I think you have more honor than that."

Captain Hob chuckled, letting out a deep croak. "No one's ever called Hob the Hobgoblin honorable!"

Max shrugged. "I call them like I see them."

"Hmm. Well, I have no love for magicians and their games, I'll tell you that." The captain reached out a clawed finger and tapped lightly on her mother's jar. The image didn't stir. "And no one deserves to be trapped like that. No creature belongs in such a cage."

He turned back to Max. "I've heard the promises Vodnik makes. I've carried men and women across the sea who gave that magician everything they had just for a chance at happiness. And do you know what I think?"

"What?"

"Happiness isn't a place. Happiness is being free. Vodnik bleeds dry the desperate who don't understand this, feeds on those less powerful than he is. He is a creature to be feared."

"Are you afraid of him?" asked Max.

"I'd be a fool not to be," said the captain. "But no one turns a member of my crew against me. Magician or no, out here on the sea I am captain!"

In two long strides he had crossed the room and flung open the door. Mrs. Amsel came tumbling into the room. She, of course, had been listening at the keyhole.

He barely spared her a glance. "Keep those jars of yours safe," he told Max. "There's choppy waters ahead."

Max hardly had time to stow the jars away in her backpack as she scrambled to follow the captain onto the deck. Harold and Mrs. Amsel followed.

The captain used his binoculars to study the oncoming ship. After a moment, he handed them to Max. Through the glass, she could see that she'd been wrong earlier when she'd assumed it was a boat like this one. The ship that bore down on them was in fact an enormous longboat, the kind she'd seen in books and movies about Vikings. Mr. Twist could be seen on deck, beating a drum to keep time as the empty oars rowed *themselves*. And there at the prow was Vodnik, his long beard trailing in the wind. Despite the distance, he seemed to be looking right at her. Max quickly pulled the binoculars away from her face and, with a shiver, handed them back to the captain.

"Necromancy," he said.

"Necro-huh?"

"Death magic. The magician uses the souls he's trapped to crew his ship."

"Okay," said Max, shivering at the thought. "He has a crew of tireless ghosts. So what do we have?"

Captain Hob smiled. "We have the best captain ever to sail this ocean, and a darn good mechanic to boot!"

He called down to the engine room, which thankfully had stopped billowing smoke. "I need everything you've got!"

A crewman poked his head out the hatch, his green face black with soot. "Could use a few more hours to do it proper."

"You have two minutes," replied the captain.

The sailor grumbled under his breath and disappeared back into the hatch. Max and her friends watched the on-coming ship get closer and closer. They exchanged nervous glances as the seconds ticked away; all the while, the captain stood there calmly humming to himself.

Almost exactly two minutes later, there was a loud clang, followed by the rumble of the engine coming to life. "All hands to their stations!" the captain roared. "Anyone falls in, you'd better be ready to swim home. Let's show this magician what real sailors are made of. Full steam ahead!"

The goblinfolk let out a cheer, and the *Leviathan* began churning up waves as the chase began.

CHAPTER SIXTEEN

You didn't need to be an expert tracker to follow ogres. Rats were good at covering their trail, since they liked to hide their numbers and use surprise as an advantage. But ogres traveled out in the open, and they seemed to go to great pains to announce their presence for miles around to anyone who'd listen. Like it or not.

For instance, Lukas noticed that rather than hide their tracks, ogres took enormous pride in both the size and the depth of the footprints they left behind. Having big feet was a very attractive trait in an ogre. Also, they were noisy when they traveled, barreling into each other in their near-constant brawling, and singing at the top of their lungs. (At least, Lukas thought it was singing. That or they were just clearing their throats.)

As for the worrisome alliance between the rats and the ogres, it was not exactly a match made in heaven. Lukas and his friends discovered this when they came across a squished-dead *something* that might have at one time been rat-shaped. So this new alliance between the rats and the ogres might not have been perfect, and that at least was cause for hope. Which was good, because up until now Lukas had been able to find pitiful little else.

They'd been following the ogres for two days, across the grasslands west of the Great River and into the Shimmering Forest. Ogres were tireless creatures and marched day or night, but they weren't fast and they often stopped to brawl or smash things for fun. Lukas hoped that if they kept following, they might discover why the ogres and the rats were working together. They might even lead them to the rat king's nest.

That was, if Lukas didn't kill Paul and Emilie first. The two had never gotten along, but Lukas had long ago become accustomed to their bickering. Paul would do something to irritate Emilie, sometimes on purpose, and Emilie would retaliate by chasing him with a stick—always on purpose. But recently their relationship had changed. Now when Emilie got angry at Paul, she *really* got angry. Sticks wouldn't do, and she'd taken to hurling rocks at him. This escalation in hostilities was bad enough, especially when Emilie's aim went wide and she pelted Lukas instead, but even worse was their behavior when they weren't fighting. In all the long years that Lukas had known Emilie, he'd never seen the Eldest Girl of the village giggle. And he'd never seen Paul, who was widely known to be shameless, blush the shade of a ripe tomato. And yet that's what the two of them did almost nonstop when they weren't trying to murder each other. They walked side by side along the trail; they sat next to each other at night when they made camp. Paul cracked silly jokes and Emilie laughed and he would grin an idiot grin and turn red. The jokes weren't even that funny. There were only so many variations on a fart joke one person could stand.

And worst of all, even more unbearable than all the fighting and laughing and blushing were the compliments. Paul commenting on how nice Emilie looked today (which was totally untrue, as the three of them were covered head to toe in dirt and Emilie's hair stuck out of her bun like crooked straw on a bent broom). And Emilie wouldn't stop going on about what an impressive tracker Paul was, ignoring the fact that tracking ogres was about as hard as telling someone which way was up.

The two of them were so busy fawning over each other or fighting with each other that Lukas might as well not even have been there. But, unfortunately, he was. The sole witness to his two best friends' unbelievable, terrifying, stomach-churning *courtship*.

Not that Lukas was jealous—far from it. Although children back in New Hamelin often teased him about his feelings for Emilie, that was only because he was the Eldest Boy and she was the Eldest Girl, and there was an expectation they'd end up together. Lukas had never seriously entertained the idea, and if he'd ever wondered if his feelings for Emilie were more than friendly, he'd gotten his answer the day he met a new girl. A girl with bright pink hair.

But he tried to put that other girl out of his mind, as she was literally a world away and, he hoped, safe. And if nothing else, watching his two friends swoon over each other confirmed something Lukas had long suspected—love was gross.

They were finishing up a short rest (unlike the ogres, children weren't tireless) when Emilie called Lukas over. She and Paul had been huddled together as he used a stick to draw in the dirt. Probably pictures of a pig farting. Again.

"Lukas," said Emilie, "look here. Paul has just had the cleverest thought!"

The cleverest thought? Lukas could remember a time not very long ago when she'd accused the scout of using his empty head to store wool—just this morning, in fact. But he bit his tongue and joined them anyway.

Paul had sketched something in the dirt, but it wasn't a pig. It was a rough picture of the Shimmering Forest and the lands west of the Great River.

"Can I see your map?" asked Paul, so Lukas dug out the charcoal-drawn map of the isle he'd re-created from memory and laid it out next to the dirt drawing.

"Not bad," said Lukas.

"Well, I know the lands this side of the river well enough, as I've spent most of my days hunting or playing in this very same forest," said Paul.

Lukas nodded. "This is what you wanted me to see? I mean it's a good map, but . . ."

"But that's not all," said Emilie. "Go on, Paul. Tell him."

Paul scratched his head. "Well, I've been thinking about the path these ogres are taking, and something about it bothers me. So I drew this, because I wanted to be sure."

"Sure of what?" asked Lukas. Paul was clever, but not

known for his problem solving, and Emilie's boasting had obviously made him self-conscious about whatever it was he wanted to say. For a moment, Lukas felt sorry for him. As Captain of the Watch, he knew how hard it was to say what you really thought when everyone was waiting to hear what it was.

"Well," said Paul. "We've been thinking the ogres are headed to the mountains, what with the rats and all. And they certainly are going in that general direction, but that's what bothers me. It's *too* general."

"I don't follow you," said Lukas.

"It's the maps," said the boy. "Maps lie. By looking at the map and the trees around us, I can tell you that we are in the Shimmering Forest, right?"

Lukas nodded again.

"But what this map doesn't show you is the twisted ropewood tree that looks like a witch's nose where I buried the jars I use for catching kobolds."

Emilie gave a little sniff and Paul reddened. He'd most recently been grounded for trying to sneak a jarred kobold into New Hamelin—a punishment Emilie had sentenced him to.

"Anyway," Paul said quickly. "We passed that tree yesterday, and that would be right about here." He pointed to a section of the dirt-drawn forest west of the Great River where they'd crossed. "Now, the reason I use that ropewood as a marker is that there's a clear game trail that cuts right through the forest to the northwest. Can't miss it."

"But the ogres did," said Emilie.

"Well, that's no surprise," said Lukas.

"No, but the rats know about it," said Paul. "I've seen tracks there plenty of times, even if they try to hide them. And this morning we passed a little pond a ways back—remember?"

Lukas did remember. He hated any body of water bigger than a drinking glass, so he'd urged them to steer clear of it. Crossing the Great River had been bad enough, but things lived in dark ponds in the forests, things that didn't care for children.

"I know that pond because . . ." And for some reason, Paul began turning red again as he spoke. "Well, I know a nixie there. I mean, we've chatted. Couple of times. Maybe."

"Maybe?" asked Emilie, her proud smile vanishing all at once.

"Anyway," said Paul, carefully avoiding Emilie's gaze. "I know that pond, and I know that it's here."

He pointed to a new spot on his map, one that was much farther west than the ropewood tree he'd marked before. Lukas took a step back and studied the dirt. Paul had been right. The ogres were generally moving westward, but not in a straight line, and not in the way that would take them north toward the mountains. At least, not by any easy route. It could be explained away perhaps by the ogres' poor sense of direction, but rats wouldn't have made such a mistake. They were ignoring all the trails, but they weren't wandering lost. They had a destination in mind; it just wasn't the one the children had assumed.

"They're not heading north," said Lukas. "They're not going to the rat king's nest after all."

Lukas held up his own map, the one he'd made from

memory of the entire Summer Isle. Maps can lie, Paul had said. They weren't as far north as they'd thought; if Paul was right, then the ogres were heading due west, which would take them through the Shimmering Forest and beyond that . . .

Paul followed Lukas's finger as he traced the path. "New Hamelin," he said.

Lukas pictured the boys of the village Watch patrolling walls, thirty feet high and solid. Those walls were proof against any rat attack. Rats, yes, but what about ogres? What could just two of those hulking monsters do to that wall, much less four of them?

"I'm so stupid," said Lukas. "Those ogres aren't going to talk to the rat king about a possible alliance, because they're *already* working together! Whoever this new rat king is, he's a lot smarter than Marrow was. He's already figured out that the rats' same old strategies just kept failing, and somehow, he's gotten the ogres on his side."

"Well, maybe only those four," offered Emilie.

"Four could be enough. Four could tear down the wall, or smash through the front gate."

"We have to warn them," said Emilie.

"Get packed up," said Lukas. "We're not stopping tonight for camp; we need to make it to New Hamelin before they do. Paul, can you find the shortest way through the forest without running straight through those ogres?"

"As sure as spit I can," said Paul.

"Then let's go," said Lukas. "We have to reach the village before those ogres do. We have to warn them that New Hamelin is under attack."

CHAPTER SEVENTEEN

Because of the thick fog, it was impossible to tell how close Vodnik had gotten. He'd been gaining on them steadily, despite the *Leviathan*'s steam engine running on full power. There was unnatural speed and strength in the magician's ghostly crew.

Then the fog rolled in, and Max worried at first that it was a part of Vodnik's magic, but the captain reassured her that the heavy fog would work to their advantage.

"We're following a weirding way now," said the captain. "We sail by instinct."

"We're sailing into New York?"

"New York, sure," said Captain Hob. "But you won't find the Winter Children in New York. You'll find them off to the side and underfoot and just out of view, hidden from the eyes of normal folk. You see, it's magic that hides them, the strongest magic left on earth. To find them you have to know the way in, the way that will take you to the city *beneath* the city. But it's treacherous if you don't know how to sail it, and dangerous to walk if you leave the path."

As they continued on, Harold and Mrs. Amsel joined Max on deck while the captain barked commands to his men. Max could feel the tension on board. The sailors were quiet, and stole fearful glances at the mist.

"I've seen fog like this before," said Max. She almost said *on the Summer Isle,* but she stopped herself. The captain had been true to his word up until now, but people reacted in unpredictable ways once they learned Max had actually been to the lost land of magic.

"Was the place haunted?" asked the captain.

"Actually, yeah, it was," said Max. Shades Harbor on the Summer Isle was literally a ghost town.

The captain nodded. "Fog like this and you know that another world is nearby, whether it's the afterlife or something in between. Either way, the walls of this world get thinner when magic is close by. But the door is still locked."

The captain fixed his stare on Max. "That's what you're looking for, isn't it? The door to the Summer Isle? For your trollish friend there, perhaps? Few more years and he won't be able to pass among normal folk, but maybe there's a place where he wouldn't have to hide. Better life to be sure than hiding in a ship's cabin all your days. Only coming out when you're well clear of land, of people in general."

After just a day at sea, Max had grown accustomed to the captain's appearance, though she doubted that others would be so forgiving. "Why haven't you tried the doorway yourself?" asked Max. "If you don't mind me asking."

"The door is locked," said the captain. "Don't see the point."

"But if you knew someone who had the key," said Max. "And if that someone offered . . ."

For a moment, the captain said nothing, then he broke out into a large grin. At least, Max thought it was a grin. Hard to tell on a face like that. "So that's why the magician pursues you. Well, you are surprising."

"We can take you with us, if you want to go."

"I appreciate the offer, but I'm captain of my own boat, and my future. Don't want anything more."

"Well, thanks for everything," said Max.

"Don't thank me yet," said the captain. "Vodnik's still out there. But I know a fellow who can guide you the rest of the way. He will be waiting for us when we make port."

❖

"Port" turned out to be a lone dock jutting out into the bay, all that was left of a much larger pier that had fallen into disuse until it was little more than a few wooden pylons slowly rotting away. It was visible only by the light of a single lamp dangling from a post, and at the end of the dock a set of well-worn steps climbed up a rocky shore before disappearing into the mist.

Beyond, Manhattan was barely visible. Though this city was Max's home, it looked alien in the fog.

As the *Leviathan* pulled up alongside the dock, a little man in a yellow raincoat and hood stepped gingerly across the rickety old boards until he reached the boat. "What's your business?" he called.

"Three passengers disembarking, Cornelius," answered the captain. "Looking for the Children."

The little man in the raincoat shook his head. "Aren't they always? Follow me, then, those who're getting off."

With that, the little man turned and started back along the dock toward shore. Max and her friends had to scramble to catch up, and the dock creaked precariously under Harold's weight. The mist had turned into a steady drizzle, and Max pulled up the hood of her sweatshirt as she waved goodbye to the captain and crew of the *Leviathan*. But the ship was already pulling away from the dock. So much for goodbyes.

"Keep right," warned the little man. "'Less you want to take a quick bath. Everything here's falling apart and no one's around to fix things."

Harold helped Mrs. Amsel onto shore, where the little man waited. Max tried to get a good look at him under that raincoat of his. He looked normal enough, if on the small side.

"Ah," said Mrs. Amsel. "After that horrible goblin boat, it is such a relief to see a friendly face."

The little man gave a gruff smirk. "I don't remember us ever being friends."

"He's not much friendlier than the captain," whispered Harold, and Max had to agree.

It was strange to be so close to home and yet feel so different. Max had hoped that they might be able to go uptown to her family's apartment before starting their search for the Winter Children. They all could've used a hot shower and a meal, and Max even fantasized that she'd get to her door and her mom would be there to greet her. And that she'd smell smoke from her father's pipe drifting into the hallway. But Vodnik was somewhere close behind, and there was no time for fantasies. Their quest had turned into a race.

"Come on!" their guide called. "We have to time this just right if you want to find the Children. You're in luck—the weather's perfect!"

Max glanced at the dark clouds overhead, at the raindrops growing bigger all around them. *Perfect for what?*

They followed the little man through the winding streets of lower Manhattan. This part of the city was a mix of cobblestone streets hundreds of years old and towering skyscrapers of glass and metal. Max had always loved that about this part of the city—that it was history and future all tangled together—but today it just added to her feeling of unease. Like they were walking in between worlds.

They were in a rush, but that didn't prevent their guide from stopping off at a bakery to buy himself an enormous bag of baguettes and bagels.

"Like bread, huh?" asked Max. The little man had enough to last him a month, if it didn't go stale first, and he even loaded Harold up with a few extra bags. He scowled at her and pointed to an inconspicuous green awning across the street, barely visible in the fog.

"There," he said.

"That's it?" asked Max. She hadn't expected the Winter Children to have a storefront.

"No, no," said the little man. "Soon, though. Follow me." He swung open the door and scurried inside, and they had no choice but to follow. Max was hit at once by the smell of roasted coffee beans and the sound of espresso machines spraying foam. Someone was calling out orders to a crowd of people in business suits typing away on their phones. "Half-caf, soy chai! Extra-shot double latte!"

"Hey," said Max, tapping on their guide's shoulder. "Why are we stopping here?"

The little man ignored her as he stepped up to the barista. "I'll have a large dark-roast soy latte."

"That'll be four ninety-five," replied the girl.

He stepped back and looked at Max expectantly. "Spent all my money on bread," he explained.

Max threw up her hands. "I thought you were taking us to the Winter Children! Not out for coffee."

"Can't quite yet," said the man. "Gotta wait on the weather."

"You mean for it to clear?" asked Harold.

"Nope," said the man. "Gotta wait for it to get worse."

The barista let out a bored sigh. "Is someone gonna pay for this or what?"

In the end, Mrs. Amsel bought three coffees, plus a hot chocolate for Harold, and the four of them huddled around a standing table near the window (there weren't any chairs at all in this coffee shop, which seemed designed to discourage comfort). Harold ignored the stares of several nosy businessmen who pointed at him and whispered. Max gave them the evil eye until they turned around.

All the while, their little guide sipped his soy latte and looked out the window. Finally, Max couldn't take it any longer. She wondered how many other epic quests stopped for a coffee break.

"So," she said. "The captain called you Cornelius?"

"That's right," he answered.

"Well, Cornelius, I'm Max, and this is Mrs. Amsel and Harold."

"You can call me Gerta," said Mrs. Amsel, but Cornelius just shrugged.

"So, you guide people to the Winter Children?" asked Max. "I mean, like professionally?"

"Yep."

"Okay, so what did you mean when you said we were waiting for the weather to get worse?"

Cornelius peeked up at her from under the hood of his yellow rain slicker. Max saw bushy gray eyebrows and an overly large nose. The hood hid his ears, which Max suspected would be as pointed as Mrs. Amsel's. "You've heard tales of travelers who've gotten themselves lost in the woods or in a terrible storm, and ended up wandering into someplace magical. Ended up having supper with gnomes or running from goblins or something like that. You've heard those stories?"

Max nodded. Gulliver. Rip Van Winkle. Her father had told her all of them.

"The key to finding the Winter Children," said Cornelius, leaning close, "is you have to get lost to find your way!

How's that for an irritating bit of nonsense? Sounds like a fortune cookie, I know, but that's magic for you."

"How long do we have to wait?" asked Harold, setting down his cup. It looked doll-sized in his massive hand.

"Not much longer," said the man. "Time enough to finish our drinks, I think."

"Then you'll take us to find the Winter Children?"

"I will," said Cornelius. "But the question I have for you is, do you really want me to?"

"What do you mean?"

"I've guided a lot of people like you," said the little man. "More than I care to count. But each time I make them stop, maybe have a cup of coffee and think real hard about what they're about to do."

"We came all this way!" said Mrs. Amsel. "We traveled with those horrible sailors and more you don't even know."

"Just think about it," said Cornelius, lowering his voice. "You, me, even the troll boy there, we all have magic in our veins, but we're also part human. Those goblinfolk smugglers, Hob and his crew, they're mostly human, too, even if they don't act like it most of the time."

That's when Max realized that Cornelius must have assumed she was an elfling, too. With her sweatshirt hood up, her ears were hidden, and she was small enough. She didn't think now was the time to correct him.

Cornelius started to whisper something, but Max couldn't hear above the sound of the espresso machine piping in the background.

"You can speak up," she said. "No one in here's going to

care what you're saying." The businesspeople had stopped talking and were too busy checking their phones to listen.

"I'm not worried about *them*," answered Cornelius. "My point is, if you go looking for the Winter Children, you're giving all that up. The human side of you. Turning your back on this world for another. Think about it."

"We'll take our chances." And that was all Max said.

"You're all the same," said Cornelius with a sigh. "Fine, it's nearly time anyway."

The fog outside had indeed gotten much thicker, and the rain coming down now made it that much worse. The buildings, cars and even her friends standing just a few feet away were barely visible.

"Right," called their guide, struggling to be heard over the pummeling rain. "Stay close and follow me. We're going to get lost."

Max and her friends did as Cornelius asked, and he led them through the curving streets, and down alleyways that seemed to wrap back around on themselves. Most of Manhattan's streets were built in a simple-to-follow grid, but not so downtown. It was easy to get turned around there, even without the storm. After a few minutes, Cornelius called back, "Anyone have any idea where we are? No? Good, then that means we're getting close."

Max had begun to wonder if the little man wasn't just walking them around in circles in the rain for the fun of it, when he suddenly stopped at a doorway. It was set into a brick building beside a graveyard with a wrought iron fence—Max could see that much through the fog. A church perhaps.

"And a port appears in the storm," said their guide. "This'll be it."

"You're sure?" asked Max. "Looks like any old door to me."

"But it doesn't lead to just anywhere," said the man. "Come on."

The door, as it turned out, was unlocked, and it opened onto a flight of stairs leading down, beneath street level. A lantern hanging on a sconce illuminated the steps for some thirty feet or so. Beyond that was darkness. Their guide took the lamp and started down the steps. "Keep close," he said. "And shut the door behind you. Don't want anyone else getting lost and wandering in here. Humans aren't welcome."

Max saw Mrs. Amsel glance worriedly at her, but Max didn't give the housekeeper time to say anything. She pushed past her and began following the little man down the stairs. If humans weren't allowed down here, it was just too bad. There was a first time for everything.

⊰ CHAPTER EIGHTEEN ⊱

The stone steps spiraled down a long shaft into the darkness beneath Manhattan. Just when Max thought they couldn't travel any deeper, she saw a distant glow that signaled there might be an actual bottom to the stairway. The light was dim, even compared to Cornelius's weak little lamp, but it might as well have been a star shining in the inky darkness.

"There," said Cornelius. "Not much farther."

Max and her friends picked up their pace to follow him, when the stairs beneath their feet began to shake as the quiet was broken by a loud rumble.

"What's that?" asked Harold worriedly. "Earthquake?"

"They say there's a dragon chained up somewhere down here and that sound is his mighty snore," said Cornelius.

Max, however, thought she recognized the sound. "Or it's the subway. We've got to be under the tunnels by now."

Cornelius shrugged. "Dragon, subway . . . whatever. Let's keep moving."

As they neared the light, Max could make out the outline of a door set into a wall of rock at the bottom of the stairs.

"That the way in?" asked Max.

"One of them," said Cornelius. "The one that happened to find us today."

"It found us? Didn't we find it?"

"Hardly," said Cornelius. He paused at the entrance and looked back at Max and her friends. "Come on. Take a look at what you came all this way to find. Feast your eyes on the hidden home of the Winter Children."

It was not at all what Max had been expecting. The doorway opened into a natural cavern so huge that the walls disappeared in darkness. But in the center of the cavern there was light, generated by a large shantytown. The buildings, such as they were, had been constructed out of old car doors, sheets of aluminum siding and other various sorts of scavenged junk. The light came from cook fires dotting the stone floor and from lanterns strung up on crisscrossing cables, leeching electricity from the world above. And people, hundreds of people, were living practically on top of one another in those squalid conditions. Some with long ears, and skin ranging from shades of green to silver, sat around the fires, looking thin and miserable. Giants too big to fit into any tent or shack huddled together out in the open. They must have been trollsons, only bigger and, well, rockier, than Harold. And there were stranger beings in the mix that Max had no name for.

"Is that . . . ," said Max, nearly at a loss for words as she took it all in. "Are those the Winter Children?"

Cornelius squinted at her. "It's been well over seven hundred years since the Winter Children returned to this world, and this here is no land of eternal summer. Everything ages. Everything dies. The elves lived long lives, longer than most, but in time they grew old and died, too. Maybe they returned to where they came from, but if so, it was only in spirit."

"Then all these people . . ."

"Don't you see? We're all that's left. Great-great-great-grandchildren. Descendants of elves, trolls, goblins and the like. You see, girl, *we're* the Winter Children now. Lost in the cold, in a world that doesn't want us. We all dreamed of a better place; we believed in it so hard that we were willing to give up everything to get there. This is what we found instead."

The elfling spat on the ground. "Welcome to the end of the line. Welcome to Bordertown."

Led by Cornelius, Max, Harold and Mrs. Amsel wandered through Bordertown in stunned silence. Faces peered out at them from darkened doorways, studying the newcomers as they passed by. Some looked desperate, but even more just looked hopeless. People with glittery skin or too-long ears or some other physical quirk that prevented them from passing as "regular folk" up above. These, the true Winter Children, squatted down here in the dark and made a life for themselves. Of a sort.

Cornelius took his shopping bags back from Harold, the ones he'd filled at the bakery, and passed out bread to families. "People come here because everyone's promised the same dream," he explained. "A place where they can live without fear. It's rare these days, but not every elfling can pass as human. Sometimes the elf blood in them just gets too strong. And then there's the trollsons." Cornelius glanced back at Harold. "Always been hard for them to pass."

Cornelius gave two baguettes to a family with tusks like a walrus's. They showered the little man with so many thanks that he needed Harold's help to pull away.

"I'll say this for Bordertown," said Cornelius. "It teaches all different sorts to get along. Misery is a powerful thing to have in common with your neighbor."

But Max saw that not everyone in Bordertown lived in harmony. She witnessed two fights that nearly broke out over Cornelius's gifts of bread.

"Do you feed them all?" asked Mrs. Amsel. The old elfling woman's eyes were full of tears as she watched the elfling children snarl at her as they passed. After so many years of hearing stories of the Winter Children, she must have felt her heart nearly breaking now that she saw the truth.

"Thank goodness, no," said Cornelius. "There's a few more of us that make deliveries from up top. We've dug wells to tap the groundwater for drinking, though baths are hard to come by. And at night, teams go up top to scavenge through the Dumpsters and such. That's risky, though. No one wants to get found out."

It was almost too much, the level of despair and disappointment that hung in the air of this . . . *ghetto.* There was no better word for Bordertown. All these poor souls were hidden away, trapped by nothing more than their ancestry. But that wasn't why Max was here, and she needed to stay focused on the real reason for her visit. They might not have much time; Vodnik could be right behind them.

She opened her backpack and took out Vodnik's little chest. She had the Key of Everything, and she might be able to help all these people while still helping herself. After all, the Summer Isle was dangerous, but it had to be better than this place. At least there they could be free.

"Cornelius, can you show us the door to the Summer Isle?" said Max.

Cornelius let out a bitter laugh. "The door's locked, girl. There's no opening it, and there's been plenty that tried. Bigger and tougher than you. Bigger than your trollson friend here."

Yes, but they didn't have the key.

"Please," said Harold. "We have come far. Can you not show it to us?"

Cornelius gave a long sigh. "Same as always. Come on, then. Let's get this over with."

They'd started picking their way through the tents and run-down shacks when suddenly a booming voice called out, "Harold? Harold, is that you?"

They looked around, searching for the source, and saw an enormous trollson lumbering their way. Unlike Harold, this one definitely took after the troll side of the family tree. His skin was rough and pockmarked like stone in places, and he had moss growing along his shoulders and atop his bald head, like a bad toupee.

"Cousin Geldorf!" breathed Harold. "You made it!" Then he leaned down to Max and whispered, "He's a lot trollier than I remember."

"Well, I'd recognize that shock of red hair anywhere!" boomed Geldorf as he scooped up Harold in a giant bear hug. Literally giant, because Geldorf was well over ten feet tall. Now that the shock of seeing him was over, Harold looked genuinely happy to have found his cousin. The two of them laughed and slapped each other on the back with good-natured blows that would have flattened an ordinary person. Of course, neither of them was the least bit ordinary, and though Max didn't know much about Cousin Geldorf, it was obvious that being as big as he was, he was stuck down here for good. There was nowhere on earth where someone like him could blend in. Even if he wanted to run away to the mountains, as Harold claimed many trollsons did, how would he get there? Like everyone else in this cavern, he'd come to a new world looking for a shining paradise and found himself trapped in a town made of trash.

Harold introduced his friends, but Geldorf already knew Cornelius well enough. Everyone in Bordertown did.

"They want to see the door," said Cornelius, and Geldorf's face darkened.

"You warn them?" he asked.

"Why bother?" answered Cornelius. "No one believes it until they see for themselves. Same as always."

By now Max was getting frustrated. "Look, I know the

door's locked, but I have the key. We stole it from Vodnik himself."

"Stole it?" said Geldorf. "Well, that's a first."

"Do you even know what she holds?" said Mrs. Amsel. "This is the Key of Everything!"

Geldorf bent down and placed a hand on Max's shoulder. He was gentle, despite the fact that Max's whole head could have fit in the palm of his hand. "Cornelius is right," he said. "You should see for yourself."

Then Geldorf and Cornelius led Max and her friends to the far side of the cavern, to a door set into the rock. A full fifteen feet high and half as wide, it was made of solid stone, only smoother than the surrounding rock and polished to a shiny finish. Etched into the center was a crude picture of a tree in full bloom.

But it was the ground in front of the door that caused Max to gasp. At once Mrs. Amsel's arm was around her, supporting her. *They'd come all this way. They'd come all this way for nothing.*

The little housekeeper was whispering to her in German, trying to soothe her, but her words cracked with emotion and barely held-back tears, because there was no handle on the door and, worse, no keyhole. Nothing but plain, smooth stone.

And littered along the ground were hundreds of small brass keys. All identical to the one in Max's hand.

Max stared dumbly down at her own key. The magician's "magic" key.

"You see," said Geldorf, his voice thick with bitterness.

"He fooled you. Vodnik fooled us all. Most paid everything we owned for it, because we thought we were somehow special. But there is no Key of Everything. Never was. It doesn't exist. All there is is this door that cannot be opened. And piles of useless, fake keys."

PART III

CHILDREN OF SUMMER, CHILDREN OF WINTER

*N*egotiation. The word tasted strange in Wormling's mouth, as it would to any rat. It was simply not a part of their vocabulary, which was necessarily limited to begin with. No room for *negotiation* in an average rat's brain already crammed to bursting with *pillage, bite, claw, betray, murder* and *steal*.

But Wormling had never been an average rat. He possessed qualities considered oddities by other rats, such as adaptability and curiosity. And now he possessed that most unusual word, *negotiation*. A word that had turned out to be an unexpected source of power. A word that had made Wormling into a king. That, and the imposing creature at Wormling's side.

Today Wormling's back hurt, but that's what came with sitting atop the rat king's throne. The last king, Marrow, had stolen the chair from the elves themselves, and though it wasn't designed with rats in mind, it had become a symbol of leadership to sit upright like an elf or human might do. Sit upright and rule.

Still, Wormling couldn't wait to get back to his private nest, where he could finally lie down. Perhaps he'd have one of the females brush the tangles out of his fur while he napped. That would have to wait, though. Wormling had kingly duties to attend to first. Two duties today, the second of which gave him a sour feeling in the pit of his stomach just thinking about it. But the first . . . The first would be a real pleasure.

Wormling leaned forward and in his whiny, nasal voice shouted, "Bring him forth!"

The main hall of the rat king's nest was crowded with onlookers, rats who'd come to see how the new king dealt with today's problem. They were attended by slave children in iron collars who'd been plucked from the village of New Hamelin over the years. A pitiful few, considering how long the rats and the children had been at war. But thanks to Wormling, that was about to change. Thanks to that one magical word.

Two well-muscled rats shoved aside the onlookers and made way for the prisoner to be brought before the king. Spitter was his name, and he'd once attended King Marrow himself, until he'd had his tail chewed off as punishment for slandering the king behind his back. And here he was again. Some rats just never learned.

"Weeeell," whined Wormling. He let the word draw out because he knew how his voice grated on the ears of others.

He liked to watch them flinch at the sound of it. "Spitter, I hear you've been saying things about your king, again. Saying things that ought not be said. Something about whether I was fit to lead."

Spitter glared at Wormling with a look of open contempt, but then his eyes flicked to the creature at Wormling's side and he took a deep breath to calm himself. Wormling had to give the rat credit for being more cautious than he'd thought. Cautiousness combined with cleverness could be a dangerous thing. Luckily, Spitter was anything but clever.

"Well, Spitter?" said Wormling. "Do you have anything to say for yourself? I'm giving you this chance to speak in your own defense." *And just enough rope to hang yourself.*

Spitter took the bait. "Do I have anything to say?" snarled the rat. "Why should I say anything? Marrow wouldn't have wasted time with talking, but that's all rats do these days, isn't it?"

He turned and glared at the crowd. "Marrow would've had the stuff to come down off that fancy chair and fight me himself! When he took my tail, at least he did it because he could best me in a fight. He did it because he was stronger than me, because he was stronger than all of us, because he was a real king!"

Spitter glared up at Wormling. "Strongest rat rules."

Wormling settled back into his throne and tried not to wince at the crick in his back. Too many eyes were watching. "What is strength, Spitter? If you mean strength like Marrow's, then you are right, I am not strong. But Marrow is dead. The fiercest fighter we rats ever bred, yet under his rule we scraped out a miserable living in these tunnels while the children of New Hamelin fattened their bellies with food grown from the ground and forged weapons of iron behind their strong walls."

"So what?" said Spitter. "You saying we should become farmers now?"

"No," said Wormling. "But we can make the farmers farm *for us*. They can forge weapons *for us*. The only thing standing in our way is their wall." Wormling stood up from his seat, and stayed on his hind legs as he addressed the entire hall now. Just like a king would. "Since I became king, we rats are free to cross the lands unhindered, and without fear of the Peddler or his roads. And more, we are stronger than ever before because we have made *friends*."

With this last, Wormling turned to the massive ogre standing silently next to the throne. Dressed in little more than a loincloth and a few necklaces of finger bones, Org the ogre was so big that he had to duck his head or else bang it on the ceiling. That was good, because Org's head was the part of his considerable body that saw the least use.

Spitter nearly cried with rage. "That's what I mean! Rats don't need ogres to fight for them. Rats fight for themselves."

And there it was. The baited trap snapped shut on poor Spitter's neck. Wormling couldn't help but smile. "Do they?" asked Wormling. "So be it. Never let it be said that King Wormling is not a fair rat. Org?"

Spitter's eyes went wide as he realized what he'd just said. "What? No! I didn't mean that . . ."

But Org was already stomping across the hall toward the panicking rat. Spitter tried to run, but the guards blocked the exit.

"Better turn and fight," said Wormling. "Rats fight for themselves, remember?"

Wormling almost couldn't watch. He really was squeamish at the sight of blood, but thankfully it didn't last long. Wormling had to call the ogre off before he left too much of a stain on the chamber floor. But it had to be done. And it had to be done publicly so that others would understand. Wormling *was* the strongest rat, because Wormling was the cleverest. Because Wormling was the meanest.

He let his gaze drift over the gathered rats for a few moments of silence before speaking again. "Our alliance with the ogres of the Bonewood will mean that everyone will share in the spoils of war. The ogres will tear down the New Hameliners' walls, and we will shackle the children in chains. I've promised Org and his people all the pigs they can eat, and when our slaves have planted new fields of crops for us, the ogres will share in the bounty. Before long, not even the elves of the Deep Forest will be able to stand against us!"

Wormling shouted, his whine carrying through the halls and tunnels. "Marrow could not offer you this! But King Wormling can!"

The rats let out a cheer. Wormling could see it in their eyes—the greed and the hunger. Rats were not an industrious race by nature, but their inherent laziness could be overcome by the promise of bloodshed and gluttony.

There would be no more challengers to Wormling's rule. For the time being, anyway.

Wormling waited until the rats had dispersed, until he was left with just a few slave attendants and Org, before he sank back into his chair. How he wanted to lie down.

"Nice speech, rat king," said a nearby voice.

Wormling sighed as he recognized it. Now came the second meeting of his day. The one he'd been dreading. "I didn't know you were there. Were you watching all along?"

From out of the shadows stepped a crooked figure dressed in a tattered skirt, heavy cloak and kerchief. Grannie Yaga, the witch of the Bonewood, hobbled across the hall until she was standing in front of Wormling's throne.

"Hello, Org," said Grannie, nodding to the ogre. "Good to see you're still hitting things."

The ogre grunted in response.

"He doesn't talk much—or at all, actually," said Wormling. "But I guess you knew that."

"Ogres don't say much, but they're good listeners," said Grannie. "Like you, Wormling. Such a good listener. That's why your dear old Grannie made you a king, remember?"

Wormling bit back a sharp reply. No one had made Wormling into a king, except Wormling. The old witch had some sway with the ogres of the Bonewood, it was true, and she'd arranged for Wormling to present his plan before the ogres without getting squashed to paste. But Wormling had *negotiated* their alliance. Wormling, who convinced the rats to side with ogres in turn. Wormling, who took all the risks.

He'd love to tell Grannie so, but she was a witch and a powerful one at that. Long years serving vicious, unpredictable kings had taught Wormling when to speak truth to those in power, and when to bow his head.

"Slaves, leave us," said Wormling.

Grannie smiled at the children as they filed out of the chamber, exposing a mouthful of splintery wooden teeth.

"Such dears. It's a shame my oven was ruined when the Peddler wrecked my poor cottage. Going to take me some time to forge a new one. Ah, but there's no use crying over milk that's already spilled. And I planted the Peddler's bones six feet underground, so now I suppose we can call it even."

Wormling waited until the last of the slaves had exited. "What can I do for you, Grannie?"

"I hears that the rats and the ogres are marching to war," said Grannie. "Laying siege to New Hamelin, are we?"

"It won't be much of a siege," said Wormling. "By now my best fighters have met up with Org's kinfolk near the Great River. Together they'll march on to New Hamelin, where they'll join with the rest of my army. I expect they'll have the wall down within a day."

"But their new king won't be leading them into battle, eh?"

"I'm not that sort of king." Wormling leaned forward in his seat. Why should the witch act like any of this was news to her? "This was the plan, yes?"

"I come to ask for a small favor. Hold off the attack. For another day or so at most."

"Why? The longer we wait, the longer the New Hameliners will have to prepare a defense."

"Them walls are coming down," said Grannie. "Don't matter what sort of defense they muster. But there might be something inside that village that I want. Something that's been . . . misplaced."

"You can have it after we've taken the village," said Wormling. "Help yourself."

"Ah, but it's a fragile thing," said Grannie. "I want the

boy Carter, you see. I want him alive, and people got a habit of dying in war. Sometimes by accident."

Wormling knew the boy Grannie was talking about. He'd been the one they were after when Marrow led a band of raiders out into the wilderness—a quest that had gotten Marrow killed. Something about the boy being important to a prophecy regarding the Piper himself. But now the Piper was free, and Wormling had assumed that the boy had outlived his usefulness. Unless there was more to him than he'd been led to believe. If so, that could be a useful piece of information. Something to be tucked away for the future.

"How'd the boy get to New Hamelin?" asked Wormling. "He was in the Black Tower last I saw."

"Our friend the Piper was sloppy in getting freed," said Grannie. "The boy and his friends escaped. Used to be that I could keep an eye on the boy with my spies, but something's hiding him from me these days. Some strong magic. Not even the crows are talking. But I know his friends are headed to the village, so he must be with them. They wouldn't leave the poor crippled boy all by himself. No, he has to be there."

Grannie said the words, but she didn't sound very sure of them. The old witch was arguing aloud with herself, and her frustration was evident. Wormling hadn't had many dealings with the witch of the Bonewood, but he'd never seen her worried. Another item of interest to remember.

"So you want me to hold off the attack for one day," said Wormling. "While you fetch the boy yourself."

"One evening's all I'll need," said the witch. "Besides, I feel a Winter's Moon nearing to rise. Feel it in my deep bones. Better to wait for the true darkness to attack, don't you think?"

Actually, attacking in broad daylight had been central to Wormling's plan. Always before, the rats attacked the village on true nights, so it became as predictable as the sunrise itself. This time, he'd hoped to catch the New Hameliners at least somewhat by surprise.

But one didn't say no to Grannie Yaga. Wormling suspected that if the witch asked, Org the ogre would just as happily squash Wormling as he had Spitter. Wormling had made allies of the tiny-brained brutes, but their ties to the witch went back many, many years. It had been a clever ploy by Grannie to use the ogres to put Wormling on the throne, and now she could use the ogres to make him do what she wanted.

But Wormling had had a taste of power, and he wouldn't be content to be anyone's puppet. He'd do as she asked for now, but the witch had given up more than she knew. She'd shown weakness—a hole in her plans—and Wormling knew how to work a hole.

"We'll wait," said Wormling, bowing so low that his snout touched the straw-littered ground. "I'm happy to do any favors for Grannie. I'm at your service."

"That's a good little king," cooed Grannie.

"Just one thing," said Wormling. "What about the Piper? Now he's free, can't he stroll up to the village and play a little tune? Charm your boy into coming outside the gate? Could save us all a lot of trouble."

Grannie's brow furrowed for a moment; then she was all hideous smiles again. But Wormling had seen the look.

"The Piper is looking for something that was lost to him," said Grannie. "Soon as he finds it, he'll be along. Trust your old Grannie. Soon the whole Summer Isle will tremble before the combined strength of the Piper, the rat king and Grannie Yaga. Our time has come. Mark my words."

"And what do you get out of it?" asked Wormling. "We rats are simple creatures with simple needs, but what about the mighty witch of the Bonewood? What does she desire?"

Wormling took extra care to keep any hint of sarcasm or defiance out of his voice. Instead, his words dripped with awe and respect like sap from a wounded tree. Still, for a moment as Grannie watched him, her hideous teeth grinding together, he worried that he'd gone too far. Then, to his relief, she let out a loud cackle.

"Why, what does Grannie want? Grannie wants what she's always wanted. She wants to care for the children, of course. I helped the Piper break free from his prison so's he could find his precious pipe, so's he could play his sweet music again. Let him play, and let all the children of earth come a-running to these summer shores!"

Then the witch turned and stared at the doorway, where the child slaves had exited. "Course it's getting colder and the sun's hanging lower and lower in the sky these days. Poor little dears will need warming up. Need fattening up! Bring me the children, and Grannie will look after them," she said, and her expression sent a shiver down Wormling's rubbery spine.

ᚦ CHAPTER TWENTY ᚦ

The Piper was cooking Carter breakfast. He'd caught a hare earlier that morning, having lured it with a charm into their camp. Now the poor creature roasted over a tidy fire. The Piper, a hawk-faced young man who looked only a few years older than Carter's sister, had his pied cloak of red, green and yellow thrown over one shoulder as he tended the fire.

There was a purplish bruise on the Piper's cheek where Carter had punched him in an attempt to get away. The escape failed because the Piper was far too quick, but Carter felt better that he'd at least gotten one good hit in. Max would have been proud.

"Where are you taking me?" asked Carter, for what seemed like the hundredth time. They'd walked far in the storm, leaving the road behind them, and now with the coming of dawn, the countryside was all thickets and scrub-land. Nothing looked familiar.

"Well, you were headed south, so that seems like as good a direction as any," said the Piper. "But I think it's best if we cut across the wild country and stay clear of the road. I'm not the only one who's been looking for you, you know."

"What do you mean?" said Carter. "Who's looking for me?" His first thought was Leetha and Bandybulb, of course, but the Piper's answer surprised him. And scared him.

"Grannie Yaga is hunting you, Carter," said the Piper.

"Me?" said Carter. He'd spent only a short time locked up in the witch's hideous hut, but the experience was enough to stay in his nightmares forever. He would not soon forget the pairs of teeth hanging over her chair, or the clatter of wind chimes carved of bone. "Why would Grannie be after me?"

"That's a very good question," said the Piper. "Why indeed? The witch and I had a bargain, and once you were delivered to me at the Black Tower, that should have been the end of it. But why her interest in you now?" He leveled a long, thoughtful look at Carter, and Carter couldn't help but squirm under that stare. The Piper looked young, but his eyes were ancient.

At last, the Piper shrugged and said, "Who knows? But you're a child of prophecy, and that's something in itself. *Only when the last son of Hamelin appears and the Black Tower found will the Piper's prison open and the children return safe and sound.* Remember? Grannie's known about your coming for a long time. A *long* time."

"I don't believe in prophecies anymore," said Carter.

The Piper chuckled. "Why not? Look at me, free as a bird, thanks to you! The first part has already come true." He winked at Carter. "Let's do our very best to see that the second part doesn't, eh? It wasn't easy leading a hundred and thirty children to the Summer Isle. Wouldn't want all my hard work to go to waste."

"One hundred and thirty-two," said Carter.

"Hmm?"

"You forgot me and my sister. You kidnapped us, too, so that makes it a hundred and thirty-two."

"Touché," said the Piper. "One hundred and thirty-two."

"So, why don't you just hand me over to Grannie, then? You're both on the same side."

"Maybe we are, and maybe we aren't," answered the Piper cryptically. "Witches can be finicky, so for the time being at least, I'm keeping you close by where I can keep an eye on you. Finders keepers and all that. But it could be a while, so you might as well eat something."

The Piper took the roasting hare off the spit and nearly dropped it as he burned his fingers. "Ow, ow!" he said, sticking his fingers in his mouth. "Better let it cool first."

Carter left the rabbit untouched. The smell was making him sick to his stomach. Or maybe it was from being this close to the Piper again. "I'm not hungry—"

"Eat!" snapped the Piper, and Carter saw a flash of the madness, the unpredictable fury that he'd witnessed back in the Black Tower. He took a single bite of the roasted rabbit, but he barely tasted it. "At least, tell me what happened to my friends."

"They're fine," said the Piper, apparently satisfied now

that Carter was eating. He frowned. "Can't say the same for my rats, though."

If the Piper was searching for an apology for any harm that came to his rats, he could forget it.

"The elf girl's name was Leetha, wasn't it?" asked the Piper.

"I hope you didn't hurt her," said Carter. "She never did anything to you."

"I told you, they're fine. My rats went running back to their nest with their tails between their legs. That was a pretty clever trick, by the way—getting yourself an army of kobolds to fight for you. It almost worked, but you forgot the most important thing."

"What?"

"I'm a magician."

Carter sighed and tried to rub life back into his leg. He'd sat in one place for too long with his brace on, and now his foot was on fire with pins and needles. The Piper was right about one thing—how could you fight magic without magic?

"So, what now?" Carter asked. "You say we're going south, but south to where?"

The Piper paused and wiped his fingers on his cloak before tossing a rabbit bone over his shoulder. "Speaking of witches, I hear you had a talk with Roga of the Wood."

So the Piper knew, and Carter's worst fears were realized. He knew where Carter had been, and he probably knew where Carter was going, and more important, what he was after. "Who told you that?"

"Roga," answered the Piper. "And she was not happy with you. Not at all."

"Why? Because I refused to be her lunch?"

The Piper chuckled. "Pretty much. Roga always had strange ideas about hospitality."

Carter had to be careful with what he said next. The Piper knew a lot, but Carter wasn't sure that he knew everything. It was easy to forget that this seemingly young man was really centuries old. And most likely insane as well.

"So, what did you and Roga talk about?" the Piper asked.

"She didn't tell you?"

"Some. Not all."

And with these words Carter began to realize why he was here in the Piper's clutches, why he'd gone through all this trouble to chase him down. Roga, Carter suspected, had told him about their talk, but she hadn't told him where the pipe was. The Piper was playing a game with Carter, trying to get him to reveal the secret location of his instrument. It was cat and mouse again, just like back in the Piper's prison, but this time Carter would play the game differently.

"Honestly?" said Carter. "We talked about your magic pipe."

The Piper's expression remained calm, but Carter could see the effect just those few words had on him. His whole body tensed up tight as wire. "Where is it?"

Carter took a deep breath and steeled himself. "I'm not telling."

From his past dealings with the Piper, Carter had expected him to shout and threaten him, maybe even hit him. Carter wasn't looking forward to that, and he didn't think he was the sort to last under torture (he didn't really think there was any sort that would), but he wasn't going to give the Piper what he wanted without some kind of fight. He'd even taken up a handful of dirt so that he might throw it in the Piper's eyes if it came to it. Not that he would have much luck fighting a magician, but it made Carter feel better to be prepared.

But instead of getting angry, the Piper turned thoughtful, his fingers steepled beneath his chin. After a few minutes of silence, Carter was getting so worried that he started wishing the Piper would just yell at him and get it over with.

"What?" Carter asked, finally. "Why are you looking at me like that? Aren't you mad?"

"Oh, furious," said the Piper evenly. "But that won't get me my property back. I've only known you a short time, Carter, but in a sense I already know you so well."

"So?"

"So I'll tell you what I think instead," said the Piper. With a flourish of his cloak he leaped up, and Carter was startled into dropping his handful of dirt. So much for that idea.

"You and your friends were headed south," said the Piper. "Then the New Hameliners split off, probably heading back to their village. You, however, kept on traveling south with Leetha. Is that where the Peddler hid my pipe? Is it in the Deep Forest? The Princess's castle, perhaps? Or somewhere else along the coast?"

"I won't tell you," said Carter.

"Why?" asked the Piper. "Afraid of what I'll do with it? Afraid that I will steal away even more children of earth and bring them here to the Summer Isle?"

"Yeah, exactly that. Isn't that what you threatened to do back in the Black Tower? The villagers of old Hamelin banished you and your mother for witchcraft, and you stole their children away as a way to get revenge. But that wasn't enough, because you're obviously crazy, and now you plan to steal away *all* the children of earth. Remember telling me that insane plan? All you need is your magic pipe, so do you really think I'm going to help you find it?"

The Piper took a step closer, still smiling, but Carter knew better than to trust that smile. His hands were clammy, and he felt sick. He tried to prepare himself for the worst.

"And what if I did bring more children here?" the Piper asked quietly. "What if I think they are better off here with me, rather than back there with all those *grown-ups*? The scolds and the hypocrites. Is the Summer Isle so bad compared to them?"

Carter wanted to laugh, but he didn't dare. Was the Summer Isle so bad? Carter himself had wondered that at first, when all he could see was the opportunity for real magic and adventure. The Summer Isle was both those things, it was true, but it was also rat creatures and witches. It was cursed winter nights that made your nightmares come to life.

"There's nothing good about this place," said Carter quietly. "Nothing that isn't a lie."

The Piper squatted next to him. "Really? Nothing good at all? Then prove it. Take that brace off your leg, Carter."

Carter reflexively, protectively pulled his leg away from the Piper. "What? Why?"

"Take it off," said the Piper. "You slept with it on. It's obviously hurting you and it would feel better not to wear it for a while, so take it off."

Carter hesitated, not wanting to do anything the Piper wanted him to do. But he didn't want to push him too far, and there wasn't any harm in it, so . . .

He unbuckled the straps secured around his shin, sighing in relief as they fell away. Then, slowly, he pulled his foot free of the plastic-and-metal brace. He wiggled feeling back into his foot.

"Good," said the Piper, and before Carter could stop him, he kicked the brace out of reach. "Now stand up."

The Piper hadn't hit him, not physically, but he might as well have slapped Carter across the face. "You're not funny."

"I'm not trying to be." The Piper stood over him and planted his hands on his hips. "Get on your feet, boy."

So this was the Piper's punishment? He wouldn't physically hurt Carter, but he would play the part of the playground bully instead. No magic, no violence, but it was torture all the same. At least, it was a torture Carter was used to, it was pain he'd carried all his life, and he knew how to carry it. He wouldn't give the Piper the satisfaction of seeing how much it hurt.

Carter scooted himself within reach of the brace, but the Piper just kicked it away again.

"Stop it!" cried Carter.

"Stand up," said the Piper. "I won't tell you again."

Fine, thought Carter, and with his good foot underneath him, he pushed himself up to standing. On one leg, precariously balanced, he looked the Piper in the eye. "This what you wanted to see? You want to watch me fall?"

Carter put his bad foot on the ground. He gave it his weight . . . and it held. His foot wasn't curled, it wasn't twisted, it was standing flat on the ground. Finally, the feeling had come back to it, as the blood returned. And there was no pain. No pain at all.

Cautiously, Carter took a step.

It held. It wasn't as strong as his other leg, but it held. He took another step, and another, and he walked—he *walked*. Then he ran. He ran in circles around their campfire.

He came to a stop in front of the Piper, out of breath and tears streaming down his cheeks. "I don't believe it."

"Believe it," said the Piper, grinning. "Because it's only the beginning."

❧ CHAPTER TWENTY-ONE ❧

N ew Hamelin was still several days away at a hard
march, but on the second day, Lukas and his friends
got lucky, and the ogres set to fighting each other.
It wasn't just a shoving match this time, or even two ogres
wrestling. This was a battle. Paul was the one to see it begin,
as he had been spying on them at the time. Now that there
were rats traveling with the ogres, it was unsafe for anyone
but an experienced scout to get close. Ogres were about as
perceptive as dirt, but rats had keen senses of smell.

To hear Paul tell it, it had happened like this: The ogres
had stopped in the middle of the day to smash some rocks
together. Smashing rocks together was a popular pastime
among ogres because they liked the sound. Stopping infuri-
ated the rats, who wanted to push on to New Hamelin, but
when an ogre stops to smash rocks you don't get in the way.
Even a rat possesses that much common sense. On a normal

day they would have smashed rocks for an hour or so, then resumed their march, but on this day the unthinkable happened and they ran out of rocks. Sure, there were pebbles around, but nothing satisfyingly smashable, so one of the ogres did a very ogre-like thing and grabbed the two nearest ogres and smashed their heads together instead.

He discovered he liked the sound.

Soon the four ogres were locked in an every-ogre-for-himself battle to see who could smash whose head. By the time Paul snuck away, the outcome was still uncertain, but he had high hopes that at least a couple of them would end up with their heads smashed in permanently. It certainly would help their odds when they reached New Hamelin.

The head-smashing brawl allowed Lukas, Paul and Emilie to put some distance between them and the ogres, and by the time they reached New Hamelin, Lukas was confident that they were at least a half day ahead of the attackers. The bell ringers atop walls thirty feet high spotted Lukas and his friends, and the warning bells were already tolling by the time the village came into view. A group of Watch boys with long spears marched through the gate to meet them on the road. Even from a distance Lukas could see Finn, acting Captain of the Watch, leading the way.

"Blast it, Finn," Lukas muttered. "He knows better than to open the gate. How can he be sure it's us from this far away?"

"He's sure," said Emilie, putting a hand on his shoulder. "He's sure."

Lukas scowled, but he knew Emilie was right. He was on edge because he dreaded what they were about to do. Finn and the rest would be expecting a happy return, maybe even news that the prophecy about Carter had been fulfilled and that they were all going home at last. *Only when the last son of Hamelin appears and the Black Tower found will the Piper's prison open and the children return safe and sound.*

The poor New Hameliners had no idea what was really in store for them.

The Watch was armed, but their spears were lowered and their faces beaming as they saw their true captain returned at last. Finn stopped several feet away and saluted. The rest of the boys quickly stood at attention.

"Captain," said Lukas, saluting him back.

"You can knock that off," answered Finn, grinning broadly. "I see you didn't get yourself killed."

"Not for lack of trying," answered Lukas.

Finn grabbed Lukas and pulled him close for a hug. The rest of the Watch joined in, cheering and patting them on the back. Finn dared not hug Emilie, but he took her hand in his and said, "Welcome home, Eldest Girl. We've missed you."

"And I you," said Emilie thickly.

"Hey!" said Paul. "I'm home, too, you know!"

Lukas shook his head. Finn was the eldest scout, and Paul had been a pain in his backside for as long as he could remember. But Finn clasped his arm around Paul's and welcomed him, too. Then he eyed the frying pan strapped to Paul's back where his bow used to be. "Don't tell me you let Paul do the cooking! It's a wonder you weren't all poisoned."

Paul drew his pan and made like he would strike Finn

with it, but everyone was laughing by this point. For a moment, it truly was a joyous homecoming. But it couldn't last.

"Where are the two strangers?" asked Finn, noticing that whereas five had set forth, only three had returned. "The girl and her brother?"

"They're safe," said Lukas. "We hope they are, anyway. We have a lot to tell you, Finn."

Finn looked concerned. "Is any of it good?"

But Lukas could only shake his head. "Let's get inside and talk there."

Finn nodded grimly, and as he turned to lead the way into New Hamelin, Lukas took his friend by the arm and leaned in close. "And, Finn," he whispered. "Double the Watch on the gate wall."

They sat around Emilie's old table in her cottage in the village square. Outside the window the Summer Tree's leaves were bright with burnt autumn colors—reds, oranges and yellows. Little ones ran and played beneath its boughs and collected the leaves when they fell. Laughter filled the square as word spread that the Eldest Boy and the Eldest Girl had returned. But inside all was quiet. The remains of a lunch of bread and cheese cluttered the table, and a map of New Hamelin's defenses had been laid out at one end.

After a few moments, Finn broke the silence. "I'll bet they come for the western walls here, and here," he said, jabbing his finger at the map.

"Why's that?" asked Lukas.

"Well, they know we'll have reinforced the front gate. We'll have extra archers, too."

"Don't think ogres are going to care much about our arrows," said Paul. "Skin's tougher than boiled leather."

"You might be right, Finn," said Lukas. "But the rats also know that short of shoring it up with a solid wall, the gate is still the weakest point. Built to open, after all."

"Do you really think the ogres are taking orders from rats?" asked Finn.

"Not orders, exactly," said Emilie. "But they're working together. I can hardly believe it, but it's true."

It was stuffy inside the cottage at midday, and Lukas wiped brown sweat from his forehead. They hadn't even stopped to wash off the dust from the road. There just wasn't time.

"So either the ogres try to break down the gate," said Lukas, "or they try knocking a hole in the wall. Both are bad."

"And how long again before they get here?" asked Finn.

"Half a day maybe," said Paul. "Tomorrow evening at the latest, assuming they don't kill each other on the way."

"We can only hope," said Lukas. "But we need to plan for the worst. Any ideas?"

No one had a chance to answer, however, as they were interrupted by the clanging of bells. Someone was approaching New Hamelin.

"Already?" asked Finn, his face turning pale.

"No!" answered Paul. "It's impossible. I mean, isn't it?"

Emilie cuffed him on the back of the head as the four

children ran from the cottage. But Lukas noticed that she was watching Paul with worry, not annoyance.

Paul was right. It couldn't be the ogres—but then who was it?

Finn and Lukas led the climb up the gate wall until they were standing on the platform the Watch used to patrol the wall. A small bell ringer was leaning out of his watchtower and pointing. "There!" he cried. "On the road!"

Lukas squinted against the midday sun and spotted a small hunchbacked figure walking slowly along the road toward New Hamelin. Emilie joined him at the wall.

"Could it be?" she breathed, and Lukas felt his heart give a leap in his chest. It was impossible, and yet now when they needed him the most, could the Peddler have returned? Might the old magician be alive after all?

Paul gave a cheer. "Open the gate! I've never been so happy to see that sour old man!"

But Lukas countermanded the order. "Wait!"

Finn and Paul shot him confused looks, but Lukas kept his eyes on the approaching figure. *Please,* he thought. *Please.* He wouldn't give the order yet, however. The gate remained closed as they watched and waited.

Lukas called up to the bell ringer in the watchtower. It was Pidge, the boy who'd been on duty the night the rats made it over the wall. He had keen eyes and the better vantage point. "What do you see, Pidge? I want details."

"It's an old man," said the boy. "Moving slow . . . wait, it's not an old man. It's an old woman!"

Emilie gasped aloud, and Paul let out a curse. Lukas kept his face impassive, but inside, his heart broke down the middle. It felt like prayers were never answered on the Summer Isle.

They watched together as the old hag hobbled into clearer view. Hunched back, long hooked nose and a mess of stringy white hair dangling from her hood. Not the Peddler, but the very witch who had murdered him. Grannie Yaga was coming to New Hamelin.

Paul reached for one of the Watch boy's bows. "Give me an arrow," he said. "One arrow is all I'll need."

"No," said Lukas. "Shooting arrows at a witch is not the same as shooting at rats. You've seen what she can do."

"Then what?" asked Paul. "We wait for her to knock?"

Lukas took a deep breath. "Open the gate. I'll meet her on the road."

The boys stared at him blankly.

"Do it!" Lukas snapped, and the great sliding pole began to grind against wood as they pulled it free.

"I'm coming with you," said Emilie. Lukas would have argued, but he knew it wouldn't do any good. Paul, however, didn't possess such good sense.

"You can't go out there!" he said. "That witch killed the Peddler and who knows how many other people over the years."

"I'm the Eldest Girl," said Emilie. "I have to go."

"I won't let you!" said Paul.

Lukas cringed, and braced himself for the verbal thwacking that Emilie was surely about to deliver. No one ordered Emilie to do anything. But, to his shock, she didn't get angry at all. She only put her hand on Paul's cheek and said, "I'll be fine. You can watch out for me from here."

Then Paul silently nodded, and Emilie scooted past Lukas on the stairs and headed for the gate. Lukas shook his head in disbelief. Some things in life were mysterious, and Paul and Emilie's relationship was near the top of the list.

Lukas and Emilie were getting ready to step through the gate when Finn climbed down to meet them. He was holding an ugly black iron sword in his hands. "Lukas, take this."

The Sword of the Eldest Boy was nothing Lukas had ever wanted, and for a time—while he was on the road with Max and her brother—he thought he'd gotten rid of it for good. Both the sword and the responsibility that came with it. But he was home now, and he'd learned that some responsibilities will only chase you if you run from them.

"Thank you," he said as he strapped the heavy blade around his waist. "Close the gate behind us, Finn. Quickly."

The boy nodded, and as Lukas and Emilie stepped outside, Paul called down from his perch atop the wall. "She gives you so much as an evil look and I'm filling her full of arrows."

"I'm counting on it," said Lukas. He tried to swallow, but his mouth felt dusty and dry.

"Let's go," said Emilie, and the two of them marched side by side down the road to meet the witch.

Lukas hadn't noticed it before now, but the Peddler's Road was changing. He hadn't seen the changes up close because they'd cut through the wild country in pursuit of the ogres, but now he could see the transformation that was taking place. Briar bushes were encroaching from all sides, and tangled vines snaked across the path, as if looking for an unwary traveler to trip. Something terrible was laying claim to the source of the Peddler's magic, and Lukas suspected that something was right in front of them.

They stopped to wait for the witch a quarter of a mile from the village gate. Lukas wanted to make sure she came no closer.

"Well, lookee here," cackled Grannie. "Coming to welcome old Yaga, are we? Ask her to sit a spell? Maybe offer her something plump to eat?"

When she grinned, she showed a mouthful of broken wooden teeth.

"You're not welcome here, witch," said Lukas.

Grannie's smile faded. "Manners, young man. Best learn to respect your elders. I'm not wearing my good teeth today, but I can fetch them."

"What do you want?" said Emilie as she put a warning hand on Lukas's arm. She was right, of course. He might as well have let Paul fire his arrows if this was how he was going to behave. But he couldn't help it. When he looked at Grannie, all he saw was the Peddler, fighting for his life, and losing.

"Well, if you're not going to invite Grannie in . . ."

"You know that we aren't," said Emilie.

"All right," she said. "Do you know what is marching your way? Them that's coming through the Shimmering Forest for you?"

Emilie and Lukas exchanged a glance. "We know," he answered.

Grannie laughed. "Ogres strong as rock and mountain. Rats clever and cruel come to put the children of Hamelin in chains."

"Rats have tried to breach our walls before and failed," said Emilie. "They'll fail again, with or without the ogres."

Grannie shook her head. "Oh, no, dear. Not this time, methinks. This time'll be different."

"So that's why you came all the way out here?" asked Lukas. "To taunt us?"

"No, you stupid boy. I came to deal. The rats have a new king, a dangerous king, ambitious, too. But he'll leave you be—if Grannie tells him to."

Lukas wasn't sure if he believed the witch's claim that she could tell this new rat king what to do—rats had never much cared what witches wanted before. But then again, rats had never allied themselves with ogres before. The Summer Isle, a land where time held no sway, was changing fast. "Even if you could get the rats to turn around, what would you want in return?"

"The Piper foolishly let the boy Carter escape from the Black Tower," said Grannie. "I want him back."

So Grannie thought that Carter was still with them, and she thought they were keeping him safe inside New Hamelin. Lukas nearly laughed in her face. He very nearly told her that Carter wasn't there, and that she'd come all this way for nothing. It would have been almost worth it just to see the look in her eyes. Almost.

Thankfully, Emilie spoke up first. "What do you want with him?"

"That's my business, pretty thing," said Grannie. "Shouldn't matter to you anyways. All that should matter to you is giving me the boy, or watch your friends made slaves by the rats. The lucky ones, that is."

Should he tell her that Carter wasn't in New Hamelin? Would that make her leave them alone? Or would it just put the boy in more danger than he already was? At least, Grannie wouldn't be out there hunting for him if she thought she'd already found him.

Lukas looked at Emilie, and a silent agreement passed between them. "There will be no deal," said Lukas.

Grannie started to argue, but Emilie cut her off. She spoke as the Eldest Girl, the one who'd led them and who'd kept them safe, Lukas included. "Do what you like, witch. But we don't give up our own. Now turn around and leave this place."

For a moment, the air between them was thick with tension as the Eldest Girl of New Hamelin stared down the witch of the Bonewood. Grannie Yaga was not used to people saying no to her. Her eyes narrowed in anger and she took a step forward, one bony hand reaching for Emilie.

Something whistled by Lukas's ear, but Grannie flicked her wrist and the arrow Paul had fired veered away, as if deflected by a mighty wind, and landed harmlessly in the road. Lukas drew his sword and planted himself between Emilie and the witch.

Grannie made another gesture, waving her crooked fingers at the sword as she had with the arrow, but nothing happened. Then the witch's eyes went wide as she got a good look at the black iron blade.

In the time before, in the old world, Lukas's father used to tell stories about the wicked creatures of the forest. The elves and the goblins, and the witches that waited to carry off troublesome boys. His father hung a horseshoe of cold forged iron over their door, to drive such evil creatures away.

The Sword of the Eldest Boy had been given to New Hamelin long ago by the Peddler himself. A symbol, but more than a symbol. A weapon of cold forged iron.

Almost cautiously, Lukas jabbed at the witch with his blade. He struck her on the wrist, barely a tap, but she screamed in pain, and the air suddenly smelled of burning brimstone. Quickly for one of her age, Grannie Yaga leaped back and hissed at Lukas.

"Curse you, boy, but I'll make you pay for that! I'll snap your bones with my good teeth!"

Sword point out, Lukas advanced on her, and Grannie Yaga whirled around as her cloak fell away, and suddenly in the witch's place was an ugly long-necked goose. It honked at Lukas angrily before taking flight, its powerful wings carrying it west over the trees of the Shimmering Forest and out of sight.

❧ CHAPTER TWENTY-TWO ❧

While Cornelius continued to make his rounds handing out bread, Geldorf invited Max and her friends back to his home in Bordertown, meager as it was. There was no weather to speak of down here belowground, so the little shacks and tents were more for privacy than anything else, but the trollsons were too big to fit into any lean-to, so they gave up privacy for community. The trollsons and the giant daughters mostly lived together in the troll quarter, on the edge of Bordertown proper. They sprawled out beneath a massive outcropping of rock, several stories tall, which possessed disturbingly troll-like features. There they sat and talked and slept out in the open. But every person needs a place to call his own, and Geldorf's was a stretch of cavern floor where he'd built a bed out of several old mattresses scavenged from above. He'd decorated a few nearby stalagmites with tattered old lampshades and hung up a faded painting of dogs playing poker.

Harold remarked at the odd outcropping overhead—from a certain angle it looked a little trollish, almost like a roughly carved statue leaning against the cavern wall. Geldorf explained that it was just old Hillbeater. As tall as a house, the poor trollson was pure second-generation, and he'd gotten so trollish and rocky that no one had seen him move in centuries. The trollsons and giant daughters still talked to him, though, just in case he appreciated the company.

Geldorf offered his guests canned beans and chocolate bars from a large stash of food that the trollsons all shared. When Harold asked how they had so much when the rest of Bordertown was going hungry, Geldorf explained that the teams who went above to scavenge for food always fed the trollsons and giant daughters first and even left them with extra. Though they wouldn't admit it, Geldorf said that the elflings and goblinfolk probably worried that if the trollsons went hungry, they might start eating the others, like their ancestors once did. Geldorf swore that he'd tried to explain how trollsons hadn't eaten another intelligent creature since his great-grandfather's time, and even then most cases had been because a trollson had lost his temper, not because of a rumbling stomach. For some reason, this didn't seem to relieve anyone very much. The extra food kept coming, and it was delivered with extra politeness.

Geldorf thought the whole business was quite funny, but when Harold scolded his cousin, Geldorf admitted that he and several of the other trollsons snuck the extra food back into the elflings' and goblinfolk's stash when they weren't looking. Bordertown took care of its own, Geldorf explained; it was just fun to watch the little folk sweat sometimes.

As they gathered around one of the trollsons' campfires, Geldorf told Max and her friends all he knew about the locked door. It was the last of its kind, the last portal by which the ancient magical creatures had abandoned the earth for the Summer Isle. It had no keyhole because it was never meant to be locked.

"That door was supposed to stay open, you see," said Geldorf as he used his enormous pinky to clean out the last of a can of baked beans. "All those centuries ago, when creatures of magic blood fled this world for the Summer Isle, this one door was left open for those who stayed behind. Just in case they had a change of heart and wanted to follow later. Or were forced to."

"The poor things," said Mrs. Amsel, dabbing at her eyes with her scarf. She was having a hard time dealing with the disappointment and shock of seeing Bordertown, and when she was upset, she needed to talk.

Not Max. Max just sat quietly clutching her backpack to her chest, and stared at the key in the palm of her hand, feeling the cavern's oppressive darkness weighing down all around her. She pulled her hood tighter around her head, partly to hide her oh-so-human ears, and partly to ward off the damp chill of the awful place.

Pink-haired girl at the bottom of the world.

"So, then, who locked the door?" asked Harold.

"The door was locked when the original Winter Children first came to this world," said Geldorf. "When one hundred and thirty elf children were stolen from the Summer Isle by the Pied Piper of Hamelin!"

"That villain!" said Mrs. Amsel. "He locked the door so they could not get home, didn't he?"

"That's the story," agreed Geldorf. "Laid a curse upon the door, and it's been locked up tight ever since."

"Why don't you tell people the truth about this place?" asked Harold. "Surely there's people, like Cornelius, who could get word out. Maybe Vodnik wouldn't be able to trick so many then."

"Been tried," said Geldorf. "But my experience is that there are certain things people just want to believe in, no matter what you try and tell them. The door to the Summer Isle is one of those things. You can tell people that it can't be opened, you can plead with them, tell them this place is a dead end, but they won't believe you until they are staring at it themselves. It's not like no one knows what a villain Vodnik really is. I knew! But I fell for his lies anyway, because I wanted to believe. I was desperate."

"I cannot imagine how one person could be so evil," said Mrs. Amsel. "An elf wouldn't be capable of such cruelty."

Geldorf laughed. "If you believe the stories my great-grandfather used to tell about elves, that's *exactly* the sort of thing they were capable of. The cruelty of elves is kind of legendary among troll-kind. Also, that they taste like chicken."

Mrs. Amsel shot Harold a worried look, but Geldorf held up his hands, smiling. "Ah, but all that gets left at the entrance to Bordertown, no worries. Old grudges forgotten, eh? Elflings or trollsons, we're all in the same pickle down here."

Max was getting tired of listening to everyone talk. Geldorf was enjoying himself, and why wouldn't he? They were probably the only new faces he'd seen in years. He couldn't resist having a little fun at Mrs. Amsel's expense, because what else was there to do down here to pass the time? But Max didn't feel like playing along.

"So, this key is useless?" she said, startling them all because she hadn't said anything for the past hour.

"Useless as me using this chocolate bar to open that can of beans," said Geldorf. "Vodnik made up a story about some magic key, and we all fell for it. Seems stupid enough now, even the name—the Key of Everything! Hah! What a bunch of suckers we all are. Take old Hillbeater there," said Geldorf, and he pointed to the trollish mountain of stone looming over them. "They say he was the very first of us to get duped by the magician. He's been down here for who knows how many centuries, and now look at him. Good for hanging your laundry from. No offense, Hillbeater!"

"But I thought trolls turned to stone in sunlight," said Mrs. Amsel. "No sun down here, yes?"

Geldorf rubbed his massive belly as he talked, and it sounded like sandpaper. "All giant Folk eventually return to the earth that made them. Sun just speeds things up, is all, but old age will do the trick, too. Same fate awaits us trollsons. That's why I'm so nice to old Hillbeater there, because someday I'll be a dumb lump of stone sitting right next to him!"

Geldorf laughed as he said it, but Max could see the hurt

in the big trollson's eyes. And the anger. He knew that he would never be able to leave Bordertown. The door to the Summer Isle was locked, and there was no place for him aboveground. He'd come to the end of the line, and he knew it.

Max had had enough. "I'm going for a walk."

"Eh?" said Geldorf. "Careful. Not everyone down here is as hospitable as we trollsons are."

Before she could object, Harold also got to his feet. "I'll go with her."

Max seriously wanted to be alone, but it didn't look like that would be possible. "Guess I can't stop you," she mumbled, but if Harold heard her, he ignored it.

They left the troll quarter, and as they explored Bordertown, Max was reminded of New Hamelin with its ramshackle buildings and twisting streets. But New Hamelin was alive, whereas Bordertown felt, if not dead, then certainly diseased. The children of New Hamelin lived in constant fear of the dark, but they countered that fear with playfulness and they celebrated the daylight. There was no daylight down here, ever. No cure for the dark. It was as miserable a place as Max had ever seen.

Harold yanked her out of the way as a pack of feral children ran in their path. They were waving sticks and shouting as they chased a city rat through the scattered garbage. Max didn't know if this was just a cruel game or they were actually hunting the rodent for food. She had no love for rats, even the ordinary rats of this world, but she still felt relieved when the creature escaped into safety beneath a pile of rotting cardboard boxes. "This is horrible."

"I've seen places like this before," said Harold. "Maybe not as big, but I've been to slums filled with magical Folk in hiding. Trollsons especially."

"Why live like this?"

"What choice do they have? Think about it. They can't get jobs, so they have no money, no home. Remember, I was living under a bridge before I met you, and I don't even look that trollish. Not yet."

"I'm sorry," said Max. "I guess I wasn't really thinking."

"It's okay," said Harold. "My grandmother Gertrude always said that feeling sorry for people is easy, understanding them is harder."

"Smart lady."

"Was she ever! Of course, she could trace her family all the way back to the Bavarian Stonemunchers, which claim to be nobility, but that's really by marriage only—"

"Harold."

"Oh. Sorry."

Max watched as the children gave up their rat hunt and wandered off in search of something else to fill their empty stomachs, or at least relieve the boredom.

"I just don't know what to do next," said Max. "Ever since I got back from the Summer Isle, I've had a goal: Find the Winter Children. I pinned all my hopes on this magical door of theirs. I thought I could get back to the Summer Isle and find Carter. We'd ask the elves or something to break the curse on my parents. But now . . ." She looked down at the backpack clutched in her hands. "I'm out of options, and there's really nowhere left to run."

"Actually, that's why I wanted to walk with you," said

Harold as he absently kicked the pile of cardboard. He was full of nervous energy, which was unusual for the normally still trollson. "It's about Vodnik."

"I know. He's still after us."

"That's not what I meant, not exactly. See, I've been thinking about what Geldorf told us about the door and all those fake keys, and there's something that just doesn't make sense."

"What?" said Max. "Vodnik's a scam artist, and he scammed all these people into believing he could get them to the Summer Isle. You saw that door—there's no keyhole, nothing. This key is useless, just like all the rest."

Harold stopped his fidgeting and looked Max in the eyes. "Then why is he chasing you?"

"Well, because we stole . . ."

"A useless fake key? Why bother?"

"Okay, but there's also my mom and dad."

"Again, why bother?" asked Harold. "Why are you so special that he had to kidnap your mom and dad in the first place?"

"He said something about not wanting people to know that I'd actually been to the Summer Isle. I guess he thinks I'll spoil his big scam."

"You heard what Geldorf said. People believe what they want to believe. They'll keep coming to Bordertown because they want to believe there's a place for them. And Vodnik will keep scamming them, no matter what you say to anyone."

"What are you getting at, Harold?"

"Why is Vodnik going through all this trouble for *you*?

If that door really can't be opened, why does it seem he'll do just about anything to keep you from opening it?"

Max thought about this. Even if people did hear her story, that way into and out of the Summer Isle was gone. It couldn't be a threat to Vodnik now. Harold was right about that much—Vodnik's actions just didn't make sense.

She pulled out the key and looked at it. A simple brass key.

"But it doesn't work," she said. "Just like all those other keys!"

"What have we got to lose?" said Harold. "While there's still time, maybe you should just try *opening the door*."

CHAPTER TWENTY-THREE

C arter leaped from one rock to the next, too carelessly perhaps, considering the gaps in between and the steep, crumbling incline on either side. A few yards ahead, the Piper called to him to hurry up. Carter could see his pied cloak fluttering behind him in the wind like a flag.

They had spent much of the afternoon climbing down a scramble of fallen rocks and boulders to what the Piper claimed was a trail through the woods below. It was hard going, with pitfalls every few feet—and Carter was having the best time of his life. His leg was still weaker than it should have been, but that would change as the muscles he'd never used before grew stronger. And besides, climbing on things you shouldn't was one of those things all boys did, and now Carter could, too.

They were continuing south, though Carter still hadn't told the Piper where exactly the pipe was hidden, and the strange thing was, he hadn't asked. Not since that first morning. By daylight they hiked through woods and scrubland, over creeks and around lakes. In the evening they would camp, and the Piper would carve a new flute from hazel wood or yew. Then he'd play little tunes and perform minor magics, such as lighting their cook fire from nothing, or summoning a wind to clear the brush off the ground so that they could have a relatively comfortable place to sleep. Every now and then he'd fail, like when he tried to stop a particularly fierce thunderstorm from pouring rain down on their heads. His freshly carved pipe split then and cracked in his hands, and the Piper was left cursing and forced to start over while the rain soaked them both to the bone.

Carter thought that the Piper might be responsible for the freakish storms that had plagued him and his friends, but the Piper claimed not to be. The weather was changing on the Summer Isle, he said, changes that were beyond even his control. Everything was changing. Carter wasn't sure at first whether he believed him, but the Peddler's Road had definitely transformed, and the weather was getting more and more extreme. It was like the land was turning wilder. The ropewood trees in this little patch of woods looked more like hangman's trees, with their looping branches that resembled nooses. Carter made sure to keep his head low whenever they passed one.

By the time Carter made it to the bottom of the rock scramble, the Piper was sitting cross-legged on the ground, examining his newest pipe as he used a branch from a horsetail plant to smooth away the splinters.

"I was wondering if you'd ever make it down from there," said the Piper. "I've been waiting forever."

Carter was out of breath from the descent and his leg ached, but it was a different kind of ache. This one felt good. "You'd be waiting a lot longer if I fell and split my head open on the way down."

"No, I wouldn't," answered the Piper, in all seriousness. "I'd just keep on by myself."

"Great. Thanks."

"I can't bring people back from the dead, Carter. No one's *that* good a magician." The Piper leaped to his feet. "Can we go on? Or do you need to rest?"

"I'm fine," said Carter. "I can keep up."

"Good," he said. "I want a brisk pace today, and with any luck we'll reach the Deep Forest by evening."

They didn't. But they got within sight of it. The massive forest of the elves dominated the horizon like a mountain range, dark and imposing, though it was still far off, and the trek across country was slow going. When evening came, they took shelter beneath an overhang of rock and lit a small fire. It didn't give off much heat, and Carter was forced to dig his woolen cloak out of his pack. It was right next to his leg brace, which he still hadn't thrown away. The brace was cumbersome and took up most of his backpack, but he couldn't quite bring himself to believe he wouldn't need it again. He half expected to wake up in the morning with his foot curled in on itself again, the dream over.

"Winter's Moon will be coming soon," said the Piper, watching Carter wrap his cloak around himself. "A day or two at the most."

Carter tried to swallow the lump of fear that rose at the mention of that long night. The darkness here on the Summer Isle had a way of taking your nightmares and making them real.

"I can help you to control your fear, you know," said the Piper.

"What?"

"That's the key to this place, to the darkness especially. Master your fear, and you master the darkness."

"I'm fine," said Carter.

"As you like," said the Piper. "You don't have to listen to my advice. But just remember, you couldn't walk on that crippled leg of yours until I told you to."

"I was never *crippled*," said Carter.

The Piper stared at him. His eyes nearly glittered beneath the shade of his cloak's hood. "I'm sorry. I forgot you don't like that word. How about *lame*?"

"Cut it out!"

The Piper chuckled. "Carter, Carter, we are never going to get anywhere if you keep letting words hurt you. I thought you were stronger than that."

"What do you mean *we* won't get anywhere?" asked Carter. He was tired from the day's march and tired of the Piper's constant taunting. "You keep acting like we're suddenly some kind of team, but we're not. I'm your prisoner, remember?"

"You don't trust me."

Now it was Carter's turn to laugh. Not long ago he would've been frightened to laugh in the Piper's face, but this was just too ridiculous. "Of course I don't!"

"Shall I tell you a secret?" asked the Piper. "That's how people learn to trust each other, isn't it? By sharing secrets?"

This must be some new game of the Piper's, but Carter didn't see the harm of playing along this time. "Fine," he said. "Tell me a secret, but don't expect me to share one in return."

"All right, then, here it is: I didn't steal the Winter Children."

"What?"

"The children of the elves were taken around the same time that I brought the children of Hamelin here to the Summer Isle, but I didn't do it. Why would I? The 'great crime' that you all accuse me of is bringing the children of Hamelin here to the Summer Isle. I say that I saved them from ever having to grow up. I did them a favor by plucking them from a world full of deceit. Why, then, would I banish the elf children to a world I abhor? My war has never been with children, human or elf."

He sounded convincing, but then that was part of his danger. Carter found it safer just to assume the Piper was lying in every case, but this one was odd. Leetha had told Carter about the missing elf children, and of her desire for revenge against the Piper. Was the Piper just lying as a way to avoid that revenge? It seemed a strange move, as Leetha was hardly a threat anymore.

"If you didn't take the Winter Children—and I'm not saying that I believe you—then who did? And why?"

"I have my suspicions," said the Piper. "But as for why—you know that the Peddler locked me up in that tower after I brought the children of Hamelin here, but he didn't do it alone. He needed the help of the Princess of the Elves, and she got involved only because she thought I was responsible for the elves' own missing children. Awfully convenient."

"So you're saying you were framed?"

"I admit to the things I've done," said the Piper. "But I haven't done everything they say I've done." He wrapped his cloak around himself and stared up at the darkening sky. "So there's a secret for you. Are we friends now?"

Not a chance was Carter's silent answer, but instead he stood up and stomped in place, trying to warm his legs and feet. "It's getting colder."

"Why don't you fetch some more wood for the fire?" said the Piper.

"Me? How do you know I won't just run away?"

"The same way I know you'll eventually tell me where my pipe is—I know you, Carter. Better than you think." He pulled his hood down over his eyes and leaned back against the rock. "Besides, you're not that fast yet and I'd catch you."

Carter grimaced. That at least was true. After a full day's march, he was so tired he didn't know if he could run at all. He'd started toward a nearby thicket when he heard the Piper call out, "Be careful of hangman's trees!"

No need to warn him about that. Still, the Piper was obviously testing him by letting him out of his sight. And despite his confidence, Carter felt like testing him back. Just how far would he let Carter go?

It was strange. A change had definitely come over the Piper in the past few days, or maybe he was just affecting a change. Maybe he was playacting for Carter's benefit, but either way he'd been less . . . threatening than before. He was still petty and impatient and even cruel at times, but Carter didn't fear him the way he once had. Which was probably dangerous as well. People who get too comfortable handling snakes are the ones who get bit.

But, still, Carter couldn't figure out what the Piper's strategy in all this was. Even if the Piper was telling the truth about the Winter Children, that didn't make him any less of a villain in Carter's mind. He may not have stolen away the elves, but he had kidnapped the children of Hamelin. And Max and Carter. If he thought he could win over Carter's trust now, convince Carter to tell him where his magic pipe was, he could forget it. As it was, Carter was only staying with him because he had nowhere else to run. That was the only reason. . . .

Absently, Carter found himself rubbing his leg as he walked through the trees. His leg, miraculously healed.

He was lost in his thoughts when he heard something rustling in the brush just to his left. A little brown face poked itself out of the grass and beamed up at him.

"Bandybulb!" Carter whispered, surprised and elated to see the little kobold's face grinning at him.

"I have been following you," said Bandybulb. "But the Piper is always watching."

"Is Leetha all right?" asked Carter. "Was anyone hurt in the fight?"

The kobold shook his head. "Leetha suffered a grievous cut on her arm. I tried to bandage it for her, but she refused. After the fifth try, she kicked me in my backside, so I think she is on the mend."

"Where is she now?"

"She is resting in a grove. She is not strong enough yet to keep up, so I bring her water and berries when I am not watching you."

"That's good, Bandybulb. Thank you."

The little kobold leaned closer and winked conspiratorially. "Are we escaping now?"

Carter looked back at the little campsite. He couldn't see the Piper from here—the overhang of rock blocked his view—but he could see the tiny glow of firelight flickering in the dusk. He could do it. He could run, and follow Bandybulb to . . . where? Assuming he could outrun the Piper, where would he go that he wouldn't be putting his friends at risk? And with Leetha wounded, he'd just be putting her in even graver danger.

Carter shook his head. "No, Bandybulb. We aren't escaping, not yet."

The little kobold blinked up at him. "Okay." He waited for a few moments, then asked, "How about now?"

"No," whispered Carter, trying to keep the frustration out of his voice. This little creature, dim as he was, had risked everything for Carter and continued to do so even now. "It's not safe, but I might have a plan. I need you to deliver a message to Leetha for me, Bandybulb. Can you do that?"

Bandybulb nodded.

"Tell her that I'll lead the Piper into the Deep Forest. If Leetha can warn the elves there, then we might be able to capture him."

"A sound plan," said Bandybulb. "I cannot pretend to understand it, but it is most certainly sound."

"Only, I need Leetha's help. I don't know what the elves will do to me if I'm caught traveling with the Piper."

"Elves are dangerous," said Bandybulb. "And they do not care for human children."

"Why?"

"Maybe you remind them of what they lost?"

Leetha had said something similar, that the elves were more dangerous than Carter believed. But he didn't see any other choice, short of leading the Piper all the way to Magician's Landing. At least this way, the only person Carter was putting in danger was himself.

"Just deliver the message, Bandybulb," said Carter. "I need to get back before the Piper gets suspicious."

"Yes, sir," said Bandybulb, and the little kobold's face disappeared into the shrubs. Just as quickly it reappeared. "And I'm glad your leg is better. I have been watching you, and you look happy. That is good!"

Then the kobold disappeared for the last time, and Carter was left alone with his thoughts. He gathered some wood and hurried back to the camp. The Piper was already asleep, his hood drawn over his face. Carter tossed a few sticks onto the fire and sat down. This plan was reckless. The Piper knew full well that the elves lived in the Deep Forest, and Carter didn't think he would just walk up to their castle and ask for his pipe back. But maybe Carter could catch him off guard. If the Piper was busy worrying about the elves, he might not worry about Carter. No, it was reckless, but it could still work.

Perhaps he'd had the analogy wrong before; perhaps

Carter was the snake, and the Piper was the one about to get bit.

But it wasn't worrying about the plan that kept him awake long into the night. It was something Bandybulb had said, about how Carter had looked *happy*. He was being held captive, so how could he seem happy? Because these past few days had been about climbing, jumping and running. Despite his protests, Carter hadn't really felt like a prisoner at all.

It was with a creeping sense of guilt that he finally lay down to sleep, after building the fire high to drive off the cold. As he drifted off, he thought he saw the Piper's eyes open beneath his hood, and he was smiling.

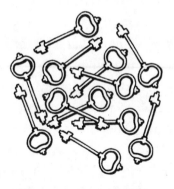

CHAPTER TWENTY-FOUR

Max sent Harold back to fetch Mrs. Amsel, with orders to gather their things and to meet her at the door. At first she walked, picking her way cautiously through the winding streets. But there was a new urgency in the air, an expectation that something was about to happen. Maybe it was just Max's imagination, a false hope born out of Harold's wild speculation, or maybe it was intuition. Either way, she was growing more and more impatient and her steps got quicker and quicker until finally she was dashing through Bordertown. She bumped into a green-skinned family who stepped out onto the street in front of her, causing the youngest to drop her raggedy doll into the mud, but Max kept going. The little elfling burst into tears, but there was barely time for an apology and there certainly wasn't time to stop.

Max had to get back to the door.

Her backpack was slung over her shoulders and she gripped the little key so hard that it bit into her palm. Buildings flew past as she ran, and it didn't take her long to reach the enormous black door. The discarded and forgotten keys crunched beneath her feet as she approached.

Max paused, her hands on her knees as she worked to catch her breath. "Okay . . . Now what?" she said.

The door was plain black rock, and the picture of the blooming tree was simple, almost childlike. If she looked closely, she could see the seams where the edges met the cavern wall, but there was no handle, no keyhole. And yet standing there felt different from standing anywhere else in Bordertown. Different from anywhere else on earth. There was something in the air, like static after a storm, only stronger. The hair on the back of her arms prickled. Closing her eyes, she tried to steel her nerves. She remembered what the captain of the *Leviathan* had said about thin places between worlds, and she knew then, without a doubt, that the Summer Isle lay just on the other side of the door. If she listened closely, she could hear the wind rustling the trees. She caught a whiff of something sweet, like flowers and honey. Eyes still shut, she reached out her hand, half expecting to feel tall grass tickling her fingertips.

"Look—there she is."

An unfamiliar voice startled her back to her senses, and her eyes popped open. Her hand was just inches from the door, but the wind was gone and all she could smell was the musty rot of Bordertown.

A crowd had gathered. Apparently, her mad dash through

the streets had gotten people's attention, because there were ten or so elflings and assorted other beings standing in a loose semicircle around her. They did not look happy.

"Oh," said Max. "I'm sorry if I bumped into you or anything. My fault."

"Look at her ears," said one of them, a plump woman with long elfling ears and skin the color of sea foam. "I told you."

Reflexively, Max reached to pull her hood closer, only to realize that it wasn't over her head anymore. It must have fallen off during the run. These people had gathered to stare at her perfectly human features, her very round ears. She thought about Cornelius's warning: *No humans allowed.*

"Um . . . ," said Max.

"What about her hair?" said another. "Pink as all."

"Shows how long it's been since you've been aboveground," answered the woman. "Pink hair's nothing unusual these days. You can buy it in a bottle."

"Um . . . ," Max said again.

"Who are you?" asked one of them.

"My name's Max."

"You're not an elfling. Not goblinfolk or giant daughter," said the woman. "And humans aren't allowed in Bordertown."

"I know," said Max. "I'm sorry I broke your rule, but I had a good reason—"

"It's not a rule—it's law," said the woman. "What happens to us if the humans above learn about this place?"

"The magic protects us," said a man with cat eyes as he stepped forward. "They can't find the way in."

"*She* found it!" said the elfling woman, pointing angrily at Max. "The law is the law. I don't care why she's here, but she can't leave."

"Look, I'm not going to tell anyone about you," said Max. "Believe me, I just came here for the door. It's because of my brother, and my parents. . . . It's a long story."

"And you'll get a chance to tell it," said the cat-eyed man. "But Maggie's right. We can't let you wander around until we sort this out."

"We can put her in the meetinghouse," said the elfling woman. "Find Cornelius, get the council together and question her there."

"Cornelius brought me here!" said Max.

"Did he, now?" said the cat-eyed man, raising an eyebrow at her. "And did he know what you are?"

Max could've bitten her tongue. She hadn't exactly lied to Cornelius, but she hadn't been exactly truthful, either. "Um, it didn't come up."

He narrowed his peculiar eyes at Max. "I think you'd better wait in the meetinghouse."

"Where's that?" asked Max.

"Center of town," said the woman. "We'll take you there."

"Look, I have friends who can vouch for me. I came here with a trollson and an elfling."

"And where are they?" asked the woman.

"Well, probably back where the trollsons live. We're staying with Geldorf."

"We know him," said the cat-eyed man.

"Yeah, well, they were going to meet me here, so maybe if we just wait . . ."

The elfling woman shook her head. "No. We will send someone to get your friends, but you'll have to come with us. The more people who see you out here, the worse it could get."

"So, what, I'm under arrest?"

"Yes!" said the woman.

The cat-eyed man took another step closer and lowered his voice so that only Max could hear. "It's as much for your protection as anything. Maggie and I are both on the town council, along with Cornelius. Trust me, you'll be safer with us."

It didn't look like they were giving her a choice. And people in the crowd had started murmuring to each other. The green-skinned family she'd bumped into were there, and they didn't look happy.

"Lead the way, I guess," said Max.

The elfling woman and the cat-eyed man walked on either side of her as they escorted her away from the door and the crowd.

"If we don't want any more attention, we'd better take the long way," said the woman warily. "That crowd could turn ugly."

The man glanced at her. "Well, if there's trouble, you didn't help things. *She can never leave.* Honestly, what's gotten into you, Maggie? Scaring the girl half to death."

"I know what I'm doing," the woman answered without looking at him. "Follow me."

Something in the woman's tone suddenly pricked at Max's danger sense. She'd assumed they would be able to talk their way out of this—Cornelius certainly seemed like a fair person, and she had friends to vouch for her. But now she got a sour feeling in the pit of her stomach, and she wondered if it wasn't too late to make a run for it. As if sensing Max's fears, the woman put a hand on her shoulder. It wasn't reassuring.

Swallowing hard, Max allowed herself to be led by the woman and the cat-eyed man, but she was ready to run at the first sign of trouble.

The woman led them through twisting streets and alleys while the man grumbled that she was succeeding only in getting them lost. Eventually she stopped outside a shack near the very outskirts of town.

"Maggie?" said the man. "This is your home, isn't it? What are we doing here?"

"Just picking up something first," she said. "I'll get the door."

"Whatever, but we need to hurry," said the man, and as Maggie opened the door, he stepped inside.

Max, however, didn't move, because as soon as the door opened, she caught a familiar whiff of something, the stink of decay.

Max turned to run, but Maggie blocked her way.

"Sorry, girl," said Maggie, and just then a pale hand shot out of the doorway and grabbed Max by the hood. She was yanked backward into the shack, then tossed roughly onto the stone floor. The door slammed shut behind her.

Max scrambled to her hands and knees, and it took a

moment for her eyes to adjust to the candlelight inside the shack. The cat-eyed man was slumped in a corner, unconscious. Behind Max, now standing between her and the door, was Mr. Twist, his dead-eyed stare looking at nothing.

And seated in a chair directly in front of her was Vodnik the magician.

CHAPTER TWENTY-FIVE

The days were growing shorter. The afternoons were still warm October afternoons, and the sun was bright enough to make Carter wish he'd brought a baseball cap with him to the Summer Isle, but it was impossible not to see what was coming. One of these days, very soon, the leaves would fall and the sun would set for real. True night was on its way.

They were crossing the Dark Moors now, miles of inhospitable terrain just north of the Deep Forest. Even with the sun shining, the moors stayed bleak and depressing. Where the ground wasn't boggy and sodden with dank water, it was rocky and treacherous underfoot. In time the moors began to give way to sparsely wooded fields, but the trees looked as unwholesome as the moors. Spindly ropewood trees crowded the path, and thorn bushes tore through your clothes and scraped your skin raw as you passed by. But the

Piper wouldn't alter their course. He was determined to avoid the road at all costs.

"You're afraid," said the Piper, startling Carter.

"What?"

"You're watching the weather. You're afraid the Winter's Moon is coming."

Carter held in a sigh of relief. For much of the morning, he had felt the Piper's eyes watching him, and he'd begun to fear that the Piper knew about Bandybulb's evening visit, because if he learned about that, then he might suspect that he was walking into a trap. Carter had been dropping hints, some more subtle than others, that the magic pipe was hidden in the Deep Forest. If Bandybulb and Leetha had done as Carter had asked, the elves would be ready for them.

Carter was terrible at secrets, but the changing weather might've given him the perfect cover. If Carter was lucky, the Piper would blame the boy's nervousness on a kid's fear of the nighttime and not on the ambush Carter was marching him into.

"Yeah," said Carter. "I don't like the dark. So what?"

"Remember what happened last time?" said the Piper with a sly smile.

How could Carter forget? On the last Winter's Moon, the dark had summoned up a creature from Carter's worst fears: a gray man—an angry spirit that feeds on children. Carter could still feel the thing's breath on his face, still smell the stink of rot and death.

"Think we'll see him again?" asked the Piper. "I'd be careful wandering away from the campfire, if I were you."

What did the Piper mean by that, exactly? Was he referring to Carter's evening talk with Bandybulb? The Piper might have been toying with him, but Carter had no choice but to play along.

"Lukas once said that the Watch boys practice not thinking about what they're afraid of," said Carter. "When night comes, I'll just . . . not think about it."

The Piper laughed. "The Watch boys *practice not thinking about it,* do they? Have you ever tried not thinking about something, Carter? Pops right into your head."

He stopped in front of Carter, blocking his path. "Don't think about a pig."

Immediately an image of a squealing pig rooting around in the muck appeared in Carter's head. He couldn't help it.

"The boys keep the darkness at bay the same way human beings have been doing for thousands of years," said the Piper. "With light. With as many torches as they can stand. And then some."

"Then I'll do as I'm told," said Carter. "I'll stay close to the campfire."

"But there's another way, Carter. A better way."

"What's that?"

"Magic."

Carter half expected the Piper to burst into laughter because, after all, the Piper was a magician and Carter was not. It would be just like him to make Carter's fears into some kind of cruel joke, but this time the Piper didn't laugh. He wasn't even smiling. He looked at Carter with an unnerving intensity, an *expectation.* Like when he'd taken Carter's leg brace away and expected him to walk.

The Piper nodded slowly. "That's right, Carter. I'm offering to teach it to you."

"Magic?" Carter said.

"Is that so hard to believe? I told you once that magic is *about* belief, especially here. The Summer Isle is infused with magic. It's as common as the air we breathe. There's magic everywhere just waiting to be used, but most don't know how."

"I can't learn magic," said Carter.

"Why not?"

"Because . . . ," said Carter, looking for the words. "Because . . . because magic is for magicians!"

"Now you sound like your sister," said the Piper. "Denying what's right in front of you. Look around you. You live in a world of magic now."

"Leave Max out of this."

"Why? Because she could never be what you are? Max didn't belong here, Carter, but you do. You have the imagination, the passion to be a magician, Carter. A real magician. All you need now is faith in your own potential. All your life people have looked at you, at your leg, and seen weakness. But I see strength."

The Piper knelt until he was eye to eye with Carter. "I understand what it is to be different. *The Son of the Witch,* they called me. All my life. And those who didn't hate me pitied me. But it's the pain that makes us stronger than them. Teaches us to overcome obstacles the rest of those fools could never dream of. All you need is practice and focus." The Piper reached into his many-colored cloak and produced a small wooden flute. Carter had seen him whittling away at it for several days now, and it finally looked complete.

"Music is my focus," said the Piper. "I'm a charmer, and I use my music to lure the magic into doing my bidding. Only, the magic here is so powerful, sometimes it comes at you like waves crashing against the shore, and if you try and take it all in, you'll drown."

"So you want me to learn to play the flute?"

"Music is *my* magic," said the Piper. "Yours will come from a different place. You can start learning right now, but to teach you *everything* I know, to make you realize your true, full potential, I need to be at my strongest. And for that, I need my magic pipe back."

There it was. The change in the Piper's behavior, the miraculous healing of Carter's leg, and now an offer to teach him magic! It all culminated in this moment; it was all a strategy to get the Piper's pipe back. He'd said it himself— he was a charmer, and he was trying to cast an entirely different sort of spell over Carter now.

Carter didn't even know how much of the Piper's offer was genuine and how much was a lie. Maybe he could teach Carter a few tricks, or maybe he was telling the truth and Carter had the makings of a true magician. Carter wasn't a warrior—he wasn't that sort of hero—but what a thing that would be, to learn magic. Real magic . . .

"No," said Carter.

The Piper's face twisted into a snarl as his calm veneer slipped away. "Why not? Don't you see what I'm offering you?"

"I won't help you get your pipe back."

"You'd be dead without me," said the Piper. "You realize that, don't you? I could leave you here in the wild, without friends to protect you, and you'd be dead in days. Because you insist on staying weak and helpless. I'm offering you the power to defend yourself, but you refuse, just to spite me. Or maybe it's something else? Maybe you like depending on other people? Healing your leg was a waste, Carter, because you're still a cripple."

If Max had been there, she would have punched the Piper in the mouth for saying that. But she wasn't there. There was no one to defend Carter but Carter.

Without another word, he turned and stomped off into the woods. For once, the Piper didn't call after him, and Carter wondered if he'd finally given up on him, or at least given up the hope that Carter would ever tell him where the pipe was. Maybe he'd just let Carter keep marching. Maybe Carter was finally free.

Free to die, alone. A voice, very like the Piper's, whispered in Carter's head as he ran through the brush, and ducked the branches of thick ropewood. If the Piper didn't stop him, where would he go? Would Bandybulb and Leetha be able to find him before some other, meaner denizen of the Summer Isle decided to have him for lunch? What if he was caught alone in the woods when the true night fell?

Carter ran for he didn't know how long, but it was long enough to get himself lost. The once-sparse trees grew thicker around him, and leaves obscured his vision. If he stopped and stood perfectly still, he could hear the trickle of water running over rocks. He must be near a stream. Well, at least he wouldn't die of thirst.

He brushed away one of the branches tickling his ear and tried to get his bearings. Perhaps he should follow the sounds of water? He turned and the branch brushed up against him again, this time scratching along his neck.

Then around it.

Before Carter could cry out, the branch, long and rope-like, coiled around his throat and pulled tight.

He was hauled off his feet, and he would have died right then except he was able to get his hands around the rope-wood so that he wasn't hanging by his neck alone. But it didn't much matter because the tree was slowly tightening its grip, squeezing the breath of life out of him. Too late, far too late, Carter saw high up in the branches the shapes of dangling skeletons, a macabre variety of woodland creatures that had met their end in the branches of this hangman's tree. As his vision began to cloud over with spots, a quiet voice beneath the panic wondered if anyone would ever know what had become of him.

Then the branch loosened its grip, just slightly, and the spots retreated as he managed to sneak in a gasp of air. At last, he could breathe, though he was still trapped high in the branches. As the rushing of blood in his ears receded, he heard music. The Piper's pipe.

Slowly, reluctantly, the tree began to lower its branches. Carter's arms were trembling, and he didn't think he could keep holding on for much longer. If he lost his grip on the branch, his own weight would strangle him before he reached the ground.

It felt like an agonizingly long time before his feet touched dirt, even though it was only a few seconds. Although the hangman's tree still fought him, its movements were sluggish, almost drowsy, and he managed to wriggle his head free of the now-loosened noose.

He collapsed to the ground. He touched his neck where the branch had snatched him, and his fingers came away bloody. On hands and knees, he dragged himself away. Away from the tree and toward the music. Against the dark trees he spotted the bright patchwork colors of the Piper's cloak. The Piper wore a look of fierce concentration, which seemed at odds with the lullaby he was using to soothe the hangman's tree. His hood was thrown back and beads of sweat glistened on his brow. He looked as if he'd been running. He didn't so much as glance at Carter. All his attention was on the tree.

Then, quite unexpectedly, the music stopped. It ended abruptly with a loud snap as the frail little flute split in the Piper's hands. The Piper looked down at his broken instrument with disgust at first, then with growing fear as the woods came alive again with the sounds of groaning wood and whipping branches, as the spell broke and the hangman's tree woke up.

"Run!" the Piper shouted, and he reached down to haul Carter to his feet, but the tree was awake now with a fury, and one massive branch swung into the Piper, smacking him across the back and knocking him to the forest floor. Another lashed out like a whip and tried to lasso Carter, but he managed to scurry free at the last second. The Piper rolled out of the way as the branch came down again, intent this time on bashing his head in. Dirt exploded from the impact, and Carter felt something tugging on his collar.

At first he thought it was the hangman's tree, but when he looked up, he saw it was the Piper, back on his feet, shoving and pushing him to standing. The Piper ran forward and dragged Carter with him, barreling into the brush. Stumbling, falling and getting up again, the two of them fled the wrath of the hangman's tree.

They didn't stop running until they were not only clear of the hangman's tree but clear of the thick copse as well. They tumbled, exhausted, to the ground in a field of tall grass, well clear of even a sapling.

They lay there for long minutes, saying nothing. Eventually the Piper took out a flask and drank deeply before offering it to Carter. The water was cool, but Carter's throat burned like fire when he swallowed. He was safe, and shockingly alive, but he couldn't get the image of those hanging skeletons out of his mind. He'd almost joined them, he'd almost died alone, just like the Piper had predicted he would. If the Piper hadn't saved him.

Someone was always saving him.

"A-a-all right," said Carter, but he could produce hardly more than a whispered rasp. The Piper leaned close to hear.

"All right what?"

Carter searched the Piper's face for a hint of gloating, for that cruel twinkle in the magician's eye. All he found was curiosity. Carter took a deep breath. His neck was in agony, but he gritted his teeth and buried the pain deep.

"Teach me magic."

❧ CHAPTER TWENTY-SIX ❧

"The most important thing you need to understand is the difference between black magic and white magic." The Piper was lecturing Carter as they trudged through a bog that threatened to suck the shoes right off their feet. The increasingly treacherous landscape meant that Carter was at most only half paying attention, which was just fine because he was pretty sure that most of what the Piper was saying was bogus. He got the sense that the Piper was making up an awful lot on the spot and calling it *the rules of magic*. Then the Piper grew irritated whenever he suspected that Carter wasn't paying attention and grew impatient if Carter asked him to repeat something. In short, the Piper was a terrible teacher.

"White magic's good, black magic's bad, right?" answered Carter as he swatted away a bog fly the size of his thumb.

"Wrong. Wrong, wrong, wrong again," said the Piper.

He seemed to take great delight in correcting his "pupil" whenever possible. "Charms are white magic. But when a water spirit, a nixie, charms some poor old fool into drowning in her lake, is that good?"

Carter was tempted to offer another example of a piper charming a village full of children into abandoning their homes and parents, but he didn't think that would go over very well. "Okay, so white magic can be used for evil, but surely black magic can't be used for good!"

"Oh, really? Let's say an ogre was rampaging through your land, destroying your countryside crops and smashing the villagers to pulp."

"I don't live in a village. I live in New York City."

The Piper flicked Carter on the forehead.

"Ow!" Carter said.

"Use your imagination," said the Piper. "The ogre is terrorizing your village and threatening your friends and family. And you happen to know this little curse that could stop the ogre's heart in an instant. Freeze it dead."

Carter shuddered. "Is there such a thing?"

"Oh, yes. It's the blackest of magic—ending a life before its time. But if it could save your village from destruction . . . Would casting it be an evil deed, Carter?"

Carter thought about this. "I . . . I guess not." Though it was hard to picture an ogre rampaging through Manhattan, he could understand the Piper's point. But the thought of doing something like that didn't feel right. Like he'd jumped into a pool of filthy water and couldn't scrub off the oily sheen. "But if I were a magician, that curse wouldn't be the only thing I could do. I'd know plenty of other spells to stop an ogre without killing it, right?"

"Not if you don't start paying attention!" snapped the Piper. "I'm trying to tell you to stop thinking about magic in terms of good and evil. It's useless."

"Okay, fine," said Carter. "So there's white magic, which is charms and life and stuff; then there's black magic, which is all about destruction and death. But if it makes you happy, I won't call them good and bad."

The Piper nodded. "That's better."

"Are there any other types of magic?"

"The elves' magic comes from nature," said the Piper. "Which mixes black and white up all together. Then there's kobold magic, I guess."

"What's kobold magic like?"

"Boring. Silly. You want a charm to find your hat, or a curse to stink up a room, go ask a kobold."

"Sounds like that would be kind of useful, actually," said Carter. "My mom can never find her keys and—"

"Then why don't you go find a kobold to teach you?" the Piper said, throwing up his hands. "Become the Summer Isle's only magician that specializes in curdling milk!"

The bargain was that the Piper would teach Carter magic, and in return Carter would lead the Piper to his lost magic pipe. Carter's side of the bargain, at least, was a lie. He still had no intention of letting the Piper get his pipe back. He was leading the Piper into the Deep Forest, where, if everything went according to plan, the Piper would be captured by Leetha and the elves. The problem was that Carter had started to wonder if the Piper wasn't lying about his side of the bargain as well. They spent their time marching and arguing, and the Piper's explanations of magic ranged from the insultingly simple to the bizarrely complex. But it was during their evenings together that the relationship started to change.

Perhaps it was just that the Piper was too exhausted from the day's hard march to be mean, or maybe it was something in the routine they'd developed that calmed him, but every evening Carter would gather the wood for the fire and the Piper would cast a charm to light it. At these times, absorbed as he was in the magic, the Piper was almost patient with Carter.

Tonight he'd asked Carter to bring back a very specific list of ingredients along with the firewood. Lichen growing on dry deadwood. A red ant. A few other curious and seemingly random things that were not easily found on the barren moor. As Carter searched, he kept an eye out for Bandybulb. The little kobold still hadn't reported back, and Carter was beginning to grow worried about the little creature. He waited for the kobold for as long as he could without raising the Piper's suspicion, and when Bandybulb didn't show, he headed back to camp.

When Carter returned, the Piper took a small mortar and pestle out of his pack and instructed Carter to dump the ingredients into the bowl. "Now grind them up into as fine a powder as you can. Let me know if your arm gets tired."

Carter noted the Piper's uncharacteristic concern for his arm, and got to work.

"Tonight we are making spark powder," said the Piper. "It can be dangerous if it spills, so take your time and be careful."

"You're not going to charm up a fire with your music?"

"Not tonight. Tonight we use something more primal. Witch's magic."

Carter stopped grinding. "You mean, black magic?"

"It's the first magic I learned," said the Piper. "Good a starting place as any."

"But we're just starting a campfire, right? What's black about that? It's not like we're killing anyone."

The Piper smiled. "Tell that to the ant you just ground up in that bowl."

Carter looked down at the mush that he'd been grinding together and made a face. If his sister, the vegetarian, were here right now, he'd be getting a lecture. "I didn't think of it like that. I mean, it's just an ant."

"It is just an ant," said the Piper. "And killing a bug is not inherently evil. Still, it is death magic all the same. That ant's life will become the spark we need to make our fire."

Carter went back to his work, but he cringed now at the feel of the mixture grinding under the pestle. "Witch's magic is gross."

The Piper chuckled. "I know. I had the same reaction when my mother first started teaching me."

"Your mother taught you this?"

"During the good years, the people of Hamelin came to

her for charms and medicines," said the Piper. "Respected her, in a way. Then when the long winter came, they needed someone to blame for their misery. Adults will betray you every time."

The Piper had told Carter the story back in the Black Tower. He told him about how the villagers had chased him and his mother out into the cold, and how his mother had gotten sick and eventually died from exposure. It was why, years later, when the Piper returned to Hamelin, he got his revenge on the villagers by stealing their children away. A childhood wound that refused to heal.

"I'm sorry," said Carter, and he meant it. Whatever else the Piper had done wrong (and there was plenty), Carter still felt bad about what had happened to him as a young boy. Who wouldn't? "I didn't mean to bring it up."

The Piper waved Carter's apology away. "It's irrelevant to what we are doing here tonight. What you need to know is this magic is called witch*craft* for a reason. If you have the gift, all you have to do is follow the recipe."

Carter still wasn't sure that he had the gift, but there was little else to do between here and the Deep Forest. And if he could learn real magic, even a little, it would be worth putting up with the Piper for a few more days. It might even help them all in the end. Carter absently touched his neck and felt where the scabs had formed over the wounds from the hangman's tree. A little magic might help him, at least. "Is that all that's different between witch's magic and the magic you cast with your music? Ingredients?"

"No," said the Piper. "It's about inspiration. A magician's magic is more mysterious. More of an art, whereas common witchcraft is a skill. A magician finds one thing that connects him to the magic, that opens a conduit to all that power, and then he uses it in place of all this crafting. For me, it's not just my music, it's my special pipe. I've had it since I was a child."

The Piper leaned over and peered into the mortar. "But I started with this. My mother taught me, and her mother taught her. You might say it's the family profession."

Carter stopped grinding. The ingredients had been ground to a lumpy powder. "You know, when I agreed to learn magic, I didn't think I would be agreeing to become a witch."

"Then we have work to do," said the Piper, "if you want to be more than that, more than just a dabbler in potions and powders. To become a magician, you have to discover your true soul. So, who are you, Carter?"

"I don't know anymore."

The Piper pulled his cloak around himself as the wind picked up. "Well, let's start with seeing if you are the kind of person who can make a fire. Take a pinch of the powder and toss it onto the wood. Just a pinch."

Carter took a bit of the powder between his fingers and tried not to think about what the powder was actually made of. Then he dropped it onto the wood. "Are you going to say some magic words or—"

Before he could finish his sentence, the little pile of wood burst into flame. It flared with such intensity that the Piper fell backward. After the initial conflagration, it settled into a warm, cozy fire.

"Well," said the Piper. "That was just a pinch, wasn't it?"

Carter nodded, staring into the mortar like he was holding a live grenade.

"Powerful mixture—that's promising," said the Piper, tossing him a small leather pouch. "Keep the powder in that. It's not dangerous as long as you're careful not to let it touch anything wooden. Good to have if you run into another hangman's tree, yes?"

Gently, very gently, Carter emptied the contents of the mortar into the little pouch.

"You see?" said the Piper after Carter had finished wiping the mortar and pestle clean of spark powder. "You have natural talent. All you needed to do was follow the recipe."

"Are you trying to tell me that all anyone needs to do is grind up some fungus and a few ants and they can make fire?"

"No," said the Piper. "You need to be a witch. Or a magician."

"Well, you—"

The Piper cut him off. "I didn't touch it. I never even handled the ingredients. Not once. It was yours from start to finish. Congratulations."

"Thanks," said Carter.

The Piper watched him for a moment. "I understand what you're afraid of," he said. "You're afraid that if I teach you magic, then that means you might end up like me."

"No—"

"You're afraid you'll go from being the hero to the villain."

Carter didn't answer right away. The truth was, the thought had definitely occurred to him, and it was why he pressed the Piper so hard on good and evil magic. If he could, he'd learn enough magic to defend himself and maybe enough to help his friends. "How much is too much?" he asked at last.

"Well, that depends on what you do with it," said the Piper. "I keep telling you, magic is not good or bad, it just is. Like a man's arm that he strengthens over time. If one day he uses it to lift up a friend who has fallen, well, that's good. If he uses it to push the friend down, that's bad. Helping hand or a fist—it's always the man, never the arm."

The Piper pulled his hood up and stared into the fire, his face hidden in shadow. "You and I have much in common, Carter. The desire to prove ourselves in the eyes of others. But you didn't grow up like I did. Hunger like a hot coal in your stomach. You didn't watch as your neighbors threw rocks at your mother, driving her into the snow. You didn't have to watch her waste away.

"I don't think there was ever any real choice for me. The magic had to be a fist. It had to be. But what you do with it is up to you. Fear me if you like, but don't fear the magic."

They ate a supper of leftover stale bread and cheese, and they said very little. Carter's head was swirling with too many thoughts to speak. He found himself clenching and unclenching his hand—open palm, tight fist. That's when he realized that he didn't fear the Piper. Not anymore. And it wasn't just because the Piper had saved his life at the hangman's tree. Carter didn't know if that made him brave or foolish, but something had changed between them in the past few days. Something important.

After dinner the Piper played a simple tune as Carter added wood to the fire.

That evening Carter lay awake a long time and stared up at the sky. Every now and then he would flex his leg, as had become his habit at night. If he lay on it wrong and it fell asleep, he would start to panic, afraid that he'd awake in the morning and it would be twisted once again. But tonight he was thinking more about the fire, and about all the Piper had said. He took out the little pouch of spark powder and turned it over in his fingers. He could feel its warmth even through the leather pouch. An unnatural warmth, a magical warmth.

The Piper had been asleep for several hours when Carter felt a little hand tug at his ear. Startled, he rolled over and found himself staring into a furry smiling face.

"Bandybulb!" Carter mouthed the name.

The little kobold nodded. "I am on a secret mission!" the kobold whispered, but not quietly enough for Carter. The Piper was only a few feet away, and Carter knew him to be a light sleeper.

He shushed the little creature with a finger to his lips. Then he whispered, "Where have you been?"

Bandybulb leaned close to Carter's ear. "Making plans. Leetha has contacted the elves of the Deep Forest. Tomorrow they will be waiting for you along the old Peddler's Road in the Deep Forest, past the Antler Gate. It will be a Winter's Moon, and the elves will use the darkness to surprise him."

Nervously, Carter looked over at the Piper. His breathing was slow and steady, and he slept wrapped in his cloak.

Carter found himself hesitating to answer. Why was he hesitating? "All right."

"Oh! One more thing." The kobold lifted one finger that had been tied with a little bow of twine. "Leetha said this was most important, so I tied a string around my finger to remember. She told me to tell you that when the elves attack, you must get as far away as possible. Listen for the owl's call three times, then three more. You must flee when you hear that signal. Otherwise, your life will be in danger, too."

"What do you mean? If they plan to capture us . . ." Carter's words trailed off as understanding struck. The elves hated the Piper for supposedly stealing their children away all those centuries ago. Leetha herself had told Carter how bitterly disappointed she was that the Piper had been locked away for all those years, only to escape again. Tomorrow night, the elves weren't planning to capture the Piper—they were going to execute him.

Bandybulb beamed up at Carter, pleased that he'd been able to remember so much very important information. Happy, the little kobold snuck off again to report back to Leetha, leaving Carter alone with his thoughts.

Carter didn't fall asleep at all that night. He stayed awake until dawn, thinking about the young man sleeping across from him, the young man who'd turned into an ageless magician and who'd caused so much misery for so many. But he had once been a little boy, and a terrible wrong had been done to him as well.

And tomorrow, Carter was going to lead him to his death.

CHAPTER TWENTY-SEVEN

The sounds started late that evening. The shouts and growls they'd heard coming from the Shimmering Forest sent the Watch boys scrambling to their posts along the gate wall, and the bell ringers climbed the high towers, eyes peeled for any movement in the trees. This was it, they thought. The ogres were attacking.

The attack didn't come, but the monstrous noises continued off and on, and the birds of the forest took to the air in fear. Even the faerie lights that gave the place its name retreated to less clamorous parts of the forest. After a few more hours, trees began to fall and the forest echoed with the sound of timber crashing to the ground. The ogres were near, but they weren't attacking. What, Lukas wondered, were they waiting for?

With the dawn came the answer. Lukas was at the gate, overseeing the effort to reinforce it with a hastily arranged barricade of tables, chairs and basically everything and anything that could be moved and stacked. When Lukas spotted Emilie running his way, he knew from her expression that she had bad news.

The leaves on the Summer Tree, the ancient oak in the middle of the village, were falling. By afternoon the branches would be bare, and come evening a hoarfrost would creep over the land as the sun set for real. A Winter's Moon would rise, and true night would fall. That's what the ogres and their rat allies were waiting for. They would attack tonight under the cover of darkness, when the wicked things of the Summer Isle were at their strongest. And now that the seasons were getting longer, there was a good chance that winter would last well past dawn. There would be frozen days and pitch black ahead for no one knew how long. It would have been a challenge to survive even if they weren't expecting a siege.

Emilie and a few of the older girls had been planning to sneak the littlest ones out of New Hamelin. They would find shelter and safety among the seaside cliffs to the west. But with the coming of winter, that was impossible now. The children of New Hamelin would survive the siege—or fall together.

Paul, meanwhile, had become an irritating expert on strategy.

"I say we charge 'em," he told Lukas as they walked the wall together and double-checked the firepots. "We paint our faces up like goblins or something, and we just charge into the forest, hooting and hollering like we're crazy."

"We wouldn't need to act crazy—we'd have to *be* crazy

to try that, Paul," said Lukas. "Hand me a few more torches, would you? I don't want anyone to run out tonight."

The scout unwrapped the large bundle of sticks he'd been carrying and counted out four pine torches, their ends freshly rolled in pitch and pig fat. "Give me a dozen archers worth their salt and those ogres wouldn't get within ten yards of the gate." Paul's bravado was mostly empty bragging, and they both knew it.

"You'll have every archer in New Hamelin up here on the wall tonight and then some," said Lukas. "Laura and a few of the older girls have been practicing shooting apples for sport."

Lukas saw the incredulous look on the boy's face. "I know, I know. But we need every person we can get. I'm putting the girls on the east wall, under Finn's command."

Paul let out a low whistle. "Girls with bows. God, I hope an ogre kills me quick."

Lukas grinned. "Just wait until you see them. Emilie has had the middle girls working all night stitching pants! Can you imagine Emilie wearing pants?"

Apparently, Paul could imagine it very well, because his cheeks turned a bright red. "She's not going to be up there, is she?"

"No," Lukas answered. He'd been dreading this moment ever since this morning, when he and Emilie had tussled over breakfast. He'd argued with her until he was hoarse, but she had her mind made up. He might as well break the news to Paul sooner rather than later. "Emilie will be at the front gate. She's taken charge of defending the inside barricade."

Paul nearly dropped his torches. "What? The front gate is where they'll hit the hardest! Once the gate falls, that barricade of footstools isn't going to hold back one angry kobold, much less *ogres!*"

"Paul, lower your voice."

"I'll tell her! I'll reason with her. And when that doesn't work, I'll lock her in the outhouse."

Lukas hadn't been any happier about Emilie's decision, but at the same time, why shouldn't Emilie take an active part in defending their home? If the barricade fell, then that meant New Hamelin had fallen as well. It wouldn't matter where Emilie was if that happened. Nowhere would be safe.

Lukas let Paul rant for a few minutes until the boy finally exhausted himself. He slumped against the wall, spent. "Blast it," he sighed at last. "If I try to tell Emilie what to do, it'll just as likely get me a black eye. Last night I tried to steal a kiss on the cheek at dinner, and she threatened to switch me in front of everyone. Then, as I was heading home to bed, she grabbed me into an alley and kissed me on the mouth— the *mouth!* I swear to heaven I don't understand that girl."

Lukas would've liked to tell Paul that he didn't understand either one of them anymore. Why were the two of them stealing kisses at all when the whole village could be under attack at any moment? Then again, maybe that was the whole reason—why wait until tomorrow when there might not be a tomorrow? Love, Lukas had just learned, would not go quietly into darkness.

"Anyway," he said. "If you want to join Emilie at the barricade when the attack comes, it's all right with me. I understand."

But Paul didn't have to consider the offer for long. "No," he answered. "You need at least one person up on this wall who can fire an arrow without hitting his own foot. I know where I'm needed, Lukas. You can count on me."

Lukas put a hand on the boy's shoulder. They'd been friendly when they started out on this adventure, but they'd come back as brothers. He thought about telling him so, but instead he just arranged the torches and set about filling the pitch pots in silence. All the while, the sounds from the Shimmering Forest grew louder as the day turned colder.

The attack came just after moonrise. The cold that true night was brutal, but no snow fell. The sky remained cloudless, and the moon glittered overhead in a clear sky. If it stayed that way, the moonlight would work to their advantage, at least—the enemy wouldn't be able to hide their numbers.

The ogres lumbered out of the trees, four massive hulks, and it was obvious at once what they had been doing all day. Two of them walked in front, carrying fearsome-looking clubs made of freshly snapped tree trunks, and the two behind hauled an enormous object made of several trees tied together. They grunted as they dragged it through the frozen grass while a horde of rats darted here and there, their night eyes gleaming in the moonlight.

The ogres had made the trees into a battering ram, and they were coming straight for the gates of New Hamelin. Paul had been right; they weren't bothering with the walls—they were going to come through the front door.

Lukas and Paul exchanged worried looks, but then Lukas shook off his fear—fear was dangerous on nights like this. The watch fires had all been lit, lanterns hung in every doorway to drive away the shadows. And the boys of the Watch, joined by the village girls, stood ready at the gate wall. Lukas, Eldest Boy and Captain, drew his iron sword and held it high for all to see. The sword had been held by every Eldest Boy before him, and every child in the village knew it by sight.

With a nod from Lukas, Paul shouted the order, and boys and girls lit their arrows dipped in pitch. The ogres bellowed their challenge, and Lukas answered it as he brought down his sword and let the first volley of flaming arrows fly like falling stars in the night.

CHAPTER TWENTY-EIGHT

The little shack where Max was being held was barely big enough to hold a small cot and a table and two chairs. One wall was covered in faded photographs of the elfling woman Maggie, the one who'd betrayed her. Only, in the photos she looked younger, and she was often standing next to a handsome young man. The people in the pictures were smiling and happy, which made sneering Vodnik look even more out of place sitting there in front of them. On the table next to him he'd placed the hideous fisherman's box, his collection of souls.

The magician ran his fingers through the tangles of his beard. "You are a slippery little thing, aren't you? Haven't made things easy on poor old Vodnik."

"How . . . How did you get here?" asked Max.

"It wasn't easy," said the magician. "But I have servants even in Bordertown. They helped us sneak in."

Vodnik opened his box and searched for a jar. "Ah, there you are!" He held one up to the light of the candle, and Max could barely see the face of a handsome young man floating in the mist. It was the young man from the wall photos. "Take Maggie out there, for instance. This soul belongs to someone very dear to her. And since there are no crows down here, she acts as my eyes and ears, and I keep this little jar safe."

"You're blackmailing her."

"Well, it would be awful for her if I accidentally dropped this, now, wouldn't it?" Vodnik tossed the jar up and caught it just before it smashed to the ground. Then he laughed.

Max hugged her backpack close, mindful of the two invaluable jars within.

As if reading her mind, Vodnik frowned. "You have something of mine inside there, yes?"

"No."

"What a terrible liar you are!" laughed Vodnik. "Try not looking down next time—it gives you away. Mr. Twist, if you'd be so kind?"

Vodnik's undead servant used his one remaining arm to snatch the backpack out of Max's hands as easily as if she were a two-year-old child. Max grabbed for it, but Twist roughly elbowed her back to the ground and Max skinned her palms on the rough rock floor.

Vodnik opened the backpack and removed the jars. He set them on the table. Her parents' souls still slept peacefully inside, each floating in a tiny swirl of mist. "Good thing you didn't try to open them yourself," he said. "It would take a powerful magician to undo the curse I've laid upon your parents without killing them in the process. I don't think a pink-haired girl with an attitude problem is up to the challenge."

Next, he removed the scroll case containing the Peddler's map. Curious, he ran his fingers along the outside and held the map case to his nose. "Now, this smells interesting. I'll need to give it a more thorough examination later." He laid the map on the table next to the jars.

Lastly, he took out the little brass key. "Why don't you keep this," said Vodnik, and he tossed the key to Max. "Think of it as a souvenir. I've got plenty."

"I don't understand," she said. "If this key's fake, too, then why did you come all this way? Why are you after me?"

The magician tapped a long-nailed finger on the table for a moment, studying her. Then he leaned forward, and his eyes grew wide, hungry. "What do you know of that door?"

"Only where it goes, and that the Pied Piper locked it with a curse."

"Yes! The very same Piper who stole you and your brother away to the Summer Isle and—now, this is most important—*returned* you home again. Such power that must have taken! Can you imagine?"

"You know what? I've seen the Piper up close and I wasn't impressed." Max almost added *any more than you impress me,* but she managed to hold her tongue.

"Regardless, you went to the Summer Isle *and* came home again. Don't you know how special that makes you?"

"Tell me."

"Long ago, when the Piper locked the door to the Summer Isle, he devised a very clever, very specific curse. He wanted to lock the door but still be able to use it himself, you see. Traditionally, this sort of magic is accomplished with actual magic keys, or secret passwords, but the Piper knew that keys can be stolen and secret passwords rarely stay secret. So he devised an ingenious curse instead.

"What separates the Piper from everyone else on the Summer Isle? His *humanity*. The Piper was the only human being to visit the Summer Isle and come back again, and in his arrogance he believed that would stay true forever. So the curse is very simple—the last door to the Summer Isle will only open for a human who has set foot on the soil of the Summer Isle. Not an elf, not a monster like me, and not a human who has never been. It will only open for someone like *you*."

Max couldn't believe it. But then she remembered what she'd felt standing outside that door. She'd heard the wind. She'd smelled the air. She'd felt like she could reach out and touch the Summer Isle, because she could have.

"Oh my God," she whispered.

"Yes," said Vodnik, grinning. "By sheer virtue of your having been to the Summer Isle once, now the door will open for you. You are the one being on this planet who can break the curse. And of course, you now belong to me. No more scams, no more pretending. Now I really do possess the only key to the Summer Isle. *You* are that key!"

Max closed her eyes and buried her head in her fists. She'd been so close. Inches away from that door, and if she'd just touched it . . .

"Good thing Maggie spotted you when she did, eh?"

said Vodnik. "And I'll tell you what, nearly losing you like that has taught me a valuable lesson."

Max opened her eyes and glared at the magician. She wondered if she was fast enough to jump up and kick him before Mr. Twist could react. Pointless, but it would feel good.

"I thought that holding your parents hostage would be enough to control you, but it wasn't. You stole the jars once—who's to say you won't find a way to do it again? You're smart, and foolishly brave, and you'd always be looking for a way to thwart me, wouldn't you? Look at you, you're doing it right now. I can see the wheels turning!"

Vodnik laughed as Max fumed. He was right. He might have the upper hand right now, but she would find a way to beat him eventually.

"No, no, you are just too dangerous to be running around *of your own free will*." Vodnik reached into his box and took out a brand-new jar. He breathed on the glass and then rubbed it clean on his shirt.

"I'll keep your soul in here," said Vodnik. "And use your body as my key. Of course, in time you'll start to ripen, like poor Mr. Twist there, but you'd be amazed how long a corpse can last if given the proper care."

CHAPTER TWENTY-NINE

The first ogre reached the front gate, and the gate held. There was a worrisome moment when the wooden planks groaned in protest as the beast shoved his massive shoulder into them, but they held. The boys along the wall let out a cheer when the ogre staggered away from the gate and rubbed his sore shoulder. But Lukas knew that the real danger wasn't from that single monster; it was from the pair carrying the battering ram.

The night had been lucky so far for the New Hameliners, as the ogres were having some difficulty getting the ram up to the gate because carrying the massive length of tightly bound tree trunks required teamwork. The ogres were fighting among themselves, even while the New Hameliners were fighting to defend their village.

The ground below was littered with dead rats, but there were more still skulking in the shadows and hiding behind their ogre allies. Paul and his archers were good at catching the rats whenever they made a charge for the wall. The rats were excellent climbers, but the Watch had thus far been ready for them. Lukas noticed that Laura and her girls were particularly adept at hitting moving targets, and he had to wonder what sort of practice archery they'd been up to, and for how long.

For his part, Lukas paced the length of the wall to check on the defenders while shouting orders and encouragements along the way. Early on in the siege, one of the ogres had gotten the idea that instead of knocking the gate down, he could simply toss the rats over the top. It apparently didn't matter to him what happened to them when they hit the ground. Lukas had to duck five screaming airborne rats before the rest of the creatures learned to stay well out of the ogre's reach.

If the siege continued to be this disorganized, Lukas hoped that they might actually make it until daybreak. He climbed down the ladder to triple-check on Emilie and the barricade. When he found her, she looked nervous, and several of the boys and girls under her charge were crying, they were so afraid. She commanded a motley crew of middle boys and girls armed with kitchen knives and rolling pins, but they would need every body they could spare to hold the barricade if the gate fell. When Emilie spotted Lukas, she forced a smile.

"That knock at the gate gave us all a fright to remember," she said, loud enough for everyone to hear. "But I'm sure that ogre will have a sore shoulder to remember for almost as long!"

"You are all doing fine," said Lukas. "Better than fine."

There were appreciative nods, and one of the smaller boys held up his rolling pin in salute. Martin was his name, and Lukas knew him to be a skilled artist.

When Emilie got close enough to whisper, she asked, "How are we really doing?"

Lukas shrugged. "Well, if they keep throwing the rats, there won't be anyone but ogres left out there to fight." This time Emilie's smile was genuine. "But I'm worried about the battering ram. If they manage to reach the gate . . ."

Lukas didn't finish his sentence because he didn't need to. They both knew what would happen if the walls fell tonight. Emilie started to say something, but at that moment there was a commotion on the wall. Lukas called up to the boys, and Paul answered that something had just flown over the boys' heads.

Lukas searched the night sky, but all he saw was inky blackness. Then Emilie let out a gasp and pointed toward the center of town. There was a shape, long-necked and winged, soaring past the hanging lanterns toward the village square.

The square was where they kept the nursery. One of the middle girls would be telling stories to the little ones, trying to keep them distracted from the fighting going on outside their village walls.

"No!" screamed Emilie, and she and Lukas bolted for the square. They'd both recognized that shape.

They got there just in time to see an ugly goose transform into a bent, haggard crone. She was at the nursery door. Grannie Yaga was coming for the little children.

They were still too far away to stop her, and the leafless Summer Tree was between them and Grannie, but Lukas called out a warning to those inside.

Grannie Yaga turned at the sound. Even by lantern light he could see the jagged grin of her false teeth. She cackled as she tossed a handful of knucklebones at their feet. Wherever they landed, a skeletal hand clawed its way up through the dirt. One of them grabbed Lukas by the ankle, and he tripped, smacking his head against the ground as he fell. He felt bony fingers wrapping around one of his wrists, pinning him to the ground. He caught a glimpse of Emilie nearby, wrestling with a pair of skeletal hands that were grasping at her hair.

Somewhere close by, children were crying.

Lukas searched the ground for his weapon, but the black iron sword was nearly invisible in the dark. The skeletal fingers were digging into his arm, his legs.

Grannie Yaga stood in the doorway, a small child in each arm. Nicholas and Hans, twins who'd been barely four when the Piper stole them from their home. They were crying.

The witch was grinning, although those hideous teeth of hers made it look like she was always grinning.

"That's close enough, Eldest Boy," said the witch. "Don't normally like my meals raw, but I might make an exception for these little sweetmeats."

"Let them go," said Lukas.

"Give me Carter, and I will," said Grannie.

Lukas cursed himself under his breath. The witch still thought Carter was hiding in New Hamelin, because he hadn't told her otherwise. He tried to yank free, but the hands held him fast by one leg and one arm.

"Carter's not here," he said. "He never was."

"You're lying. Don't give up your own just to keep that boy safe."

Then Lukas's other foot brushed up against something hard lying in the grass. The sword was there, and it was within reach.

"Eh-eh," the witch warned. "The Peddler may have charmed your nasty little sword against poor Grannie, but I will kill these two sweet babes if you try to use it. By the hairs of my chin, I will."

"I swear Carter isn't here!"

Grannie cocked her head and considered this. "Perhaps just one, then. A curse to stop the heart. Painless. If you let one die, then I'll know you're telling the truth."

"No, take *me*!" a voice shouted.

Lukas turned and saw Emilie back on her feet. Her kerchief was gone, and it looked like a clump of her hair was missing—her scalp was bloody where it'd been yanked out—but she'd managed to free herself from the undead hands. "If you need to kill someone, kill me," she said. "Just let the little ones go."

"So many choices!" Grannie Yaga sighed. "There will come a day when I'll get to choose who I like when I like. Oh, yes, my dears. And it's coming soon. Very soon. If the Piper has his way, this land will be swarming with stolen children, and there's no Peddler to fence old Grannie in anymore, eh?"

"Please let them go," pleaded Emilie, stepping closer.

"So hard to decide," said Grannie. "Let's see. How do you children do it? Ah, yes. *Eeny meeny miney . . .*" She pointed a bony finger at one of the twins. Hans, Lukas thought it was. "Sorry, dumpling. You're moe."

But at that moment there was a thundering crack, one that shook the very buildings. It was the sound of tearing, splintering wood, followed by the bellowing cry of ogres. Everyone, even Grannie, looked toward the gate.

Everyone except for little Hans, who looked right at the finger in his face and bit it.

"Ow!" screamed Grannie, dropping the twins to the ground. "You nasty little thing!"

The twins scrambled to their feet and ran to Emilie as fast as their chubby little legs would carry them. She met them halfway and scooped the pair up in her arms.

"So be it!" said Grannie, glaring. "I'll have all three of you."

With his free hand, Lukas wrenched his body around. Something popped in his shoulder, but he ignored it as his fingers found the pommel of the Sword of the Eldest Boy. The cold iron felt good against his palm, and he brought the blade down on the bony hand that held his other arm. The instant his blade made contact with the bones, they crumbled to dust. He remembered Grannie Yaga's reaction to the sword, how it had seemed to burn her. Apparently, it could break her magic as well.

Grannie pointed her bleeding finger at Emilie and the twins. Emilie turned her back to the witch and pulled the twins close, trying to shield them with her own body.

Lukas dragged himself to his feet just as she was completing the deadly spell. He was too late.

But Paul wasn't. Lukas felt the arrow fly by his face, barely missing him, and he heard the witch's cry as it found its home in her eye socket.

The sound of the gate snapping was nothing compared to the scream Grannie Yaga let out. It was pure agony and rage.

Lukas glanced over his shoulder to see Paul standing directly behind him, loading up a second arrow. "Emilie, run!" he said.

Emilie grabbed the twins and did just that as the witch yanked the arrow free and snapped it between her fingers. Half her face was covered in black blood. Her one good eye was wide with fury.

"Lukas, get out of the way!" said Paul. "I've got another shot!".

But this time the witch was ready for him. "Paul, get down!" shouted Lukas, but the scout was too busy lining up his aim. Grannie Yaga finished her deadly curse, only this time her finger was pointed at Lukas and Paul.

A rush of freezing air enveloped Lukas, and for a second it threatened to steal his breath as he felt an unnatural chill coursing through his veins toward his heart. But then the iron sword in his hand grew suddenly warm, and that warmth chased away the cold. The sword had deflected Grannie's curse.

The witch gave a yell of frustration as her killing spell failed to stop Lukas's heart. Under his breath, Lukas muttered a thanks to the Peddler, and he ran toward Grannie, his sword raised high.

But the witch was already transforming back into her goose form. Before Lukas could reach her, she'd taken flight, disappearing into the night just as the air was rent with another bone-shaking crash. The ogres were breaching the gate.

Lukas turned to see Emilie standing stock-still in the middle of the courtyard. The twins were hiding behind her skirt.

"Emilie!" said Lukas. "We have to go! The ogres are at the gate. We have to reach the barricade."

But she wasn't listening. She had her hands over her mouth, as if to hold back a scream, and she was staring at something behind Lukas.

He followed her gaze until he saw a still shape lying on the grass near the Summer Tree. A boy who looked so peaceful he might have been sleeping, but he wasn't.

The Sword of the Eldest Boy had saved Lukas from Grannie's deadly curse, but it hadn't saved the boy standing directly behind him. It hadn't saved Paul.

PART IV

THE WINTER ISLE

CHAPTER THIRTY

"Did you know Mr. Twist's soul was the very first I ever jarred?" asked Vodnik. "I should've retired him centuries ago, but I suppose I'm just too sentimental."

Max felt the silent servant stepping up behind her. She was trapped between Mr. Twist and Vodnik, with nowhere to run.

"My point is," said Vodnik, "you and I will have many happy years together."

"No, wait!" said Max. "I'll cooperate. You don't have to do this!"

The magician drew a short-bladed knife out of his coat pocket. "Too late. Don't worry, it'll only hurt at first. A drop of blood in the jar is all I need."

Then he began to sing:

Beware the reeds along the shore
For the old magician sleeps no more.
He'll prick your thumb with a stick,
And you'll belong to Uncle Vodnik.

Max ran. Not back toward the door and freedom. Instead, she charged Vodnik himself. The magician reared back, surprised, and brandished his knife, so Max did the only other thing she could think of and went for the magician's box instead.

"No!" Vodnik snarled as he realized too late what she was doing. All those jars, all those innocent souls, neatly arranged from left to right, with the newest jars on top. So Max reached deep, and grabbed the oldest-looking one, so old that it wasn't even made out of glass, just a small clay jar with a wax-sealed lid, tucked away near the back.

Max lifted the jar high above her head.

"Stop her!" cried Vodnik.

"One more step and I smash it!" said Max. She had no idea if her threat would work, but this little clay jar was old—centuries, probably. Max prayed that she'd chosen the right one.

Vodnik glared at her, his beard quivering with rage, but he stayed where he was. "I lied," he snarled. "I don't think I'll make this quick at all. Unless you put that down!"

Max glanced over at Twist and saw a strange transformation overtaking the undead servant. His normally unfocused eyes were fixed upon the jar in Max's hand. His stoic face softened, and his lips turned into something like a smile.

Vodnik roared as he lunged at Max with the knife, but somehow Mr. Twist had gotten in between them, blocking the magician's attack.

A raspy whisper rose up from Twist's throat, from vocal cords that hadn't been used in ages. "Do it," he said.

Then Max smashed the jar against the hard stone floor. The brittle clay exploded in a cloud of dust, and a tiny wisp of mist hung in the air for just a second before disappearing altogether.

All semblance of unnatural life went out of Mr. Twist. Luckily, he fell on top of Vodnik instead of Max, and the magician collapsed beneath his weight. Vodnik did not, however, drop the knife.

Max scooped the Peddler's map and her parents' jars into her backpack and bolted for the door just as it was opening. The elfling woman, Maggie, peeked her head inside.

"Master Vodnik, is everything okay—" She didn't have time to finish because Max barreled straight into her without stopping. The surprised woman hit the ground hard, but Max didn't stop.

A quick glance over her shoulder revealed that Vodnik had gotten free of Twist's now-useless corpse and was chasing her, knife in hand. Rage had distorted the magician's features into an almost inhuman mask, and with his wild beard, and eyebrows protruding like two horns from his head, he looked more monster than man.

There wasn't time for Max to get her bearings, so she just chose a direction and dashed through narrow streets lined with leaning shacks and wide-eyed elflings. Several of them pointed at her as she passed by—apparently, word of the pink-haired human girl was spreading—but even more began to notice Vodnik. There were gasps of recognition as the magician pushed his way through the milling crowds, but if he was aware of them, he didn't care. All his spite was focused on Max.

Soon Max found a landmark she recognized, and she reached old Hillbeater just as Vodnik was gaining on her. Unfortunately, she didn't see her friends anywhere, and the great stone statue offered little protection from the magician and certainly no place to hide.

Max put her back against one of the statue's thick legs and turned to face her pursuer. Vodnik snatched her by the arm with one hand but left his knife hand hidden in his coat.

"I have a jar in my pocket," he growled. "Fight me and I'll slit your throat and steal your soul right here."

Vodnik's crazed eyes bored into Max, but what he did not see was the mob who'd followed them. There were still fearful faces among them, but the fear was turning to anger. As the elflings and trollsons crowded around, Max heard mutterings of "Vodnik . . . Vodnik . . ."

Finally, Vodnik heard it, too, and he glanced over his shoulder at the mob. A look of concern flashed over his face as he counted their number, but then he bared his teeth and brandished his knife, and the mob hesitated. He twisted Max by the arm and pulled her close but kept his blade leveled at the crowd.

"What is this?" said Vodnik. "You mixed-blood Border-towners trying to show some spine? Think you're tougher than old Vodnik?"

A few of the bolder ones actually nodded. That was

exactly what they were thinking. Meanwhile, at the back of the crowd, Max saw Geldorf's mossy head poking up above the rest and Harold and Mrs. Amsel pushing their way toward the front.

"I am here for this human girl," said Vodnik. "By your own rules, she doesn't belong here anyway." Still, the crowd edged forward, like the tide threatening to overturn a jetty of rocks.

The magician's eyes darted this way and that, searching for an avenue of escape even as he sneered at the mob. "You dare threaten Vodnik? Which one of you will be first? I'll cut your throat and jar your soul for my collection!"

The magician was in an even greater fury now, and he actually took a threatening step toward the crowd, causing them to retreat a few feet. "I am Vodnik the magician!" he shouted. "Who wants to stop me? I'll bleed the whole lot of you dry if I have to!"

No one came forward to answer his challenge. Geldorf's face was a battle between hate and worry, but Harold held the mighty trollson back. Max's friends were afraid for her, afraid what Vodnik might do to her if the mob attacked.

"No one!" roared the magician. "No one can dare challenge me. Now let me pass!"

Reluctantly, the crowd started to break; even as they cursed the magician's name, they opened a path for him. Vodnik had just started to shove Max forward when she heard the sound of grinding stone from somewhere behind them. It was subtle at first but quickly amplified until the cavern echoed with it like an avalanche of rock.

Vodnik turned back, and what he saw made him falter

for just a second. Max didn't hesitate. She shoved with all her might and broke the magician's grip on her arm, throwing herself clear in the process. She landed hard on the rocky ground and rolled onto her back just in time to see a massive stone foot lifted high above Vodnik's head.

Hillbeater the sleeping stone trollson had awakened, and he wasn't afraid of Vodnik's puny knife. Harold and Mrs. Amsel acted fast and grabbed Max by her arms, dragging her clear. Vodnik screamed a hateful cry just as Hillbeater brought his enormous foot down, silencing the magician forever.

Hillbeater didn't move from that spot. Slowly, and with a loud rumble of rocks grinding, he sat down right where he was, and went back to sleep. In minutes, he was just a new hunk of stone, a statue that marked the magician's unfortunate grave. The crowd didn't cheer. Most stood there dumbly, unsure of what to say or do next, until finally Geldorf broke the silence.

"I'd say old Hillbeater looks better there anyway." Then the trollson let out a mighty laugh as he slapped his fellows on the back.

Harold and Mrs. Amsel helped Max to her feet. "Are you all right, dear?" asked Mrs. Amsel, fussing over Max and offering her a handkerchief.

"I'm fine," said Max. Vodnik was gone, but if she'd been just a second slower in getting out of the way . . . She looked back at the sleeping statue and shuddered. Best not to think about it.

She quickly checked her backpack to make sure the jars were intact. She felt her own horror start to melt away when she saw her friends' concerned faces. "I'm really okay. Really. In fact, I think I'm kind of great." She broke into a huge grin.

Mrs. Amsel and Harold shared a dubious look. "You sure you didn't bump your head, *meine Liebe*?"

"We need to get everyone together," said Max. "The elflings, the trollsons and giant daughters—everyone. Tell Geldorf to put the word out to everyone in Bordertown."

"What word?" asked Harold. "What do you want us to tell them?"

Max took the little brass key out of her pocket and looked at it for a moment, then she turned her palm over and let the key fall to the ground with a tiny clatter.

"Tell them to meet us at the door," she said. "Tell them to pack their things because we're all leaving Bordertown. . . . Tell them I've finally found the key."

CHAPTER THIRTY-ONE

New Hamelin was falling. With each impact, the ogres' battering ram opened new rents in the thick gate as the wood splintered and buckled at the seams. It wouldn't be long now. Lukas paced in front of the barricade, shouting orders to shore up this section of the gate or add a few more fighters to that stretch of wall. Meanwhile, the boys and girls chose their shots carefully as they tried to conserve their dwindling supply of arrows.

Lukas would not think about Paul. He would not think about what the witch had done or his own mistake in letting her believe Carter was still with them. If he'd just told her the truth the other day . . .

No, he would not think on it. He could not. If they survived this night, he would hand the Sword of the Eldest Boy over to Finn for good. Lukas had never wanted the responsibility, and tonight he had proved he didn't deserve it. For the time being, it was still his, but the sword felt heavier than ever before in his hand.

He made a dash for the gate as he spotted an evil-looking rat squeezing through one of the gaps the ogres had made. Though probably a head taller than Lukas, the creature managed to contort its body just enough to make it through the narrow opening. Like many of the rats they'd fought, this one carried a weapon—a twisted dagger. These rats fought tooth and knife.

The creature hissed in warning and raised its blade as Lukas closed on it. He was vaguely aware of the archers on the wall above shouting for him to move out of the way, but he ignored them. With a cry, Lukas swung his sword wildly at the rat's head. Had the creature been at all practiced with its knife, it could have stabbed Lukas in the heart before the boy had a chance to finish his swing. But the rat hesitated, and Lukas's sword struck home. The rat fell over dead at Lukas's feet.

Within seconds, two middle boys came running to the gate with a wooden plank, which they began hammering over the open gap. For a moment, the ramming outside stopped as the ogres started arguing among themselves again. That was a blessing, because that new plank wouldn't withstand another attack. The gate was being held together by splinters and luck.

Lukas turned as someone shouted his name. Emilie had climbed down from the barricade. She looked red-faced and furious. She'd also been crying.

"What in heaven's name do you think you're doing?" she asked.

"Killing a rat that made it through the gate."

"That's what the girls up top are for! Any one of them would've had a clear aim if you hadn't charged into their way. You very nearly got yourself killed for nothing."

"I wasn't in any danger."

"I saw the way you charged at it," said Emilie. "You were like a little boy trying to swat a fly with a broom. You're lucky you're not dead."

Lukas glowered at her. "Get back behind the barricade and let me handle—"

Emilie cut off Lukas's sentence with a slap to his face. A hard one.

"Just because Paul is dead, I will not let you toss your life away!" She grabbed Lukas by the collar. He could see the strain on her face, the barely suppressed tears. She was like that gate—still holding together, despite the damage. "*We* don't matter, Lukas. Emilie and Lukas don't matter tonight, but these children need the Eldest Girl and the Eldest Boy!"

Lukas wanted to argue. He wanted to shout and curse and slap Emilie right back, because she was right. A knot of shame stuck in his throat, and he didn't have the words to respond, so he simply nodded.

Emilie called the boys away from the gate area where they'd finished patching the hole and ordered everyone back behind the barricade. The ogres had stopped their arguing, and the fighters on the wall were desperately letting fly the very last of their arrows as the beasts readied their final attack.

Lukas helped Emilie scramble back over the top of the barricade, and turned to look at the frightened faces of the boys and girls beside him. There were a few older boys of the Watch who'd been called off the walls when it became clear that the attackers were focused on the front gate. But most here were middles, boys and girls who'd never seen fighting up close. On true nights like this, they normally stayed huddled safely in their little cottages with the lights burning until dawn. Lukas didn't have any words for them. He knew—they all knew—that if the thick wooden gate couldn't keep the ogres out, then this makeshift barricade wouldn't, either. But what else was there to do but try?

They waited for the crash, for the final blow that would bring the whole gate down. It never came. Instead, Lukas heard the Watch boys and girls up on the wall shouting to each other. Finn was calling his name.

Leaving Emilie at the barricade, Lukas ran to the ladder. Finn was waiting for him at the top, offering him a helping hand. "I don't know what to make of it," the boy said.

"Make of what? Are the ogres fighting again?"

"No," said Finn, and he pointed to the Peddler's Road. The bright, clear moon lit the night well enough that Lukas could make out a crowd of shapes coming up the road, and his heart immediately sank in his chest. Another army was marching on New Hamelin. A line of massive figures in the front, some as tall as, if not taller than, the ones at the gate, were charging forward at a full run.

"We're finished," said Lukas softly.

But Finn shook his head. "That's not what *they* think. Look at the ogres."

For the first time, Lukas looked down at the battle-field. The front gate was lit with a flickering orange glow from the flaming arrows that littered the ground. Some had burned out, but many more were still smoldering, making the ground look like a crop of torches. Rat bodies were everywhere, and the Watch had even managed to bring down one of the ogres with about a hundred arrows. But none of that mattered right now. Right now Lukas was watching as the ogres dropped the battering ram and stood there, dumbfounded. The rats that were left turned their weapons around and faced the charging line of newcomers.

"What are they doing?" asked Lukas in amazement. "Are they getting ready to fight their own reinforcements?"

"There!" shouted a voice. It was Pidge, the bell ringer, in his tall lookout tower. "Do you see her? Out in front! Look!"

It wasn't until the approaching army reached the line of firelight that Lukas was able to get a good look at the human girl leading the charge. Coming to the rescue. A girl with bright pink hair.

CHAPTER THIRTY-TWO

When Max saw the fires burning around New Hamelin, she was afraid they'd arrived too late. From the moment the first Bordertowners stepped foot on the Summer Isle, they'd been able to hear the sounds of distant fighting. In singles, pairs or even clumps of whole families, they stepped through the Black Door, and it was like stepping into a bitter frost. Expecting summer, they found a winter's night instead. Of course, Max knew at once what was happening; she'd been through true nights before. Even so, as she stepped through the doorway and felt the crunch of frozen moss beneath her feet, as she saw the silvery moon high overhead, her confidence faltered and she wondered if she'd made a terrible mistake leading them here.

But then she'd spotted the drifting lights of the Shimmering Forest, and the Peddler's Road beyond that, and at once she knew where they'd emerged. When the Piper stole Max and her brother, they'd been found in the Shimmering Forest, asleep on a bed of furry moss. It was to this very glade that the Black Door had opened. On this side, the door blended in perfectly with a dense copse of trees at the edge of the glade, and if it hadn't been wide open, it would have been hidden to the naked eye. As Captain Hob would have said, this was one of the thin places where the worlds almost touched.

If they were near the edge of the Shimmering Forest, that meant they were close to New Hamelin, which was good. But it also meant that it was probably New Hamelin where the sounds of fighting were coming from, and that was undoubtedly bad. Very, very bad. It meant that New Hamelin was under attack.

Max tried to hurry the stream of Bordertowners through the door, but it was proving difficult, as most stood around dumbfounded once they stepped through. The elflings, trollsons and goblinfolk had fled their cavern city for the fabled Summer Isle, but what they found was a frozen forest at night. It would take hours for the whole of Bordertown to make it through, and Max's gut warned her that New Hamelin didn't have hours.

So she searched the confused faces until she found Harold, Mrs. Amsel and Geldorf. Mrs. Amsel, bless her, was already organizing groups of elflings to make campfires and erect tents on this side of the door. She'd even put on several pots of tea.

That was well and good, but it was the trollsons Max needed now. Quickly she explained to Harold and Geldorf what she feared was happening, that the one human village in all of the Summer Isle was under attack. The one safe haven that the Bordertowners could count on might not be there come dawn. Geldorf, still antsy because he hadn't gotten any licks in on Vodnik before Hillbeater squished him, was up for a fight. And with Harold's help they quickly assembled a group of thirty or more trollsons and giant daughters, a rough-looking bunch of thick, gnarled faces and stony fists. At seven feet tall, Harold was easily the smallest of the lot, which meant that poor Max came up to most everyone else's shins.

Nevertheless, she led the way. Leaving Mrs. Amsel to manage the rest of the Bordertowners, Max guided the small army of trollsons and giant daughters out of the Shimmering Forest and to the Peddler's Road. The road had changed since she'd last seen it—it was now filled with brambles and vines—but Harold and Geldorf cleared the trail with ease. In the distance, Max could see the glow of fires ringing New Hamelin. She could hear the roars and the sounds of wood splintering.

She urged her companions to pick up the pace.

When they got close enough to see the bodies littering the field outside the village, Max nearly cried out in alarm. But then she saw that the bodies belonged to rats. So, so many rats, but there were even more still living, swarming about the base of the village walls. And there were other beasts, three hulking masses of muscle even bigger than Geldorf. They were clustered at the gate, and a fourth lay unmoving among the dead.

"Ogres," Geldorf whispered in awe. "I heard stories but

never thought to lay eyes on one." Upon seeing the carnage, Max expected the trollsons to have second thoughts. Instead, Geldorf just shot her a heady grin and cracked his stony knuckles. In contrast, however, Harold's face was a reminder that Max's large friend was still just a boy. Max could see the fear in his eyes as he gazed down upon the battlefield. Still, he didn't falter. No older than Carter, but just as brave.

The trollsons let out a savage yell and charged straight into the attacking army of rats, who'd by now seen the newcomers and were setting up their lines of defense. The charge sounded so ferocious that Max wondered at Geldorf's claims that the trollsons of today were ordinary civilized folk. By the looks of it, they still had a bit of monster left in them, and for that, Max was glad.

The rats, faced with dozens of roaring trollsons, broke easily. Half turned tail, literally, and ran, while the rest scrambled to put up some kind of counterattack. Trollsons mostly swatted them aside, and giant daughters bashed heads together. Their orderly charge quickly degenerated into a massive street brawl. In all the dust and smoke, Max quickly lost track of Harold and Geldorf, but she had a *sense* that their side was winning.

All the while, she dodged fighting bodies and pushed on toward the village gate. What if her friends were inside? What if Lukas and Paul were up on that wall? What if Emilie was inside? But most important of all, where was Carter?

Just as Max stumbled over the body of a slain rat, a towering shape appeared out of the smoke. At first she thought she'd found Geldorf, but soon enough the creature stomped into full view and Max saw that this was no trollson. This was one of the beasts who had been hammering away at the village gate: an ogre. Layers of blubbery muscle hung on thick arms and legs. Beady eyes in a too-small head narrowed as they spotted her. The ogre let out a gurgling growl and reached for her.

Max ducked out of the way and rolled. Too late she realized that she was unarmed, though she doubted even a spear would do any good against this behemoth. For a moment, the ogre stood there confused, staring at the spot where Max should have been. Then he turned and caught her trying to sneak away, and let out another growl as he lurched for her a second time.

But by now Max was far enough away to make a run for it, and so she turned to sprint and . . . found herself face to kneecap with another of the massive monsters. This ogre was even larger and just as ugly as the first, and he let out a pleased rumble when he saw Max. She was trapped between the two.

Max thought she was dead for sure, but the ogres hesitated. They eyed her. Then, warily, they eyed each other. Like two children who'd discovered a treat fallen on the floor between them, each was waiting for the other to make the first grab. Two enormous girl-eating children.

Max had a crazy idea, and before she could talk herself out of it, she actually turned and backed up toward the first ogre. "Fair's fair," she called. "He saw me first!"

The first ogre's massive brow furrowed in bewilderment, and then he broke out in an evil grin. He thought he was in for a tasty snack without having to work for it. But

Max had been counting on the second, larger ogre being just as dumb and twice as greedy. Sure enough, the second creature snarled and barked out something in an ugly guttural language—at least, Max thought it was language—and then he charged.

Max barely avoided getting trampled underfoot as the two monsters began to pummel each other over the right to eat her. She dodged their tree-trunk legs and ran for it. She ran as fast as she could. She left the wrestling ogres well behind her and made for the gate.

It was clear by now that the rats were in full retreat. The two ogres eventually stopped punching each other long enough to see that they were now outnumbered, and then they, too, fled for the forest. A third ogre lay unmoving. Geldorf stood over the body, his nose bloody and several teeth missing, but he was smiling broadly. The trollsons had enjoyed themselves immensely.

Max found Harold at the gate, and he gave her a quick hug. He at least had emerged from the fight more or less unscathed. Max peered through the smoke at the child defenders up on the wall. Far from letting out a cry of victory, they looked haggard and worn, unsure of what to think of their strange saviors. She searched their faces until she found someone she recognized. It was Lukas. When their eyes met, he smiled, but it was a smile full of heartbreak. His dirty cheeks were streaked with tears.

Carter wasn't there. Max knew her brother, and she knew that no force in existence could have stopped him from joining Lukas on that wall.

But Carter wasn't there.

CHAPTER THIRTY-THREE

Tonight's winter felt even colder, despite the lack of snow. The previous Winter's Moon had arrived with a blizzard, but this night was still and dry and brutal. The land lay under a crust of killing frost that glistened in the moonlight, and the frozen grass crunched beneath their boots as Carter and the Piper stepped off the moors where the Peddler's Road bordered the Deep Forest.

The Piper refused to let them carry their torches any farther. Too many elves about, he warned, even on a true night. Elves did not fear the dark like humans did, nor were they fond of fire, and if Carter and the Piper entered the forest with torches blazing, they would alert every elf for miles. So they paused there at the edge of the trees, and enjoyed the last minutes of their torches' light and warmth.

They stood at a crossroads, and before them was a gate hung with animal skins and antlers, which barred the road south into the elves' domain. Bandybulb had told Carter to lead the Piper past the Antler Gate, and this must surely be the one. The roads west and east were not closed, but they were no more inviting. The Peddler's Road had grown even wilder since Carter had last seen it. How much longer before there wasn't any trace of it at all?

The Piper stared at the road and wrapped his pied cloak tight around himself. "It's all happening so fast. I don't think this winter will be over come dawn."

"My friends told me that Grannie Yaga killed the Peddler," said Carter. "Is that why his road is disappearing?"

The Piper nodded. "The road fueled the Peddler's magic, and in return the Peddler maintained the road. They were connected, and together they kept the evil on the Summer Isle in check."

Carter mentally added, *Evil like you.* But even as he thought it, he wasn't sure he believed it. The Piper was a villain, to be sure, but now that Carter had spent time with him, it became harder to think of him as evil. Misguided, arrogant and dangerous. Insane, maybe. But evil? He wasn't sure anymore, and that thought alone chilled him more than the winter's night.

"The Peddler taught me, you know," said the Piper. "I was his apprentice once, long, long ago. I think I'll miss him."

"But you sent Grannie Yaga after him, didn't you?" asked Carter. "That was the deal, right? She captured me and brought me to the Black Tower, to you, and in exchange you made some kind of deal to help her get the Peddler. You knew that the Peddler would help my friends try and rescue me, and you knew that to do that he'd have to leave the protection of his road."

"It's true I lured him into the fight," said the Piper. "But that doesn't mean I wanted him to die."

"What did you think was going to happen?"

"Can you believe I was hoping that he would win? The fight would have given me enough time to escape my prison, and in any case, after battling Grannie Yaga he'd have been too weak to try and stop me. He should have been strong enough to defeat Grannie, though. He would've been if he hadn't also been protecting your friends."

Incredible as it was, it sounded as if the Piper was blaming Carter's friends for the Peddler's death. Carter knew that the Piper and the Peddler had a long history together. That they'd even come to the Summer Isle together. The Piper claimed to have once been the Peddler's apprentice, but it was the Peddler himself, helped by the Princess of the Elves, who'd locked the Piper away in the Black Tower. That was his punishment for stealing away the children of Hamelin, and the children of the elves. It was hard to believe that the Piper was now grieving over the Peddler's death.

Though he didn't talk about it, Carter still believed that the Piper planned to steal the rest of earth's children away and bring them to the Summer Isle. As insane as it was, the Piper claimed that he was doing them a favor. But Carter knew better. The Piper wanted revenge on a world that had scorned him. Carter had to assume that the Peddler would try to stop him again, if he were alive.

No matter how he felt about it, the Peddler's death meant there was one less obstacle in the Piper's way—Carter wouldn't forget that. Whether he'd intended to or not, the Piper had led the Peddler to his death, which made him culpable. Now the Deep Forest was just on the other side of that gate, and waiting somewhere in those trees were the elves. It might be Carter's best chance to stop the Piper, but did it also make him culpable for whatever fate lay in store?

Their torches were burning low, and the Piper grew impatient and stamped his out in the frost-covered grass. Carter hesitated, and not just because he feared the dark.

"What's the matter?" asked the Piper. "Afraid of what might be waiting for you out there at night?"

That wasn't the only thing Carter was afraid of, but he nodded anyway.

"True nights play with our fears, Carter. That's true of everyone, but it's particularly dangerous for a magician. Our imaginations summon some pretty ugly things." The Piper flicked him on the forehead. "Your own mind works against you."

"Ow."

"So don't let it," continued the Piper. "Magicians must also be disciplined. If you feel something coming for you out of the dark, push back against it with your willpower. Be stronger than the dark."

"But what if I'm not? What if I don't have any willpower? I mean, I always eat dessert, even when I'm so stuffed I'm gonna barf. I can't help it."

"Carter, you have to believe in the magic, and in yourself. Belief is the key to a magician's power. I know what it is to be different. To have people stare at you. To call you names.

I know that to survive you have to believe you're stronger than all of them; it's the only way to win."

"I'm not trying to win anything."

"Of course you are!" said the Piper. "Life is always about winning. You and I have a truce now—I teach you magic, and in exchange you show me where my pipe is hidden. I will hold you to your end of our bargain, but then you'll be free to do as you like. Of course, I have much more to show you. I promised to make you into a magician, and that's what I intend to do, as long as you don't get in my way."

"And what if I do get in your way?" Carter asked cautiously.

The Piper's eyes glinted in the moonlight. "Then may the best magician win."

And just like that the Piper admitted that despite everything they'd been through in the past few days, very little had really changed. Carter had seen glimpses of another side to the Piper, the human part of him, perhaps, and whether Carter believed it or not, the Piper believed they were alike. The Piper had made it hard for Carter to hate him. But the Piper was still set on retrieving his magic pipe, and he assumed that the lure of magic would be enough to make Carter cooperate. The Piper thought Carter wanted to be a magician more than anything, more even than stopping him. Carter had wondered, in his guiltiest moments, if the Piper was right.

The Piper deserved to be locked up; he didn't deserve to die. But if he succeeded, every child on earth would be in danger. Carter made up his mind. He would do everything he could to keep the Piper alive—beg the elves for his life, if that's what it took—but he couldn't let him go free.

"The pipe is in the Deep Forest," Carter lied. "Past the Antler Gate, we have to follow the road for a while, but it's not far."

The Piper cocked his head at him. "You're sure?"

"Yes," said Carter. "Roga said so."

"Then in we go. Stay close to me, and I'll protect you. If we somehow get separated, remember what I've already taught you. Be stronger than you think you are."

Then he snatched the torch from Carter's hand and ground it into the frost-covered road, smothering the last of their light. "Let's go."

The forest was quiet except for the hunting calls of night birds and the rustling of small animals keen to avoid them. The luminous moon overhead provided light enough to see by as it filtered down through the bare branches, and the thick boughs gave welcome shelter against the howling winter wind. The road inside the forest was not as ruined as it was elsewhere, which was lucky because the ankle-high blanket of fallen leaves would have made sinkholes and tripping vines even more treacherous.

They didn't talk much, but the Piper hummed quietly under his breath, and Carter found the tune soothing. It didn't calm him exactly, but he felt the hysterical edge of his fear melt away. He suspected there was some magic at work in the Piper's little song, but for once Carter didn't mind being under his spell.

As they walked, Carter's mind wandered back to the campfire and what he'd done—he'd performed real magic. By leading the Piper into the forest, into the elves' ambush, Carter was giving up on learning any more. Even if he kept the Piper alive, his dreams of becoming a magician himself would be over. Imagine it—Carter Weber, a magician! What would Max have said? She might have been jealous at first, but she probably would have been relieved not to have to stick up for him. His days of being bullied would be over. And his parents? Carter wondered if there was a spell to make your mom and dad fall in love again.

His thoughts snapped back to the present when he realized the Piper had gone silent. He'd stopped humming.

"Is there something wrong?" asked Carter quietly.

"I don't know," said the Piper. "I'm wondering that myself. I mean, we've been wandering through these woods for an hour at least and you haven't said a word about where we're *really* going. We're supposed to be searching for my pipe, but it seems more like you're waiting for something."

"What?" asked Carter. "What would I be waiting for? I told you, Roga said that your pipe was here in the forest. I'm just not sure where exactly . . ."

His words trailed off as he heard an owl hoot somewhere nearby. Three distinct calls.

"What's the matter?" asked the Piper. "It's just an owl."

The owl hooted three more times.

Carter threw himself to the ground just as something whistled over his head, and the Piper let out a cry as an arrow lodged itself deep into his shoulder. All at once the trees came alive with bodies swinging between the branches. Lithe, shadowy shapes leaped from above and landed on the road in front of and behind them. The elves' eyes shone like the eyes of night predators in the dark.

The Piper fell to one knee and his wounded arm hung uselessly at his side, but with his other hand he lifted his small flute to his lips and managed, with shuddering breaths of pain, to blow a single harsh note.

In answer to the Piper's call, a sudden torrent of wind tore through the trees, blowing up leaves into a blinding whirlwind and knocking the elf attackers to the ground and the rest from their perches in the trees. And it blew Carter off the road entirely. He tried to stand, but blinded by the flying debris, he stumbled and fell and found himself sliding down a steep embankment. He rolled through the underbrush until he landed roughly at the bottom of a dry creek bed. He was covered head to toe in scratches, but at least he hadn't broken anything. He figured he must have tumbled thirty or forty feet through brambles and over sharp rocks and hard roots. The distant sounds of battle echoed from the top of the ravine.

Carter pulled himself up to sitting and examined his surroundings. It was darker down here, much darker than up on the road, where the trees were thinner and the moonlight could reach. A few feet away from him, lying on its side across the creek bed, was a toppled, rotted tree. The broken roots reached up like grasping fingers, and in the hollow beneath the trunk was a black patch that not even moonlight could touch.

In an instant, Carter realized he was free of the Piper. The ambush had worked, but he was also alone. He thought about calling out for Leetha. Maybe she was somewhere in the trees nearby. But if so, she was probably deep in battle. Plus, Carter was loath to make any more noise than necessary. Something about that fallen tree and the dark space it sheltered unnerved him.

He took a deep breath, trying to calm his nerves. He couldn't let his fears run away with him.

He heard a snapping, like the breaking of twigs. And another. His heart beat even faster against his chest as he peered at the hollow beneath the log. Was there something moving there?

No! he told himself. *There's nothing there. There's nothing there.*

A pale hand, twisted and clawlike, reached out from beneath the tree. A body took shape; a painfully thin creature all covered in rags came crawling out of the darkness.

A gray man.

Carter was lost. No one was here to save him this time, not even the Piper. Carter had seen to that.

He scrambled backward from the creature and tried to get to his feet, but his legs were shaking so badly he could barely stand. He searched frantically in his bag, feeling around for a weapon, anything, but all he could find was his leg brace. It wouldn't do much harm, being mostly plastic to begin with, but he still brandished it like a club.

The gray man rose to his full height. A spindly demon in the dark, with arms outstretched.

"I'm stronger than you, I'm stronger than you." Carter repeated the words, but they sounded hollow to his own ears. As the gray man came closer, Carter gripped the brace tightly, until the buckles bit into his palms, just as they'd bit into his leg for all those years. All those years of walking when the other kids ran. All the people staring. All the names. All those years that Carter had survived, *thrived,* in spite of it all. In spite of the brace. "I'm stronger than you."

Be stronger than the dark. Carter was holding the reminder of his strength. His armor.

"I'm *so* much stronger than you!" cried Carter as tears streamed down his face. And he believed it.

Then the gray man was gone.

By the time Carter had climbed out of the ravine, the battle was over. He could see, through the trees, the Piper kneeling, his head bowed in defeat. Elves tended to wounded comrades, and some were not moving at all. Two watched over the Piper with their blades bared. A third, Leetha, stood in front of him. She was holding her long knives in her hands.

"Piper," she was saying. "For the crimes you've committed against our people, and against this land, and for the death of the Peddler, we sentence you to death."

The Piper lifted his head, and his hood fell away. But he didn't look at Leetha; instead, he looked past her into the trees directly at Carter. It was too dark to see the Piper's face, but Carter could feel those eyes on him.

Bandybulb had warned Carter that the elves might hurt him, too, if they found him with the Piper. At the very least, they would take Carter prisoner for trespassing in their domain. Not even Leetha would be able to protect him from that. The plan had been for him to escape in the chaos of battle. That had been the plan.

Plans had a way of going awry on the Summer Isle.

"Stop!" Carter cried.

The elves whipped their heads around to look at him, and one drew back an arrow and aimed it at his heart.

"No!" said Leetha, and she held up a warning hand. "I know this human boy; he's the one who led the Piper to us."

The elf relaxed his bowstring, but he kept the arrow cocked. His eyes were unfriendly, suspicious.

"Carter, you don't belong here anymore," said Leetha. "You don't want to see this."

"Don't kill him," pleaded Carter. "Can't you just lock him up again?"

"So that he can escape again?" said Leetha. "He must pay for his crimes. Truly pay, once and for all."

The elf with the bow growled and showed his fangs. "Who is this boy who begs for the Piper's life? A changeling child?"

"I'm sorry, Carter," said Leetha. "This has to be."

The Piper stared at Carter, his face expressionless.

Carter's hand drifted to his belt, and he found the little pouch of spark powder he'd used to light their campfire. His first magic. The Piper had warned him not to let it touch anything wooden. Gently Carter loosened the drawstring.

Leetha looked at one of the elves standing guard over the Piper. "Do it."

As the elf drew back his blade, Carter hurled the entire bag of spark powder into the trees over the elves' heads. At once, the branches exploded in flame. Every piece of wood the powder touched went up in a magical fire. The initial flare was so bright that it blinded the elves, ruining their night vision. And they tripped over each other as they ducked out of the way of the falling burning leaves. It was into that sudden inferno that Carter ran. He shoved Leetha out of the way and safely away from the flames, and then he grabbed the Piper by his cloak. He hauled the Piper to his feet, but was surprised to see that he could stand without any help. His wound must not have been as bad as it looked.

Together they dodged the fire and made for the safety of the darkness. As they ran, Carter heard Leetha calling his name.

"Carter, wait!"

But he didn't stop for her. He pulled the Piper after him, and together they fled into the night.

They ran until the fire's glow became a distant spark of light. The Piper played a small tune to hide their tracks, but as he did so the notes sounded flat and hollow. Carter saw that the little flute was cracked and warped, its magic nearly spent from the battle. But it was enough to aid in their escape, and they ran until they were finally clear of the trees. Clear of the Deep Forest. Clear of Leetha and the elves. Clear of any paths but the one Carter had chosen.

CHAPTER THIRTY-FOUR

Max had never been to a funeral before. It felt sort of like a going-away party. There was food and drink and even laughter as people took turns telling funny stories about Paul's antics. Lukas's story about the fart cushion Paul had slipped under Emilie's chair got a really good laugh. But there were a lot of tears, too, and when Emilie got up to speak, she broke down before she could get any words out, and Max had to help her back to her seat, and she kept her arm around her for the rest of the service.

They buried Paul in the town square beneath the Summer Tree. His name was carved into the tree bark and the letters filled in with smelted iron so that they would never fade.

But New Hamelin couldn't afford to grieve for long. The gate had to be rebuilt, and a decision had to be made about what to do with the hundreds of Bordertowners that had suddenly appeared, wide-eyed and bewildered in their new magical home.

Lukas put the trollsons to work felling trees from the Shimmering Forest, and plans were drafted to expand New Hamelin's walls. The village would have to double in size to accommodate the newcomers, but anyone who wanted to join the village would be allowed to do so, human or not.

Between the business of the refugees and Paul's funeral, it was nearly two days before Lukas and Max had a chance to properly talk alone. They shared a small breakfast of cheese and sliced apples on the gate wall one morning, wrapped in blankets to ward off the cold. The sun shone weakly in the sky, and snow flurries drifted along the morning wind. It had been two full days since the battle, and spring had yet to arrive. The days stayed cloudy and dim, and the nights were true nights. A change had come over the Summer Isle. A real winter had come at last.

"Maybe it'll last for just a few months, like a normal winter does," said Max. She stomped her feet to warm up her toes. "I'll need warmer socks, though."

"I wish it would at least snow," said Lukas. "It would be nice for the little ones to get to play in snow in the daytime. I can't remember the last time I threw a snowball at someone."

"I'd kick your butt in a snowball fight."

"I won't argue with you."

Max gave Lukas a *Well, that's settled* nod and smiled. The wind picked up, and she had to clutch her blanket tighter to keep it from blowing away. "Do you really think the cold will never end?"

"I don't know," said Lukas. "Something's broken on the Summer Isle. We saw it out there on the Peddler's Road; you can feel it in the air. It's like when the Peddler died, all the good parts of this place got weaker."

"Do you think there's a way to fix it?"

"I hope so," said Lukas. "But I'm no magician. I wouldn't even know where to start. We'll just have to learn to live with the cold for a while longer at least."

He handed her a slice of apple, and Max ate it without enthusiasm. It tasted bland and watery. A winter apple.

"So, it's final?" asked Max. "You're all staying?"

"It's not normally how we do things, but last night we put it to a vote. We'll set Watch boys to guard the door you discovered, keep anything nasty from using it, but the New Hameliners won't be leaving the Summer Isle until all the children can leave together, and that means rescuing those who are being held as slaves by the rat king. And that means finding Carter, too."

Max nodded. She'd expected as much. The Black Door may not have been a door back to the thirteenth century, but it was a door away from this place, and they'd just begun to explore its secrets. But the children of Hamelin had waited almost eight hundred years to escape the Summer Isle; they were prepared to wait a little longer.

"So, when are you leaving?" asked Lukas.

"Tomorrow," said Max. "Emilie's packing me a bag. She says it's good to get her mind off Paul. Wants to stay busy."

"Going to be a dangerous journey to the Deep Forest. Even if you stick to the road."

"I'm getting used to it by now."

Lukas frowned. "I'm sorry we let your brother go on without us. I really did think he'd be safer with Leetha and the elves."

"Don't worry about it," said Max. "If I know Carter, he's probably running through the Princess's halls playing knights and castles, and stuffing his face full of . . . whatever elves eat. Besides, I need to talk to the Princess. They say she's got magic, and I need a little magic right now. I need her to break my parents' curse."

Max absently patted her backpack. She'd wrapped her parents' jars in an extra layer of wool to keep them warm. It was probably a silly gesture, but it made her feel better. "Maybe she can explain what this winter is all about, too," she said.

"Maybe. I guess we'll find out when we ask her."

"Lukas, no . . ." Max looked at the boy. She'd known this was coming.

"I'm going with you."

"You can't," said Max. "You've got your hands full here with your own people and now, like, a hundred refugees making camp outside your walls. What if the rats decide to attack again? And what about your friends that are being held by the rat king?"

Lukas shook his head. "Emilie is a better leader of New Hamelin than I could ever be. And I really don't think the rats will try anything for a while. Not while Geldorf and the trollsons are around. Plus, we need to prepare before we try and rescue the missing New Hameliners. After the defeat here, the rat king will be on guard. The trollsons have agreed to help, but first we need to rebuild our defenses. Finn and Emilie can handle that. I made a promise to you, and I aim to keep it."

"But you don't have to do this."

"I know." Lukas pulled the Sword of the Eldest Boy out of its scabbard and held the ugly blade up, pointed to the sky. "I was going to give this back to Finn, but I think I'll hold on to it for a while longer. The journey won't be dangerous just because of rats and ogres, Max. Grannie Yaga came here looking for Carter. I don't know why, but she wants him back. Which means that if we go looking for him, there's a good chance we will run into her again." Lukas gripped the sword handle with both hands. "I'm counting on it."

Max didn't like the edge in Lukas's voice, but she understood it. Grannie Yaga had a lot to pay for. So did the Piper.

"You know," she said after a moment, "I knew you were going to come."

"Of course."

"No, I mean ... I'm bad at saying it, but I mean *thank you*."

"I know what you meant."

"But this time, I've got the map and I'm in charge."

Lukas gave her a look. "Really?"

"I've kind of gotten used to it."

Lukas nodded. "Fine. Well, then, *Captain*, when do we leave? Dawn tomorrow?"

"Noonish. In honor of Paul."

Lukas smiled, and the two of them finished their breakfast on the gate wall. Max watched a tiny flurry of snow blow past her cheek and out across the ruins of the Peddler's Road. She quickly lost sight of it as it was carried by winter winds past the Shimmering Forest and beyond.

A single snowflake spun in circles away from New Hamelin and above the treetops, until it rose high on a mighty gale, joining with others of its kind as they blew eastward. When it came back down to the ground again, it was part of a storm that battered the eastern shore of the Summer Isle. The first snowstorm of this new winter.

Carter pulled his wool hood tighter around his ears and tried to breathe some warmth into his stinging hands. The Piper, as usual, bragged that he could barely feel the cold. When Carter complained about it, the Piper told him to just ignore it. Magicians couldn't let themselves succumb to something as trivial as the weather. Carter wanted to kick him.

But this morning was too bitter cold even for the Piper, and when he returned with an armful of firewood (it was his turn), they both grew frustrated when they were unable to get the damp wood to light. The Piper was carving a new flute, but it wasn't finished, so he couldn't use magic yet to light the fire, and Carter had used all his spark powder in their escape. So they ate a cold breakfast of leftover rabbit as they shivered inside the cave where they'd hidden for the past several days while the Piper's wounds healed.

But he was better now, surprisingly so, and in the morning they planned to venture forth, staying clear of the trees whenever possible. While the Piper finished his breakfast, Carter sat near the cave entrance, studying the leg brace cradled in his lap. He could feel the Piper's curious eyes watching him, even though he didn't say anything.

"It's a reminder," said Carter. "That's all."

"Is that all?" said the Piper. "I'll make a magician out of you yet, Carter."

Carter nodded, but he didn't look at the Piper. He didn't want him to see the blush of shame on his cheeks. He didn't regret saving a person's life, even the Piper's, but he did regret how he'd had to do it. Leetha was his friend, and he'd betrayed her. And he worried about what was to come. It was now more important than ever that the Piper not discover the hiding place of his lost pipe.

"So," said the Piper. "Are you coming with me to Magician's Landing?"

Carter gave a start. He looked up to see the Piper wearing the most infuriating grin.

"Your face looks like a donkey's when you get surprised, did you know that?" said the Piper. "You have an ass's face, Carter, you really do—"

"You knew all along!" said Carter. "Roga told you where your pipe was hidden and you knew all along!"

"Of course," said the Piper. "Roga wasn't at all happy with the way you slipped away. She was in such a rage that she would've spilled any secrets."

"Then why go through all this . . . this whole charade? You let me lead you into the Deep Forest for nothing."

The Piper grew suddenly serious. "Not for nothing, Carter. Not for nothing. Just look around you. The Summer

Isle is changing. For the first time in a very long time, the balance has tilted in favor of evil. But evil hasn't won, not yet. And that means war is coming. One last war. Winner takes all—that's what life is about, remember? And I want you on my side."

"And what side is that?" asked Carter.

"The only side that matters," answered the Piper, and he grimaced as he sat up straight. He was healing fast, but the arrow wound still bothered him. "Can I tell you another secret? Grannie Yaga stole the Winter Children away, Carter. She stole the Winter Children and laid the blame on me, I'm almost certain."

"But why would she? That only caused trouble for you."

"That's the question, isn't it? The old witch is playing her own game, and she won't tell me all the rules. She's been around forever, you know, and she plots constantly. Who do you think I got the magic mirror from? The mirror I used to bring you and your sister here, the one you shattered. It first belonged to Grannie, and I believe she used it to steal the elves' children away. There were never many portals. The mirror was one. The Black Door back on earth is another, but I locked that one up tight ages ago. There's no one back there who could open it, unless . . ." The Piper's words drifted off as he seemed to be thinking of something. Something bothersome. Or someone.

"It doesn't matter," he said, shaking his head. "I'm telling you this about Grannie because she's up to something, and until I know what it is, I'm keeping you far away from her. The only reason she hasn't found you yet is that my magic is hiding you from her spies. But she's searching for you. She's desperate to find you."

Carter shuddered thinking about the old witch and her oven. He knew the old folktales of Yaga, and of witches in the woods and what they did to children. Rats and hangman's trees were nothing compared to that.

"The way I see it, you have a choice to make," said the Piper. "Walk away from me now and take your chances with Grannie. Or you can come with me south to Magician's Landing and continue your magic training. Learn to defend yourself. Who knows, maybe you'll figure out a way to stop me from getting my pipe back after all. . . . Or maybe you'll decide you don't want to. Come with me or be hunted by the witch. What will you choose, Carter?"

In that moment, Carter hated the Piper as much as he'd ever hated anyone. Lies and betrayal came as naturally to the Piper as breathing, so why should Carter believe anything he said? It was different for Carter; he'd recently had to learn those skills. Much to his shame.

He grabbed his bag and stormed out of the cave, fully intending to march right into the Deep Forest alone, witch or no witch. But then he realized that he was still carrying his brace. Suddenly it represented everything that he used to be, before he'd woken up on the Summer Isle. It wasn't just a reminder of the pain he'd suffered; strangely, it was a reminder of a happier time, before his life had been upended. That was the saddest thing about feeling happy—you don't truly appreciate it until it's over.

The Piper was right. Carter couldn't leave. But not

because of Grannie Yaga. He'd saved the Piper's life, and that meant that now more than ever the Piper was his responsibility. His problem. He'd started this quest to find a way home for himself and the children of Hamelin, and the Piper still represented the best chance they had. But that didn't mean that the Piper had gained the upper hand. Something *had* changed between them. It had changed in Carter.

The Piper had told him that his pain was his source of strength, but he was wrong. Carter's strength was something else, the thing that had allowed him to endure the pain, to weather it. It was the thing Carter possessed that the Piper couldn't understand. A tragedy, really, because the Piper had never known it himself.

Carter closed his eyes, and as he breathed in the winter air, he felt it chill his lungs. In his mind's eye, he pictured his family. His mom and dad. Max. He focused on them, his true armor, his barricade against the years of pain. He pictured the people who loved him, and he felt their strength flow through him.

Then he pictured the little pile of wet sticks, the failed campfire at the Piper's feet.

The Piper let out a little cry of surprise as the pile of sticks suddenly burst into flame. A small fire, but it burned hot, despite the sodden wood.

A fire created by magic.

The story will reach its conclusion in
The Piper's Apprentice

THANK YOU

I'd like to thank Team Hamelin over at Knopf, Stephen Brown and Kelly Delaney. And their fearless team leader and my wonderful editor, Michelle Frey, who makes my stories better, always. A big thanks to Kate Schafer Testerman, who's been my agent for almost ten years, and a friend for longer than that. And, of course, I have to thank my family, Alisha and Willem, who usually get the dedication page, but this time I didn't want it to go to their heads.

ABOUT MATTHEW

Matthew Cody is the author of *The Peddler's Road*, the first book in the Secrets of the Pied Piper trilogy, as well as the popular Supers of Noble's Green trilogy: *Powerless, Super,* and *Villainous*. He is also the author of *Will in Scarlet* and *The Dead Gentleman*. Originally from the Midwest, he now lives with his wife and son in Manhattan. You can visit him on the Web at matthewcody.com.